MORE PRAISE AND CRITICAL ACCLAIM FOR THE
BESTSELLING ST. JUST MYSTERY SERIES:

Death of a Cozy Writer

Winner of the Agatha Award for Best First Novel
Chosen by *Kirkus Reviews* as a Best Book of 2008
**Winner of the Left Coast Crime/Hawaii Five-O Award
for Best Police Procedural**

"[A] delightful homage to the great novels of Britain's golden age of mysteries."

—Nancy Pearl, NPR commentator and author of
*Book Lust: Recommended Reading for Every Mood,
Moment, and Reason*

"Malliet's debut combines devices from Christie and Clue to keep you guessing until the dramatic denouement."

—*Kirkus Reviews*

"Detective Chief Inspector St. Just and Detective Sergeant Fear of the Cambridgeshire constabulary conduct a lively investigation that underscores how the lack and the love of money might be at the root of society's ills."

—*Publishers Weekly*

"Malliet's skillful debut demonstrates the sophistication one would expect of a much more established writer. I'm looking forward to her next genre-bender, *Death and the Lit Chick*."

—*Mystery Scene Magazine*

"The connections made by St. Just are nothing short of Sherlock Holmes at his most coherent. A most excellent first mystery!"

—*Midwest Book Review*

Death and the Lit Chick

"Malliet's satirical take on the mystery scene is spot-on."

—*Publishers Weekly* (starred review)

"Malliet excels at stylish writing very reminiscent of the golden age of British mysteries. A real find for old-school mystery fans."

—*Booklist* (starred review)

An absolutely delicious skewering of the world of mystery publishing and its none-too-savory denizens, *Death and the Lit Chick* is even wittier and more skillfully constructed than her Agatha Award-winning *Death of a Cozy Writer*."   —Denver Post

"Delicious. Malliet is laugh-out-loud funny in describing the cadre of crime writers encountered by the sometimes-flustered St. Just."

—*Mystery Scene*

"A good choice for readers who enjoy intelligent cozies and traditional mysteries."   —*Library Journal*

"An entertaining diversion."   —Kirkus Reviews

"Readers who enjoy all things British, as well as a good whodunit, will find these novels just the ticket."

—*Free Lance-Star* (Fredericksburg, VA)

"The writing is A+ smooth, clever (in the good sense) and a pleasure to read."   —*Cozy Library*

"*Death and the Lit Chick* shows why classics never go out of style . . . Malliet belongs on your bookshelf."

—Reviewing the Evidence.com

DEATH
at the
Alma Mater

DEATH

at the
Alma Mater

G.M. Malliet

MIDNIGHT INK
WOODBURY, MINNESOTA

First Edition
First Printing, 2010

Book design and format by Donna Burch
Cover design by Lisa Novak
Cover art: Certificate © Istockphoto.com/MB Photo; Scroll © Istockphoto.com/
    Felix Möckel; Gargoyle © Istockphoto.com/Jan Rihak
Editing by Connie Hill
Interior map by the Llewellyn art department

Midnight Ink, an imprint of Llewellyn Publications

Library of Congress Cataloging-in-Publication Data (Pending)
Malliet, G. M.-
   Death at the alma mater / G. M. Malliet. — 1st ed.
     p.   cm. — (A St. Just mystery ; #3)
   ISBN 978-0-7387-1967-2
   1. University of Cambridge—Alumni and alumnae—Fiction. 2. Cambridge (England)—Fiction. 3. Murder—Investigation—Fiction. I. Title.
   PS3613.A4535D42   2010
   813'.6—dc22   2009040815

Midnight Ink
Llewellyn Publications
2143 Wooddale Drive, Dept. 978-0-7387-1967-2
Woodbury, MN 55125-2989 USA
www.midnightinkbooks.com

Printed in the United States of America

For Bill

CONTENTS

ACKNOWLEDGMENTS

I would like to thank the following people for their graciousness in allowing me to make calls on their time and their invaluable expertise:

Leslie Dunn

Andrew Peden

Stephen Redburn

Dale Steventon

My special thanks go to expert Thomas Edwards for his thoughtful review and commentary on the parts of this story pertaining to rowing and sculling. As always, any mistakes are entirely my own.

While the University of Cambridge, England, of course exists, St. Michael's College does not. I have randomly placed St. Mike's on a make-believe plot of land backing onto the River Cam, and preempted the architectural features of several famous colleges to serve the needs of St. Mike's and of my narrative.

All members and staff of this imaginary college are likewise figments of my imagination.

CAST OF CHARACTERS

Dr. D.X.L. Marburger—Master of St. Michael's College, University of Cambridge, England. His best-laid plans to replenish the college's dwindling coffers are rapidly undone by murder.

Mr. Bowles—College Bursar. A canny man with an uncanny eye for the bottom line.

The Reverend Dr. Otis—College Dean. A wooly-headed lamb among the wolves?

James Bassett—Knighted for his services to literature, Sir James is less than gallant when his former wife joins the weekend's festivities.

India Bassett née Burrows—Lady Bassett has never been the jealous type, but this weekend may test her limits.

Alexandra (Lexy) Laurant—She may still carry a torch for her ex-husband, but everyone wonders: What exactly does she plan to do with it?

Gwennap Pengelly—A celebrity crime reporter, she'll do anything to get the scoop.

Hermione Jax—An academic who revels in her reputation as a bluestocking of high moral standards and long memory.

Constance Dunning—An American who complains about everything. Murder ruining her holiday is simply the last straw.

Karl Dunning—Constance's financier husband, necessarily a man of infinite patience—or is he?

Augie Cramb—An American dot-com millionaire and St. Michael's alumnus, he has old, and often fond, memories of his college days.

Sebastian Burrows—A golden lad with little use for the weekend's visitors, especially since they include his parents.

Saffron Sellers—Sebastian's girlfriend. A hardworking undergraduate, has she learned too much for her own good?

Portia De'Ath—St. Just's inamorata. Once again, her fine romance takes a back seat to murder.

Geraldo Valentiano—A millionaire playboy with little interest in the victims he often leaves behind.

Detective Chief Inspector Arthur St. Just—As usual, he's called in for a case that requires unusually delicate handling.

Sergeant Garwin Fear, Dr. Malenfant, and Constable Brummond—DCI St. Just's assistants in solving the most baffling of crimes.

William Trinity—The college's Head Porter.

Mary Goose—College chef.

Kurokawa Masaki—A brilliant student with his head always in the clouds, but he notices more than he lets on.

Jason Wright—Rowing coach.

Marigold Arkwright—College bedder.

"In Xanadu did Kubla Khan
A stately pleasure-dome decree,
Where Alph, the sacred river, ran
Through caverns measureless to man
Down to a sunless sea."

—SAMUEL TAYLOR COLERIDGE

Webster was much possessed by death
And saw the skull beneath the skin.

—T. S. ELIOT

ST. MICHAEL'S COLLEGE, UNIVERSITY OF CAMBRIDGE

View of Rear Grounds

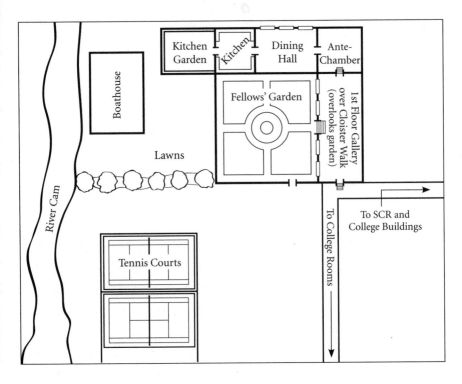

ALMA MATER

FOUNDED AROUND THE TIME King Henry VIII was selling off "his" monasteries, St. Michael's College of the University of Cambridge spreads in haphazard fashion by the River Cam, a model of functional medieval architecture wedded to Tudor bombast and, later, Victorian excess.

The University itself, of which the college is a part, was formed by a group of tearaway scholars escaping the wrath of the townspeople of Oxford, where clashes had ended with two students being hanged for murder, which incident should have given everyone in Cambridge pause. But by this time—the early 1200s—the inhabitants of Cambridge had survived the Romans, the Saxons, the Vikings, and the Normans, and, perhaps numbed into apathy at the sight of yet more new arrivals, rashly allowed the fledgling seat of learning to take hold.

St. Mike's, as it is inevitably called, is one of the lesser-known of thirty-two Cambridge colleges—a former Master liked to insist it was as well known as Trinity, which is like saying Marks and Spencer is as well known as Harrods—and it has never, even from its earliest days, been among the wealthiest of colleges. Indeed, it has more than once in its long history flirted with financial disaster. One early benefactor, having promised the college a substantial legacy, on the strength of which promise the college incurred various debts, was found on his death to be worth only £23. There were many other such incidents as the college slumbered its way through the centuries, betraying either a touching naiveté or a rampant incompetence on the part of those entrusted with St. Mike's care.

The college was, however, given a boost in early Victorian times by an infusion of funds from the will of a wealthy owner of smoke-belching smokestacks in the Midlands. A painting of this scowling, mutton-chopped benefactor hangs, like an old-fashioned ad for castor oil, in pride of place in the Hall—one of the conditions of his bequest. But this benefactor's funds, too, had long since gone to repair the crumbling brick and clunch of the chapel, and by the late 1980s exuberant but doubtful investments in the stock market and offshore hedge funds had shrunk the college's coffers still further. The stone walls, chipped in places and worn to a gloss in others, continued to flake and wear like a favored old coffee mug, and the college remained a constant source of anxiety for the Bursar and others in whose care she was entrusted. (Although named for a male saint, St. Michael's is female, as are all the colleges, and a high-maintenance female, at that.)

So it was that as the twentieth century neared a close, the then-Master decreed "Something Must Be Done," and the answer came back from the Senior Combination Room, as it had done since time immemorial: "Let's hit up the old members for donations."

Something resembling energy infused the normally antebellum spirit of the SCR. Brochures were produced on one of the college's antique computers, and pleas personally signed by the Master were mailed out by the hundreds. This campaign met with little success (a thunderous silence, in fact), so much so that the suggestion of one wag—that the fundraising brochure be illustrated by a photo of a starving student holding a tin cup—was taken under serious consideration for as long as two weeks. Finally another idea was broached: Why not tempt graduates back to the college during the summer for a St. Mike's Open Weekend? The initial thought was that college members of specific years of matriculation would be invited, but over time it became the custom to carefully screen the guest list to include only the most successful—in monetary terms, that is—graduates. (One weekend in 1991 creative artists spawned by St. Mike's were invited, an experiment that was never to be repeated, as the artists proved not only to be living in less-than-genteel poverty, but to have accepted the invitation in the hope of being offered stipended Fellowships. They ended up alleviating their disappointment by making chip shots on the college's manicured lawns and dressing the statue of the College's Founder in women's undergarments. One specialist in "Found Art" left behind in his room a large tortoise. The hysterical bedder who discovered it was instrumental in instituting the ban on artists' weekends at St. Mike's. A specialist in tortoise biology easily being located—this was Cambridge, after all—the tortoise was duly adopted and lived to a ripe age somewhere in the region of North Piddle.)

The Bursar was generally assigned the task of combing through the lists of members who, for good or ill, had made their mark on the world, and had been well compensated for the marking up. He gradually began to notice that 1988 had been a bonanza year for such luminaries at the college—that over the course of the past twenty or so years, several of the members who had matriculated or were in some way attached to the college in that year had achieved success and, more to the Bursar's purposes, accumulated great wealth. It seems 1988 was one of those times, not unlike the Renaissance, perhaps, when the world burst with new ideas and energy before subsiding once more into its habitual indolence. In any event, the Bursar soon had a short list of worthies—the Master had asked that the gatherings be kept to under ten members, since spouses and guests were also encouraged to attend—and the college Fellows were duly summoned to hear the announcement concerning the upcoming festivities, to which most of them would not be invited.

("Good Lord, the idea is to get the old members to donate, not to revive any horrid lingering memories they may be harboring of the place," the Master had been heard to say. "No, the Fellows must be told in no uncertain terms: They are to stay away from the visitors unless instructed otherwise.")

Over the years, a regular program had evolved to keep the targeted visitors suitably entertained. They would be invited to partake of a dinner on a Friday and a special buffet lunch in the Master's Lodge on a Saturday, with a tea that afternoon and a Choral Evensong followed by a formal dinner in Hall, watched over by the portraits of the colleges' Masters down through the years (portraits which had gotten bigger and bigger in an unspoken competition for Most Beloved and Important, so that the march of centuries, if not progress, was easy to trace). On Sunday would be a Sung Eucharist in the Chapel. As a special treat, the Library and College Gardens would be flung open, with lectures offered by the College Archivist and the Head Gardener, and an exhibition of College Silver would be mounted in the Senior Combination Room. An added highlight—a veritable pièce de résistance—was a tour of select student rooms, all carefully purged beforehand of traces of graffiti, scraps of unwashed clothing, seminal Marxist tracts, and empty liquor bottles.

In short, it always promised to be a weekend of the most stupendous dullness for any but the most steadfast and loyal alumnus or alumna, but in fact it proved over the years a surprisingly popular and successful venture, especially among the Americans, especially once a tasting of the College wines was added to the program. The Secretary of the College Wine Committee, an attractive man with a gift for smooth repartee, was on hand to answer questions on these occasions, where cases of College port and sherry were offered for sale, with free shipping thrown in for the Americans.

If all went according to plan, purse strings (and tongues) would be loosened, and the coffers of St. Mike's would once more fill to overflowing.

This, in any event, was the plan, a plan that had been successful, in varying degrees, for many long years. It has since been largely agreed that no one could have foretold the calamitous events which took place during the particular reunion that is the subject of this story.

No one, after all, had ever suggested that the alumni of St. Mike's be invited back for a murder mystery weekend.

A HIVE OF ACTIVITY

It was the upcoming Open Weekend that was the subject of a special meeting of the College Bursar and the College Dean, convened by the Master in his dark, Tudorish study one unseasonably warm evening in late June. The wealthy graduates were due to start arriving on July 4, and despite problems with the antique plumbing that had prompted some last-minute rearrangements and tested the bedders' patience, everything looked set for a memorable weekend—more memorable, as has been mentioned, than anyone could have anticipated.

There was a general bustle of activity as the three settled in their accustomed places. The Master, having surveyed his small assembly with his habitual look of contempt, took his own seat at the head of the rectangular table, first flinging aside imaginary swallowtails like a concert pianist. He then offered his brethren a wintry smile, folded his hands in his lap, and turned with a nod in the general direction of the Bursar.

Ten minutes later, a student with the cheek to peer in through the mullioned windows of the study would have seen that the Bursar was just reaching the end of a list of projected events.

"Let's see now. Croquet set up on the lawn. Tennis courts and equipment made available. Yes, I think that's it for the sporting activities. If they want to hire a punt they can easily walk into town. We could offer them access to the sculls..."

"They're getting too old for that, although they won't think so," said the Master, a man long-boned, pale, and gray, like something thrown up on the tide. He was the kind of person who even if forced into jogging togs would manage to look as if he were wearing a suit and tie. He had a wife, rumored to be sickly. She was seldom trotted out, looking when she was like a spouse at the press conference of a politician who has just been caught in a prostitution ring, appearing dazed and disoriented as if shot through with tranquilizer darts.

"It's a young person's sport. I'll not have the weekend spoiled by the sound of rescue sirens piercing the night air," continued the Master.

The Dean—the Reverend Otis—nodded his agreement, the overhead light glinting on his polished head and setting his dandelion hair aglow, giving him a halo of sorts.

"No, indeed. We wouldn't want sirens to spoil the fun," he said in his earnest way. "Will there again be a tour of the Gardens following Wilton's lecture? I do so enjoy that." He tapped fingertips together in a happy little pitty-pat of anticipation. He was a man who talked slowly and with extreme care, searching for each word, examining each thought before releasing it dove-like into the air. "Like a man with a bullet lodged in his head," the Master had been heard to say, most unkindly, behind his back.

Ignoring him, the Master again turned small, watery eyes the color of tarnished silver on the Bursar.

"The dining arrangements?" he asked.

"Yes." The Bursar flipped open a new folder. This one was red to signal its importance. "Afternoon tea in the garden of the Master's Lodge, weather permitting... a four-course dinner with wine in Hall at eight p.m. on Saturday accompanied by musical entertainment provided by our more talented undergraduates" ("When you find some, just be sure they're told to be well out of the room before pudding is served," the Master interjected. "One can never know how they'll behave.") "... followed by a gathering for port, chocolates, and coffee in the Senior Combination Room. I say," the Bursar looked up from his spreadsheet, "do we have to give them chocolates? This is getting rather expensive." The Bursar, true to his calling and training, was a man with a keen eye for the bottom line.

"Yes, Mr. Bowles, we do. Belgian chocolates." The Bursar's hand flew to his mouth to stem a cry of horror. He had been planning, as the Master had rightly surmised, to fob the guests off with something from the Christmas sale bin at Sainsbury's. "This is no time to be penny wise," continued the Master.

"'And is there honey still for tea?'" quoted the Reverend Otis.

"No!" said the Bursar, nearly shouting.

"We're going to be asking these people for donations in the hundreds of thousands of pounds," said the Master. "We're frightfully lucky to have alumni who have done so well for themselves."

He added this last sentence grudgingly, for the Master, who was a tremendous snob, was also extremely sensitive to the fact that St. Mike's was a college so small and obscure as to be invisible in the pantheon of notable Oxbridge colleges. He longed to be Master of a college in the grand tradition, to be able to boast of famous scientists and diarists nurtured upon the college's bosom, but it was not to be. Neither a Nobel laureate nor an Archbishop of Canterbury had ever swollen the college's ranks. Not even a prime minister. St. Mike's, although hundreds of years old, at the darker moments of its history had been remarkable only in that so many third-rate minds had managed to assemble under one roof.

When the Master looked at the competition—Peterhouse, founded 1284; Queens', 1448; St. John's, 1511—it was with the sinking sense of inevitability that however many centuries St. Michael's was in existence, and even if it one day managed to produce a Nobel Prize winner or two, it would never belong truly in the lineup of really old, really famous colleges. Even at two thousand years of age, it would remain young and somehow, forever, not quite the done thing.

Somehow this train of thought led him to face another anxiety that had been niggling at the corners of his mind for some time.

"That old business of the scandal," he began. "I'm a bit concerned, you know."

"Quite," said the Bursar, catching him up immediately. "When I saw how the guest list was shaping up, I did wonder whether ..." As noted earlier, the Bursar, tasked with providing a list of candidates suitable for a genteel shakedown, had realized the students living in college in 1988 had turned out to be a remarkably successful lot. So he had subtly altered his usual methods of assembling his list: Those invited for this particular Open Weekend had not necessarily matriculated in the same year and were in fact a collection of former graduate and undergraduate students of varying ages.

"That kind of thing can't be encouraged," said the Master.

"Not for one single moment. No indeed," said the Bursar.

All of this was moving right past the Dean, like leaves scattering before a gentle breeze.

"Scandal?" he said, his gentle eyes wide. "I don't recall anything like that."

The Master was not surprised. There could be nightly orgies and Black Masses on the High Table and the Reverend Otis, almost childish in his innocence, would be the last to notice, or to understand what was transpiring if he did notice.

He gave the Dean a shriveling glance and said, "Well, you were here at the time, and they made little secret of it. It's incredible that even you didn't notice the drama."

Typically, the Dean took no offense at the "even you."

"Let's see. The year 1988, you say...I think I do remember something about it now. The blonde woman, wasn't it? Two blondes, actually—isn't that right? It was all so long ago. Surely..." He didn't finish the sentence. Otherworldly or not, it registered with the Dean that having all the players in such a story under one roof might make for an uncomfortable time, at least for some. Determined, as always, to put the best face on things, he continued, "Surely all is long forgiven now."

The Master and the Bursar wiggled raised eyebrows at one another over the Dean's head. Everyone except the Master held the Dean in the highest regard but he was without question the most useless Fellow about the place.

The Master said, "Even without that particular complication, I do so hope there won't be any friction. These old boys—and now, of course, girls," he added, mournfully, placing an emphasis of distaste on the word. He was one of the old school that remained unreconciled to the admission of women to Cambridge. He might have been discussing an infestation of mice. "These old-boys' get-togethers... I do wish we didn't have to be bothered, really—bound to be trouble, however minor."

"Why do you say so, Master?" asked the Reverend Otis, again wide eyed, this time at the thought that anyone would choose strife when peace was such an easy alternative.

"Because," the Master replied with exaggerated patience, knowing it was breath wasted, "only a certain type is drawn to these weekend reunion events, don't you see? People with something to prove, people with something—whether a spouse or a car—to show off, people with ..." His voice trailed off.

"With?" prompted the Bursar.

The Master had been about to say, "People with a score to settle." The thought had emerged in his mind full blown, unbidden. Uncomfortable thought. Thank God he had not spoken it aloud. The Bursar was a solid man, if a bit excitable at times. As for the Dean, well... The Dean had been born to demonstrate the meaning of the word "suggestible."

"Nothing, nothing," the Master said now. "I do rather wish the whole thing were over and done with this time, I must say."

"Soon enough," said the Dean beaming on him kindly. "Soon enough."

ARRIVISTES

It was early July, usually nature's cue for everyone to have long since decamped a University town for the beaches, the lakes, or the mountains. But Cambridge is so much more than a University town. For every student who leaves, five tourists tumble out of trains and buses and other conveyances to take his or her place. This yearly migration and renewal system is a welcome tradeoff for most of the town's tradespeople, students by and large having no money.

The curved staircase in the entrance hall of St. Michael's College also seemed to smile a greeting, sweeping up from either side of the walk-in fireplace to the landing—a landing from which the Master liked to issue the occasional sonorous proclamation; a landing which had been the scene of many an impromptu, ribald undergraduate performance. The elegance of the carved wood balustrade, the stained glass depiction of the college arms, and the thickness of the carpeted stairs were lost on most of that weekend's visitors to St. Mike's, however, occupied as they were with their own thoughts. Even the sight of the academic gowns hanging on pegs in the entrance, reminders that they were entering an established if not hallowed seat of learning, went unnoticed and unremarked. Besides, they had seen it all before, years before, several times a day over the course of their studies.

Two of the visitors, Sir James Bassett and his wife, having arrived not by train but by Bentley, were already in their assigned room in the Rupert Brooke wing, continuing a conversation that had begun in London and kept them occupied all the way down the M11 to Cambridge from their much-admired townhouse (which, to their mutual delight, had been featured just the month before in Tatler). Rather, they were in India's room, the college never since its monastic days (and never until the last trumpet sounds) being organized for couples. Sir James would spend the weekend in the room next door to his wife. Needless to say, there was no adjoining door.

"What I don't understand," Lady Bassett was saying now, and not for the first time, "is how you could not have realized?" She held up a gauzy peignoir in a shade of dusky rose and gave it a good shake, staring at it critically as if she couldn't quite decide what to do with it. This was likely true, as she was not used to unpacking: She always left all that to her maid. She gave the garment one more critical squint, then rolled it in a ball and stuffed it inside one of the drawers of the room's massive oak bureau.

"I mean, you must have known she was going to be here," she continued.

She held out to him a sheet of paper letterheaded with the college's crest. Shook the list at him, rather, as if it were another puzzling garment from her suitcase. It contained the names of people attending the weekend gathering. With one finger, which trembled with outrage, she pointed at the offending name halfway down the list: Lexy Laurant.

Foolish of me not to have told her before, Sir James thought now. That was a miscalculation. But he'd been hoping to avert or at least delay the scene that was almost certain to arrive. He'd really doubted Lexy would attend, and couldn't believe it when he saw the name on the final, official list. Even now he thought there was a chance she might not show. She'd claimed an undying hatred for the place at one time. It was the type of dramatic statement Lexy was given to. He spoke the thought aloud.

"She spoke of her 'Undying Hatred' of the place, India. Capital U, capital H. I never dreamed she'd even reply to the invitation." He shook his head ruefully. "Dear old Lexy. Always one for melodrama."

"Yes, dear old Lexy," repeated India.

"She may not show up."

"She will, if only to annoy me. If I'd known, I wouldn't have come. I'll spend the whole weekend avoiding her, or being forced to pretend how thrilled I am to see her. And after the letters she's sent you, I would think you would be less than thrilled, too."

Sir James sighed. "I know. She can't help it, you know. She gets depressed, and she was used to thinking of me as someone she could talk openly with. 'Share her feelings,' is I'm sure how she'd put it."

"You shouldn't have burned those letters she sent. I have a bad feeling about this. It's like she's, well, stalking you. Us."

He took her hand in his, and traced the blue veins showing against the sun-warmed skin. He didn't think India's concern was whether or not he loved her—that she knew. India was not a woman given to jealousy, one of the reasons he had grown to love her more than life. But he told her now, just in case.

"You know you are my life, my heart, and my soul. Don't worry. It's only for a couple of days. It will be fine."

She disagreed, but she kissed him anyway.

———

Several doors away, the topic of this marital conversation had indeed shown up and was removing her clothes from the scented tissue in which her maid had wrapped them for the trip. She wasn't thinking of Sir James, however, or even of India (who she refused, in any case, to think of as Lady Bassett. Stuff that). She was thinking of all the bullshit mantras her astral therapist had given her. She'd tried, really she'd tried. The gods and goddesses knew she'd tried. But what good had it done, really?

May good befall me. Sure, fine, all right.

May I be fit for perfection. Well, she was already a size four, wasn't she? She worked out every day. Her clothes and hair were perfect, and widely imitated. She was perfect. It wasn't helping, though. None of the Eastern religions, in fact, seemed to have grasped the essence of her particular set of problems.

Most annoying and useless of all were the little platitudes. You must learn to be in the moment, Madame Zoerastra had told her, completely missing the point. It was the moment that Lexy so often couldn't bear to be in. The past was better, painted rose-colored over time as only Lexy could manage. And dreams of the future were way better.

It was the Now that sucked.

In the distant and unexplored recesses of her mind, she knew her unhappiness was, on its surface, irrational. She lived in a big, white Kensington townhouse of light-filled rooms offering views into the gardens of her millionaire neighbors. She had a hectic and well-documented social life. She had, if not friends, people she could call on to take her places. She was young and admired. Sought-after, even. What more could anyone ask?

Leaning into the mirror, she took stock: bright red lips, flawless white skin, bright blue eyes. Check. Blonde hair feathered about her face and neck in a much-imitated style that had become her trademark. Check. Uncapping a tube, she darkened the cherry red stain on her full lips. Thoughtfully, she pressed her lips together as she snapped the cap back into place.

She'd tried the traditional therapists, as well. This had advantages; they could write prescriptions, for one thing. But it wasn't, she told herself, like scoring pills for a party or whatever. Not an addiction.

Doctor Mott, one of the traditionalists, had told her she must confront her demons of the past. But some demons were best left undisturbed, surely? Even Lexy knew that. Let sleeping dogs lie. That was the ticket. What was important this weekend was that everyone see that she was over it. She really was, too. The water had long gone under that bridge. They'd see her with her dishy Argentine, who was unpacking next door at the moment and no doubt flexing his muscles as he did so. The man flexed his muscles as he brushed his teeth, for God's sake. If seeing her with Geraldo didn't signal to the world the end of her interest in that poo-wipe James and his donkey-faced wife, she didn't know what did.

She reached into one of the elastic pockets lining either side of her suitcase. These, she'd packed herself. She pulled out a sheaf of financial statements that had come in the post from her broker just as she'd left for Cambridge. Yes, that would need seeing to this weekend. Keep an eye on things. Never completely trust the experts—one would have to be a fool to do that. Stashing the pages back into the pocket, she rootled around some more. Success.

She unscrewed the cap from a plastic vial, shook out a tablet.

One extra couldn't hurt. It was going to be a long weekend, after all.

———

"Part of the thrill of the whole weekend is that we're all allowed to use the SCR, a room from which we were roundly banished when we were students here," Gwennap Pengelly was saying to Hermione Jax. The women were sitting on a bench in the Fellows' Garden, basking in the filtered sunlight. "Personally, I can't wait. I may take off my shoes and run barefoot through the carpet. And to have allowed us the use of this heavenly garden! They must really be quite hard up for donations. Before you know it they'll be letting all of us walk on the grass, Fellow of the college or no." She paused to adjust the tortoise-shell slide holding back the caramel-colored curls from her square face. The teeth of the thing bit into her scalp; it felt as if it were cutting off circulation to the brain. What price beauty.

Hermione, who held Gwenn's intellect in no high regard, might have agreed. She was shocked at hearing this truthful assessment of the college's financial situation spoken aloud, and merely said repressively, "No indeed. I believe the Master's only thought is that we should all enjoy ourselves."

"Make a change then, won't it?" Seeing her companion's aghast countenance—she'd forgotten how Hermione worshipped the Master—she tried to jolly her along. Always rough sailing with Hermione, but still, worth a try.

"Hermione, my dear old thing. You don't seriously think any of us is fooled by this invitation? One only has to look at the guest list to see we're all what the Americans would call 'loaded.' Am I supposed to pretend this was a random sampling of old members drawn up by the Bursar? Names drawn from a hat? No indeed. Much better, really, that we all know what we're in for. It will save ever so much need for subtlety and subterfuge on the part of the Bursar. I've brought my chequebook in anticipation."

"Really, Gwenn." Hermione stroked the nubby arms of her sweater, as if smoothing her own ruffled feathers. "You needn't always say whatever comes into your head, you know."

"Why ever not? It's an inclination that made me a telly reporter, and a jolly good one. And a highly compensated one, to boot."

Again, disapproval settled over Hermione's lugubrious face. Such things were never spoken of when she was a girl.

"Which brings us full circle," Gwenn continued. "I don't think for a minute I was invited along to help this lot parse the Dead Sea scrolls. Neither were you, even though you're probably the brightest of the bunch. Why pretend otherwise?"

Hermione, unused to praise—in fact, unused to any attention whatever, flushed, tongue-tied. But no matter. Gwenn swept on.

"You saw who else is coming, of course. How do you think that's going to play out?"

"You mean Sir James and Lady Bassett, of course," replied Hermione. "And Lexy. Yes, I still have reservations about that. I did mention it to the Master. He doesn't seem to have fully realized until it was too late that there might be … a problem."

"Too right. To invite both the ex-wife and current wife to a gathering under the same roof with the husband. Well. Bound to end in tears, especially if Lexy hasn't changed much."

"Lexy was always given to letting her emotions rule, yes. But not without cause in this case, as you know."

"I never understood, really." Giving up on beauty for the moment, Gwenn removed the slide and massaged her scalp, sending her curls flying in all directions. "James leaving Lexy for India. It was like trading in a new Rolls-Royce for a beaten up old Land Rover." But he'd gravitated, quite obviously, to his comfort level, she thought. People did.

"How long do you think they'd been at it before Lexy found out?" she wondered aloud. "Did anyone ever hear?"

"Really, Gwenn! It's hardly our business."

"Oh, come on. It was the scandal of the year, if not the decade. Don't pretend you aren't just a bit curious. All I ever heard was that Lexy discovered the pair of them—in flagrante, no less—and went ballistic. I never quite got the details; it was all hushed up so quickly and I never got a chance to speak with Lexy in private about it before she—before they all—left. Too bad—there's quite a story there."

"You wouldn't!" Hermione stared at her friend in staggered disbelief. Gwenn shrugged her thin shoulders impatiently.

"Who wouldn't? Once they're all dead and gone, the truth might just out. The only thing preventing me now, really, is Lexy. I always felt sorry for her, somehow. India is a different story. She was a troublemaker always."

"Certainly, there was always a man involved," agreed Hermione, caught up, despite herself, in remembered outrage. "What basis there could have been for the attraction—indeed, that struck many as a mystery. Pheromones?" she wondered, calling on remembered reading in her botanical research.

"Yes, certainly something primitive like that was in play," replied Gwenn. "But I would call it an uncanny ability to get into the head of your victim—it's the only possible word, other than 'target'—and charm the pants off of them." She smiled, a slow lazy smile of reminiscence. "I suppose I mean that literally. India always had this ability—seldom wasted on the likes of me or you, I assure you—to talk on whatever subject most interested the object of her affection. It's as if she herself doesn't exist—all bug eyes, and little interjections of 'ooh' and 'ah' at the relevant points in the narrative. I'd say she had no personality at all but of course she has the most powerful personality I've ever come across. Not to mention, destructive. That son of hers is much the worse for her brand of mothering, if you ask me. That's one unhappy kid. I ran into him earlier on the stairs, looking like thunder."

Hermione nodded. "Sebastian is a bit of a worry."

They sat in silence a moment, contemplating the possible future for the handsome if troubled offspring of their former fellow student.

"Have you spoken with Karl yet?" Gwenn now asked.

"No. I saw him and Constance arrive, but they must have gone straight up to their rooms."

"He's probably somewhere trying to work the ring out of his nose."

Hermione allowed herself a delicate snort. She always enjoyed Gwenn's company, almost despite her better instincts. That two women so exactly opposite should have remained friends was something Hermione always wondered at and, in her way, was grateful for. She had few friends: No one, if she but knew it, felt they could quite live up to her high moral standards. Gwenn, because she didn't care, didn't try.

"She does rather lead him around, doesn't she?" agreed Hermione now. "Always has done."

"I've seen Chihuahuas with more courage than Karl."

Hermione nodded.

"And I've seen Rottweilers better disposed than Constance."

———

Constance and Karl Dunning were in the SCR, taking advantage of the rare freedom of the place, he to admire the woodwork and she surreptitiously to take a peek inside the walnut drinks cabinet.

"They do all right for themselves, these Fellows," she said, assessing the paneled walls, the oil paintings, and the two deeply embrasured windows that looked out over the front of the college. Their window seats held padded tapestry cushions, depicting the college shield (goats and unicorns rampant), that had in 1951 been the project of the then-Master's wife.

From the open windows of the SCR came the sweet fragrance of flowers and newly shorn grass and the faint "thwump" of a tennis ball in play. Tall leaded windows on the opposite side of the room were merely decorative.

"As for our rooms," Constance continued, "I've seen better accommodation in a stable."

"There are parallels in Christianity, of course," said her husband mildly.

"What?"

"Oh, nothing, nothing. Take a look at this. That's a genuine Chippendale or I miss my guess."

She nodded, gray eyes judiciously weighing and measuring, oversized round earrings gleaming. She smoothed her skinned-back dark hair, which she habitually wore shellacked into a tight chignon at the base of her large skull, and straightened the knitted jacket of her suit.

"There's mold somewhere in this room," she announced. "And in my room upstairs. I can feel it, seeping into my pores. My allergies—"

"There's mold in most Cambridge rooms. It's probably what prevents the buildings from collapsing altogether—it acts as a sort of glue. Oxford's far worse, I hear."

"And the food! Remember what you said about the food! It's all not going to be what we're used to."

"No, indeed, my dear."

"We should leave now!"

"Sweetest, it's only for a few days."

"I'll be in a hospital by then, I tell you. And, my room is going to be freezing at night. There is no heat coming out of that contraption on the wall. But—you just don't care, do you?"

"Darling, I told you: The heat is at the optimum setting already. The thermostat must be broken. But it's only for the weekend. Besides, it's summer. Could be much worse, and probably usually is." He gave her a hopeful, benign smile.

She leveled at him a venomous look from beneath high-arched eyebrows.

"Do I look happy?" she asked him.

As there was no need for reply, wisely, he made none.

"Then have it seen to," she commanded. "Ask the Porter or someone."

People wondered how Karl stood it, and why. He would be mortified to hear some of the theories and rumors that had been bruited about over the years, most of them originating with Gwenn Pengelly. Gwenn had read widely of the tales surrounding the Duchess of Windsor and her baffling hold over HRH. The story had been spread around the time of the abdication, and had gained rapid currency, that Wallis had picked up some diabolical sexual techniques during her time in China, and that she had used these to ensnare the future King. For some reason, foot fetishism was the most agreed-upon outlet for the Prince's ardor.

But the truth, probably in the case of HRH and certainly in the case of Karl Dunning, was much simpler. Karl, introverted and shy, had been lonely when he met Constance. Insanely lonely and, thanks to his financial acumen and various inventions for which he held the patents, wealthy. Constance, with the sure instincts of her kind, had spotted the weakness and gone in for the kill, unawed by either Karl's social status or his intellect, where lesser egos had been deferential to his genius. Far from resenting his entrapment, Karl remained grateful and deeply attached to his wife, recognizing the neediness behind the constant demands. He was one of those people who needed to be needed. Most would have agreed that according to his lights, he'd found the perfect match.

"Just get through the weekend, my dear," he said now. Her unhappiness made him almost physically ill, so attuned was he to her moods. "Get through just these few days, and I promise you a week at the Ritz in Paris that you'll never forget. Whatever you want is yours."

She didn't have to pause for thought. She kept a mental list of her latest wants constantly updated.

"You know I've had my eye on that cocktail ring…"

"Anything."

"All right, then. But don't expect me to enjoy myself for a moment."

"You're a saint, Constance."

AULD ACQUAINTANCE

As the instructions accompanying the invitation to the alumni weekend had explained, there would be an informal meal in Hall Friday night, to be followed by a formal dinner on Saturday night. Saturday day would be taken up with lectures, tours, and chances to reminisce. Augie Cramb, late of Austin, Texas, debated the choices as he walked along Sidney Street, past Sidney Sussex College, his footsteps carrying him ever farther away from St. Mike's. He'd much prefer a pub meal and a chance to chat up the locals to what, however "informal," would surely be the grinding bore of a meal in Hall. Even when he'd lived here as a graduate student for the two long years it took to get his Master's, he'd avoided meals in college like the plague they often were. It wasn't the pomp and circumstance of college life he was after, but to get to know the people. He regarded this natural inclination as the secret to his success. He understood the little man. It was the nobs he couldn't fathom. Besides, the weekend was going to be awkward enough in spots without his having to go out of his way to have meals with the others. He was here to sightsee. Sightsee he would.

He pulled out his personal navigation device, although he knew the way perfectly well. Augie, who had made and conserved his fortune during the dot-com bubble, loved gadgets, and this small new GPS seldom left his side. He punched in the name of the pub he remembered from nearly twenty years ago. Nothing. Maybe it was another victim of the pub closings that were swamping England. More than fifty per week were shutting their doors, he'd read somewhere. The smoking ban and cheap supermarket booze had done for them. It was the real end of the British Empire as far as Augie was concerned.

Well, there was always The Eagle on Bene't Street. That pub was so famous, so beloved of scientists and World War II buffs, it would be around even if the city fell. Heck, if there were ever any danger of the Eagle's closing he'd buy the place himself.

He set his steps towards Petty Cury, turning there to walk towards the river. He kept his eyes on the GPS screen, not realizing how this inhibited his ability to see any actual sights. So engrossed in his gadget was he, in fact, that he had collided with Sir James before he knew it.

"Oh, I say, I'm jolly sorry," said Sir James.

"Jamie, my boy!" shouted Augie in surprise. Several heads turned to see what the commotion was about. Augie, from the wide open spaces of Texas, where a man was free to yell all he wanted, saw no need to moderate his speech.

Sir James, hugely affronted at the familiarity (his knighthood was a source of immense pride and had been awarded not before time, in his opinion), smiled somewhat frostily and turned to his wife.

"You'll remember India, I think," he said, his voice deliberately kept low in the vain hope Augie Cramb would follow suit.

"Indy!" shouted Augie. He clapped her on the upper arm hard enough to send her flying into traffic; she was just prevented from such a fate by her husband's quick thinking. Grabbing her, Sir James set her to rights. Unlike her husband, India could not be bothered to hide her antipathy: Augie Cramb had always been a buffoon, and while age had not withered him—he had to have put on two stone, and all of it around his middle—custom, she felt sure, would quickly stale his infinite variety.

"It's my GPS." Augie was explaining now, in excruciating detail, the device he held to within a few inches of James' nose. "It uses satnav—satellite navigation—see? I just love this thing."

This thang fumed India silently. Oh, my god. To think at one time she had found this prat worth putting on net stockings for.

"Then you punch in the address, see? And look, it's even got a world travel clock with time zones, a currency converter, a measurement converter, a calculator . . ." James, to his credit, looked on with every appearance of polite interest. James, who could not insert a battery in the electric toothbrush and had no wish to learn how. That was what servants were for. "I was headed for the Eagle," Augie went on. "The GPS tells me where to turn. You should get one of these things. Tells you where you are."

"I know where I am," said Lady Bassett.

"And surely," said James, hesitating, "you remember the Eagle? We all spent many an afternoon there during our wasted youth."

Augie sighed. "That's not the point. It's that … well you see … I can't miss it this way." Reluctantly, he pocketed the little device. Difficult to explain the thrill of technology to two people probably still wedded to their ABC railway guides. "Why don't you two kids join me for a drink?"

James and India, fighting to keep the looks of desperate horror off their faces, spoke simultaneously:

"We're due for drinks with the Master."

"We're having drinks with the Bursar."

India gave her husband a subtle stomp on the instep. It would have been bearable if she hadn't been wearing heels.

"They'll both be there," she finished brightly. "The Master and the Bursar, you see. Dreadfully sorry. Some other time, perhaps." She did not allow her voice to end on an upward inflection that would turn the last sentence into a question. She would have drinks with this ruffian colonist when hell froze over and not before.

"Sure," said Augie. They thought they were fooling someone but he knew better. The friendlier he tried to be, the more these bluebloods looked down their noses. He didn't get it. Folk high and low were friendly where he came from.

And it's not as if the three of them didn't go way back together …

"Sure," he said again. "Catch up with you later."

———

"I wonder when it'll be safe to go back. They're everywhere. Including my parents. Could this get any worse?"

Sebastian Burrows stood at the rear bar of the Eagle. After countless visits he had become oblivious to its history and the golden ambience created by its warm yellow walls. The famed ceiling, its darkened surface scorched with the writing of British and American fighter pilots, went unnoticed and unremarked.

"Insult to injury, I agree," said Saffron Sellers. She stood behind the bar in jeans, a knee-length T-shirt, and iridescent green eye shadow.

"You want another?" She indicated the pint at his elbow. "Manager'll never know. He's out somewhere with the missus; they won't be back until business picks up around five."

"Sure, why not?" Sebastian shoved the glass in her direction. Having a girlfriend who tended bar had its perks. Besides, he wasn't officially in training right now.

"Have you seen Lexy yet?" he asked Saffron's turning back.

"Oh, yes. I caught a glimpse," she sighed, expertly pulling his pint. "She's amazing." Saffron had lost the struggle with the knowledge there was something slightly shameful about her avid interest in their distinguished visitor. It was like having a movie idol visit the college. Not that Lexy had ever done anything but be Lexy. She had no discernable talent except for being a lesser member of the minor nobility who happened to be stylish and hugely photogenic. For some people, that was enough. By a little-understood process—little understood even to the reporters and reviewers who followed her every move—Lexy's presence at a restaurant meant years-long success for that restaurant, however marginal may have been the meal she'd eaten there. Her being seen wearing a particular designer's dress spelt triumph for the designer and steady employment for the knock-off designers.

Sebastian, reading the longing in Saffron's eyes—she was the most transparent of creatures, Saffy—laughed, with a mockery that was not quite gentle in his voice. "She's famous for her hair-style, isn't she? Why on earth would you care about that?"

Ruefully, Saffron ran a hand through her own tousled, multi-colored mop—a mop she styled herself, often with a straight razor.

"You wouldn't understand," she said.

"Anyway, the parents aren't half in a twist about her being there. What's odd is, I guess I'm sort of related to her. What do you call your stepfather's ex-wife?"

"I don't think there's a name for it."

"My mother has a few names for it," said Sebastian. "None of them suitable for printing in a family newspaper. She hates Lexy's being here."

"It is jolly odd."

"I wonder if Lexy thinks there's a chance of breaking the pair of them up?"

Saffron shook her head solemnly: Dunno. What the oldies got up to in the name of amor was beyond her ken.

Sebastian had his own reasons Lexy, and the other visitors, made him uncomfortable. Just one was the unhappiness Lexy caused his mother, and James—although Sebastian cared less about the happiness of his stepfather. But he liked James, really. For a stepfather, James was all right. Like all old people, James tried too hard to get Sebastian to like him, asking about his studies and his professors and trying to show an interest. But James, had he but known it, didn't have to try quite so hard. He seemed to make his mother happy. That was good enough for Seb.

Besides, James wasn't stingy. Sebastian had to give him that. All Seb ever had to do was ask, and money would flow into his bank account. If he asked for a fiver, James would hand over a hundred-pound note. It drove Sebastian mad, actually—he didn't want handouts, although sometimes he had no choice. It was bribery, besides. Seb knew that: Here's a hundred, now go away. But like most young people, Sebastian wanted to be independent, not relying on money from the wrinklies. Money like that always came with strings attached. He was hoping very much at this moment his independence day wouldn't be far off.

"…It's brilliant," Saffron was saying. "You're a genius, Seb."

Sebastian hoisted his pint, acknowledging the compliment.

"Working like a charm so far."

Saffron's attention was distracted just then by a new customer. She hadn't seen or heard him come in, treading lightly in an expensive pair of trainers. Now he sat patiently at a far corner table, some old guy wearing a weird shirt with pointed pockets and mother-of-pearl buttons—the kind of pockets that snapped shut instead of buttoning in the normal way. A cowboy shirt, like she'd seen on the telly. Howdy! He wore an enormous belt with a buckle the size of a tea saucer. This had to be an American. Jeez, they grew them big over there. He was taller than Seb, who was well over six feet.

"Shhh," she said to Sebastian.

She walked over to see what Matt Dillon wanted.

BLOCKED

PORTIA DE'ATH WAS WORKING on her thesis. At least she sat, pen in hand, surrounded by books, notebooks, papers, and other tools of the academic trade. On one side of her desk sat a laptop, its cursor blinking balefully, like the countdown-to-doomsday screen in an old science-fiction movie.

"Psychopathy," she read aloud portentously from her notebook, "as a predictor of violent criminal recidivism among the various age groups of a prison population has been shown to be … Shown to be correlated with a tendency … A tendency towards and documented history of …"

She threw her head down on the desk and, after a moment, tilted it slowly to glare at the clock on the wall.

Oh bugger, bugger, bugger it. I don't even know what I'm saying anymore. Her thesis topic—basically, the reasons old lags became and remained old lags—had all seemed so important to her at one time. Now she cursed the hubris that had made her think she had something to contribute to the academic discussion.

With a deadline bearing down, she could barely summon up the interest to finish the thesis, let alone remember why she'd started such a long, painful, and expensive process in the first place.

What on earth was wrong with her? She had her heart's desire. The basics: food, clothing, shelter. The esteem of students and colleagues—well, most of them. A sense of self, hard won though it had been. The success of her novels, bringing both satisfaction and financial reward. And now, the man with whom she was, without question, going to spend the rest of her life. The gods having their little senses of humor, they'd sent a policeman, no less. She and her policeman had met, in fact, over a murder in Scotland. Hardly a propitious beginning. But very quickly she'd known, without second-guessing the knowledge, without a shred of reflexive self-doubt: This was it.

She had returned from the mystery conference in Scotland, had a break-off dinner with Gerald, and then she'd waited to hear from Arthur St. Just, the Cambridgeshire DCI who had run off with her heart. And waited. Feeling more like a conceited fool each day, she'd waited.

Breaking it off with Gerald had been the right thing to do, and inevitable in any case. That was all right. But … where was St. Just? That detective with the burning eyes, as she'd come to think of him. The man whose integrity seemed to surround him like a force field, compelling her to reexamine all her preconceived notions about the police. She found him absurdly attractive, like a matinee idol of the thirties, his face all craggy planes and angles, the kind of face that photographed so well in black and white.

What now? she had wondered. Was she to be reduced to blockbuster, bodice-ripper prose?

But she couldn't have been wrong. She knew she had not misread the signs, misheard the words. She'd begun keeping a journal, so unique had it been in her experience to long for the sight of another human being in this way. She felt she'd go mad otherwise, for she wasn't the type of woman to confide in girlfriends. Then she'd torn up the journal, afraid of its discovery.

And so she'd waited some more, "focusing" on her thesis. And then, a little over three months ago, and one week after her return (it had seemed no less than two years), a handwritten letter had arrived on embossed notepaper: Would she do him the honor of having dinner with him at St. Germaine's? She should have known. Arthur St. Just was an old-fashioned man. No phone calls for such in important occasion: no less than a formal invitation would do. He'd arrive on time with flowers, wearing his best suit and aftershave, driving a newly washed and hoovered car.

She'd played hard to get for all of three minutes, then she'd dialed the number he'd provided.

After that, with very little fuss or soul searching, Portia had settled into their relationship, although settled was the wrong word. Rather, she quickly had reached a near-constant state of ease and contentment. There was no drama between them, and no cause for it. She knew he would appear when he said he would. There was no angst. He loved her with a clear, unwavering, forthright, and simple intent, which she soon reciprocated, likewise without reservation.

Smiling at the thought, she pulled the manuscript of her latest DCI Nankervis novel from the right bottom drawer of her desk. Her mystery writing, she knew, served as an escape from the opaque, brocaded prose of her dissertation, and from anything else that might be troubling her. Time and again her mind returned to her inspector, working his way through a complex investigation in the jagged peninsula of England known as Cornwall. It was all far more engrossing—and more solvable—than the high rate of recidivism. She was stymied, she knew, by her belief that she had to present an elegant solution to the problem in some kind of thundering, resounding conclusion—some humane and all-encompassing answer. That there was no real solution to all the ills of society she had become more and more convinced, the more she researched the mind-numbingly tedious and long catalog of essentially fruitless research, which always seemed to conclude with the sentence: "More research is needed." Ah, well, it kept the academics employed. "The poor you will always have with you," Jesus had said, and Portia wondered if he weren't quite correct about that. He may as well have added, "And crime, too."

She reread her pages of the day before, and then began writing a scene where her detective was interviewing a suspect in a restaurant in Cornwall. He was supposed to have conducted this interview in the suspect's home, but as Portia could think of no reason the suspect might offer to cook the detective a meal on the spot, or any reason he would trust the suspect enough to eat it, she felt a restaurant scene was called for. She had DCI Nankervis order roasted scallops with a vermouth sauce, slow-roasted lamb flavored with rosemary, fried zucchini, and scallion-potato puree. For the pudding course, a Tarte Tatin.

Not surprisingly, when she put down her pen and paper an hour later it was because hunger had derailed her train of thought. Dinner tonight in college might be better than the norm, she thought, given the arrival of the weekend guests and the Master's desire to impress; but also given the usual low standard, that might not be saying much. The vegetables would still be boiled to a consistency suitable for a toothless baby, and for pudding there would be something involving tinned fruit, as if summer had never arrived.

Portia's natural gourmet tendencies had been brought into full play by the poor choices available in college. She had a tiny kitchen in her college flat, from which she had managed to coax some miraculous results, the most memorable to date being Peking Duck, which duck had hung in her window to dry for three days one winter as part of the process of producing the famously crisp skin. (She had daily expected a knock on the door asking her to remove the duck but no knock had arrived.) She kept a wine rack in her front hall closet stocked with the best vintages she could afford; she had once macerated fruit for fruitcake under a chair in her sitting room. Her supervision students had kept remarking on the wonderful smell, not knowing it was coming from underneath them.

Perhaps a quiet Indian takeaway in her room would be the better option than dining in Hall, she thought now. Tomorrow night, the big gala dinner to which the Master had invited her—nay, commanded her to appear—might be marginally better, but the college "chef," as she was now called, would still be in charge, so how much hope was there, really, for a lean portion of meat not disguised by a vile Mystery Sauce?

Now thoroughly famished, thesis completely forgotten, Portia wandered off down the corridor to retrieve a power drink she'd left in the common refrigerator, praying it would still be there.

They had a food thief in college—several, probably, so she knew the chances were against her. But—she checked her watch—the college bar would be open now. She could buy something to bring back to her room, enough to carry her over until she could get to the shops.

She was in the area of the college designated for use by unmarried Fellows—a relatively modern add-on, circa 1780, connected by a long corridor to the main building. The circa 1980s, Gulag-style dormitories for the undergraduates, of no architectural distinction whatsoever, were tucked firmly behind a screen of trees, well away from the main building. The youngest students, who called it Cell Block Nineteen, were roundly encouraged to stay there, where they reigned in squalor, according to the Bursar, like wild monkeys surrounding the main compound. But their Junior Combination Room was in the main building.

Portia's steps carried her past the open door of this JCR, a room not unlike the waiting rooms of airports in many a third-world country, generations of slothful, untidy students having rendered redecoration pointless.

Three students, having apparently escaped the cell block, sat watching the start of a DVD, laughing as they tried unsuccessfully to fast forward through the government's copyright violation warnings. One of them, a young man who she remembered gloried in the name Gideon Absalom, began reciting his own version of the warning, adding additional, personalized threats.

"We'll take your wife and your children!" he sang. He stood and began dancing in an exuberant style, part hoochie koo, part Michael Jackson. "We'll confiscate all of your property!" Here he leapt, spinning, into the air, landing en pointe with all the precision of a ballet dancer. "You'll spend your life in prison!" he cried. The rest joined in the chorus, throwing their arms wide: "So don't fuck with us!"

In spite of herself, Portia, trying to slip past unobtrusively, let out a loud splutter of laughter. Gideon, seeing her, took a bow, smiling as he doffed an imaginary hat.

Ah, to be young again.

She continued towards the central staircase in the main entrance hall, where she nearly collided with the Bursar, and where she had her usual Stepford Wives-caliber exchange with him. Quite voluble in some circumstances, Mr. Bowles seemed not particularly comfortable around the female sex, which added to the stiltedness of most of the conversations Portia had had with him. He was quite a formal man, most at home, she thought, in black tie. Even his dark, slicked-back hair and rounded belly added to the illusion that one was addressing a penguin of good breeding but limited vocabulary. His embonpoint seemed to be increasing with his status as a pillar of the college, she noted. He must dine out frequently as a guest at other colleges; it couldn't be because he enjoyed the food on offer from St. Mike's kitchen.

"How are you, m'dear?" he asked her now. He was the kind of man who called women m'dear, especially when he couldn't recall their names. "Lovely day, isn't it?"

"Oh, yes," she agreed, falling into line. "Quite."

"Will you be at the dinner tomorrow?"

"Oh, yes, of course. Quite looking forward to it. Just popping into the bar and then back to work on the thesis!" she said heartily.

"Quite, quite! You may find one or two of our visitors there. Pay them no mind."

"Quite!"

The college bar, like all such amenities, was the heart and soul of the college. It nestled in a room just off the main entrance hall, near the Great Hall, and with a view over the front grounds. Small and cozy, it was surrounded on three sides by leather-padded benches; the bar itself ran the length of the fourth wall. It was largely intended for use by the undergraduate and graduate students, and although college Fellows were in theory welcome to mingle, they (horrified by the very idea) preferred to do their drinking in the sanctuary of the exclusive SCR at the far side of the Great Hall.

There was only one other person in the bar. Somehow she'd become aware of his presence in college without having actually met him. Big and tall, with a voice to match. It was Augie Cramb, returned from his visit to the Eagle and changed for dinner. He was playing about with what looked like a GPS gadget, poking and prodding at its screen.

"Howdy," he said, by way of greeting.

She smiled and nodded, hoping to grab a Coke from that night's bartender (the college kept the students on a rota) and make her escape.

The man was beside her now, one large paw extended. His costume—there was no other word—was a grab-bag of influences, with a tuxedo shirt, jacket, and bowtie paired with black Levis and a cowboy belt. The Wild West meets Brideshead. At least he'd left off the chaps.

"Augie Cramb."

"How do you do. Portia De'Ath."

"You from around here?"

She turned to accept the Coke from across the counter and said, "Only in a manner of speaking. I'm a Visiting Fellow of the college."

Augie's jaw dropped. "You don't say?" He gave her a playful punch on the arm, nearly spilling her drink. "But, wouldn't you be called a Visiting Gal?" He threw back his head and laughed uproariously at this witticism. Portia smiled tightly and said, simply, "No."

Augie threw a fiver on the bar and, taking her arm, led her towards one of the benches. She had two options: Struggle madly as if she were being kidnapped by pirates, or politely acquiesce. The British in her acquiesced.

"I was here as a student, about twenty years ago. They didn't have fellers that looked like you then, I can tell you that."

"What were you reading?" she asked politely.

"Law. Damned silly waste of time—it was my daddy's idea. I always knew I was going into business. Anyway, they sent me an invite for this alumni weekend and it made me nostalgic, you know? Thought I'd come see how the old place was holding up."

"And what are your impressions?"

"They could use an influx of cash, is my impression. Money's being spent for show, but the infrastructure is coming apart. They're gonna lose the chapel roof if they don't act fast. 'Course I know that's why we were invited, and I'm happy to oblige."

"I see. You're in construction, then?"

This caused another explosion of laughter. He had a truly infectious, puckish laugh, like someone who looked at all of life as suitable material for a comedy. Portia, despite earlier misgivings, found herself warming to him.

"Lord, no," he said at last. "I just have lots of money, you see. I'll let someone else repair the roof. It's why we're all here, this group, this weekend. We're all loaded."

He didn't appear to be bragging, just stating a fact.

"Anyway, I've been looking forward to this weekend for months. Even though flying is less a pleasure these days and more like being evacuated from a country where rioting has just broken out."

"Do you know all the visitors this weekend?" Portia asked, taking a sip of her drink.

"Yep. Funny thing, that. We had a bumper crop of success stories, I reckon. Most of us what-you-call 'matriculated' at different times, but our years at St. Mike's overlapped. I suppose you've heard of Lexy Laurant?"

Portia grinned, nodded. "Yes, I've also heard of Weetabix."

"Exactly. Everyone knows Lexy, if only from the newspapers. Anyway, I haven't seen her myself yet. She's here with some playboy type in tow, so the bedder who does her room tells me. That's because her ex-husband is here, too."

"You don't say…"

"And his wife."

"Oh. Awkward, that."

Another playful bop on the arm. "You can say that again, Visiting Gal." Much as she liked him, she was pretty certain if he called her that again she'd wrest the GPS from his hands and beat him about the head with it. "I remember James—Sir James, as I suppose we must now call him," Augie went on, oblivious. "Everything dress-right-dress with that one. Always knew which fork to use. La-di-da. I saw him and the missus just this afternoon. Too grand for the likes of me, a'course. But I'll tell you what..." Here he lowered his voice confidentially, decreasing his range to half a mile. "I knew them when. Maybe that's why they've no time for me now. You reckon?"

"I reckon." At the entrance to the room stood an attractive woman of perhaps forty years of age, of medium height but, in Portia's estimation, dangerously thin. The woman's most remarkable feature was her abundant coppery crown of curly hair, which seemed to take on a life of its own as she bounced into the room. "Hello, Augie," she said. "Long time no see."

"Gwenn!" he shouted. Augie leapt up and the curly head vanished momentarily inside a bear hug.

"I'm sure they've no time for me, either," she said, once released. "Especially since I'm one of those reporters covering Lexy. Hello." Here she aimed a hand in Portia's direction.

"I recognize you from the news, of course," said Portia. "I should say, from the news desk on the telly—channel YTV, isn't it?"

Gwenn Pengelly, nodding, continued:

"I'll be writing a worshipful little piece on Lexy, of course. Too tailor-made for the likes of me, this weekend."

"I have to admit I'm curious," said Portia. "What was she like? I mean, back before she became so well known?"

Augie having returned with a drink for Gwenn and a refill for Portia, Gwenn addressed the ceiling, apparently with the effort of remembrance.

"Lexy was lovely," she said at last, "and she didn't really know it then. Maybe she doesn't know it now. Always carefully turned out, nicely dressed and all that. But it was as if she were dressing to please everyone but herself. Had a gorgeous figure and could have gotten away with anything. But she somehow always chose to wear what would give the least offense to the majority. She was the only one at the annual Garden party who wore a hat to match her outfit. You see the kind of thing I mean—the Queen wears clothes like that. It's only later she began to acquire her reputation as a fashion icon."

Portia, realizing Gwenn's description told her little of Lexy's character, in which she was more interested than in her clothes, merely asked, "And Sir James?"

"Oh, yes, as Augie says, we have to get used to Sir-ing him now, don't we? What was he like? Good looking, gifted, polished. Lexy, never slow on the uptake in these matters, was after him like a shot. Then India went after him, or he went after her. India won the toss. Quite the scandal, wasn't it, Augie?"

But Augie, fiddling with the settings on his electronic device, appeared less than interested in this ancient news from the romance front.

"Urghmph," he said.

As often will happen, one of the subjects of their gossip walked through the door just then. He nodded to the group—was it only guilt that made some of them think it was rather a cool nod? But having been served his drink, he walked over to join them. Portia's first thought was that Gwenn's assessment was right: Sir James was handsome in a rather retro, drawing-room comedy sort of way. Intelligence shone from his somewhat hooded eyes, separated by a large Roman nose. His wealth quietly announced itself via his impeccable grooming and the cut of his suit, cunningly designed to make him look both broader in the shoulders and leaner through the waist than he likely was. An embryonic paunch had been discretely disguised and even rendered acceptable by a tailor of some cunning: the Savile Row version of the Aloha shirt.

Just then a woman entered on the arm of the Bursar. Sir James turned towards her, his face transformed by a welcoming smile. Portia had the fleeting impression of a comfortable-looking, middle-class woman, but one who had been made up for a Cinderella outing—she was appearing in the "after" photo so beloved of women's magazines. Her style of dress, like Sir James', was of an impeccable pedigree, but somehow Portia suspected she'd be much more at home in trousers, sweater, and boots. The woman continued chatting with a clearly besotted Bursar as Portia wondered at the woman's appeal. From what she could overhear, the Bursar was talking about accounting methods and balance sheets. Portia heard him call her Lady Bassett. Sir James' wife, then. She looked completely enthralled in the conversation, and the Bursar's chest visibly puffed out as he warmed to his theme before such a rapt audience.

With the influx into the small room, Portia felt this was her chance to depart. She did not want to in some way get sucked into dinner in Hall tonight. Too much work to do on my thesis, she thought, without a trace of irony.

But her escape was momentarily blocked by the entrance of a vision of angelic beauty. A woman wearing a gold lamé dress that clung like a mermaid's skin stood in the doorway. Portia, svelte as she was, wondered how many hours in the gym were required to produce a figure that could have been sculpted from marble. Adding to the illusion of flawlessness, the woman's complexion, thick as cream, might never have seen the sun; her hair had been artfully arranged into a haloed perfection of light-and-dark blonde strands. This could only be Lexy Laurant.

The goddess, on entering the room, looked immediately, as if instinctively, at Lady Bassett, who offered a weak grimace of acknowledgement on her own freckled, lived-in face. It was probably meant to be a smile, but seemed somehow hostile, even threatening. Lexy returned the grimace, and gave Sir James a passing, haughty glance. Then, with a sniff, she turned heel and shimmered away.

It was altogether a somewhat childish performance, and someone—no one was later sure who it was—was heard to mutter: "God, but don't you just want to choke her sometimes?"

———

It was much later that night that Portia saw, or rather heard, Sir James and his wife again. Portia had gone out to collect her takeaway, brought it back to her room (along with the guilty indulgence of a fairy cake from the Elizabeth Barrett Bakery), and watched the BBC on the telly as she ate. Then she'd turned again to working on her novel, and several hours passed without her noticing they'd gone. She'd sat until the room grew quite dark except for the cone of light cast by the desk lamp against the burnished wood of her writing table.

"An atmosphere of tension," she wrote, then crossed out "tension" and wrote "fear?" She looked at the words in her notebook, bought new that evening from Heffer's. Why did she feel that so strongly, she wondered? The words had come unbidden, unrelated to the novel. Try as she might, she could not shake off the sudden sense of a fatal change, as of tectonic plates shifting beneath the buildings of St. Mike's.

She stood and stretched out the ache from the back of her neck, and shook the writer's cramp from her hands. A walk before retiring was needed; maybe she'd ring to see if St. Just was still at work. She knew the college dinner had ended—along with the perfumed night air, several voices had wafted up through her open window as people left the Hall. She'd smiled as she overheard someone say, commenting on the meal just consumed, "That was pureed spinach, I'm nearly certain, but what was the fowl? Was it seagull, do you think?" The Bursar had struck again. Meals in Hall tended to feature gristle flanked by minute traces of meat. It was the reason so many students became vegetarians. In most cases, it had nothing to do with regard for their friends in the animal kingdom. Oddly, the Bursar was not offended by the unremitting student complaints about the food. To the contrary, he regarded it as the highest compliment to his ability to feed a large number of people for a pittance—a veritable song of praise to his incessant ingenuity.

Portia walked downstairs, past the SCR, now filled with visitors gathering for their after-dinner port, and headed towards the Fellows' Garden. It was where she often walked, regardless of the weather, to settle her mind at the end of the day.

She'd forgotten the visitors had been granted access to the Fellows' Garden that weekend, and came upon the couple by surprise. The door into the garden stood open, and they didn't see or hear her, too engrossed were they in conversation. Instinctively, she stood back until she was hidden from their view.

They sat on a bench that was screened by a trellis, the vines trained into the shape of a heart. The Garden itself was in the design of a French Parterre, with low plantings divided by gravel footpaths and the whole surrounded by walls cloaked in English ivy. The large Garden was overlooked by a first-floor gallery over a cloister walk, with the gallery leading to the dining hall.

"It's just a feeling I have, James." The aristocratic, nasal tones of Lady Bassett were unmistakable. "It would be better if we left. I'll just claim a mysterious virus—you know the kind of thing. We can make it right with the Master at a later date."

"Perhaps you're right, India," His answering voice, low and soothing, also carried clearly to where Portia stood.

"Do you mean it?"

"If it makes you happy, of course I mean it. I'll have a word with the Master. It's just a bit awkward, that's all."

"I'll tell you what's jolly well awkward is Lexy's being here. I think it's one of her blasted games, James, I really do. She so loves creating a scene. Don't you remember?"

He shifted. Something in her tone seemed to have affected him. He sat for a long moment, looking at her, then took her hand in his.

"Let's talk about it in the morning," he said, his worry clear in his voice. "If you still want to go then, we'll leave."

He stood suddenly. Portia, afraid of discovery, shrank back and started to slip away. Just then, she saw something flash in the shadows of the cloister walk, the shape of a woman in a dress of gold lamé—a most unsuitable costume for undercover observation (and surely a bit of overkill, even for dinner in Hall).

Portia also had the sense that someone else was watching this little tableau of spies and espied. She felt rather than saw a shadow draw back from a window in the library overlooking the Garden, a window which stood open to the summer breeze. A lack of privacy was always a feature of college life. Making her escape, Portia nearly collided with someone as she turned a corner, heading for the main stairs.

"I'm looking for Lexy," the man said, exactly as if everyone in the world would know whom he meant, as much of the world would. Fully taking in Portia's appearance, he smiled appreciatively. "But you'll do," he said. He was a broad-shouldered, dark-haired man of muscular build. His broad smile displayed perfect white teeth, and he spoke perfect English with an overlay of accent from the Southern Hemisphere. He announced that he was Geraldo Valentiano, as if this, too, were a name she would recognize.

"I haven't seen her," Portia lied, without quite knowing why. It had almost certainly been Lexy in the gold lamé—what were the chances another woman would be wandering the college in a similar dress?

"She's probably mooning about the college somewhere. She told me she always did that when she was upset, even twenty years ago."

"Upset?" asked Portia.

"You don't want to know. She's been moody since we got here, and it's looking like it's only going to get worse. Now she's disappeared immediately after dinner, and I've half a mind to leave her and go back up to London. If she had been a proper wife to James none of this would have happened, anyway. Are you free?"

Portia, not knowing if he meant free as in available, or free as in no charge, felt that one answer would suffice for both.

"No," she said, brushing past him and up the stairs. Good heavens, she thought, letting herself into her flat. Much more of this and I will have a thoroughly jaded view of men. She thought with more than a little longing of St. Just, her eyes lingering on the most recent bouquet of flowers he'd brought her, which stood in a vase on a table in her front hall. A single petal had fallen on the table. She wondered if he were still at work so late.

She looked up at the sky, spotted a bright star, and wished upon it. But her prayer wouldn't be answered just yet.

LIGHTING UP

THE NEXT DAY WITH its full schedule of lectures and tours passed without incident, and Saturday evening arrived. Sebastian and Saffron were in her room in St. Mike's, where they had just made love, and they lay rather self-consciously folded in one another's arms. They had seen magazine ads, mostly for perfume, of how this pose of sybaritic abandon was supposed to look: glistening, tangled limbs and tousled curls; heads thrown back to gaze into one another's eyes in spellbound, satiated adoration. But because Sebastian did not adore, only Saffron held her head at this awkward angle. And it was much too cold in her room for abandoned limbs.

"Time to go," he said.

"I know," she replied, too quickly. Her voice, which she had tried to train since meeting Sebastian into the self-confident bray of the upper classes, usually betrayed her, this time breaking in the middle of the two short syllables like a schoolboy's. She cleared her throat and aimed for a lower register.

"I have work to do," she added firmly but unconvincingly. He was making moves to get out of bed. Think of something to ask, quickly.

"How's it going with the parents? Have you seen them today?"

"Yes. It was ghastly. Bloody Lexy being here is causing no end of strain. I've even wondered…"

"Wondered?" she asked, treading gently, gently. It wasn't like Seb to "share," as the American students would say. These few sentences were as gold to her. She didn't want to rush at him, make him clam up.

"I told you. I've wondered if she has some vague hope of getting back together with my stepfather."

"There's a cracked idea." Saffron gave a gentle snort of contempt, to mask her guilty realization of how similar were their situations, hers and Lexy's. The Americans would probably tell them both it was time to "let go and move on," and they'd be right. How easy it was to spout brainless platitudes.

"Isn't it just? I really don't think James would be that mad, but you never know… he's such a stick; I never understood what my mother sees in him, really… I wish she'd go away… stay away from them. If anyone hurt India, I swear…"

Saffron, thrilled at these disjointed disclosures, wisely kept quiet, but she was thinking, not for the first time, that Sebastian could be a bit of a mummy's boy. He'd do whatever it took to make his mother happy and keep her that way. The thought of James leaving his mother to reunite with the gorgeous Lexy—she could see it made Sebastian livid.

"Maybe you could have a word?" she suggested tentatively.

Sebastian, no longer listening, swung his legs over the side of the bed and reached for his rucksack. He had brought his kit with him to save time. He always did that. She knew how much rowing meant to him—she was reconciled to the fact he wanted that Blue more than he wanted anything, certainly more than he wanted her—but couldn't he at least pretend reluctance to leave? Maybe it was time, fretted Saffron, to start a slimming regime. She had put on a couple of pounds lately ... The words of a Tracy Chapman song went through her head, as they often did when she thought of Seb:

Maybe if I told you the right words

At the right time you'd be mine.

"Couldn't you ..." she began. Don't say it.

Sebastian began pulling on his rowing shorts and shirt. He reached for his warm-up top.

"Couldn't I what?" His back was to her, which made it easier. Whatever you do, Don't Say It.

"Couldn't you stay, just a bit? This once?" Oh, fuck. She knew better than this. She had no mind left when it came to Seb. Fuck fuck fuck it. Keep your face still and flat. Don't let him see.

He turned. He wasn't angry, as she'd feared. It was worse. From the condescending, pitying smirk on his face, Saffron had her confirmation that those were not the right words. Those were precisely all the wrong words, lined up in the wrong order, and said in the wrong tone of voice. And definitely at the wrong time. Full points.

It was his leaving a bit early that had thrown her off, she thought. Otherwise she'd have been smart enough, calm enough, to keep her mouth shut.

Sebastian said nothing, just knelt to tie his shoes. Then he picked up his rucksack and headed for the door. As he was leaving, he threw over his shoulder the three little words that made her heart, which had plummeted like something thrown through an open trapdoor, lift again with hope.

"See you tomorrow."

But his tone was dismissive, like a king ordering the removal of a chamber pot, and she worried over this for a long while, playing and replaying the whole scene in her head. Rewind. Couldn't you stay? Oh my God, what had she been thinking? Play ... just a bit? This once? Rewind. Just a bit?

Anger, the only fitting response to his boorish behavior, never entered into it. The option of never seeing him again wasn't a choice that existed for Saffron. She was too amazed, too in awe, that Seb had ever looked her way in the first place, let alone chosen to spend time with her.

That the awe was the reason he would leave her one day—that she knew already.

———

The path to the boathouse skirted the sanctum of the Fellows' Garden, so Sebastian missed witnessing any scenes that might be playing out there. He walked instead along the outside brick wall of the garden, even though he had long since learned how to take a forbidden shortcut through whenever the coast was clear. With all the visitors, he doubted the favored meeting spot would be clear tonight. He passed by Gwenn Pengelly—he recognized her from the telly. She was headed away from the tennis courts towards the main building. She seemed to want to engage him in conversation so he just gave her a wave of his hand and kept going.

He looks dark, she thought. Obsessed. Too serious for his age, that one.

Sebastian quickened his pace. Having dawdled, he was late now. He had his routine, and it seldom varied; it unsettled him when it varied. He hadn't missed a day on the water except when a red flag warned of foggy or windy conditions, or the stream was running too fast. First, he's have a warm-up in the gym, including a spot of weight-lifting and a stint on the much-despised ergometer, then he would carry the single scull from the boathouse and feed its awkward length into the river. He would lock in the oars and, grabbing both oars in one hand, step lightly into the narrow scull, maneuver expertly into the seat, and secure his feet onto the footboards.

Nearly an hour later he was ready to set out. The weather being warm, the air heavy, he had brought with him a drink bottle, which he slotted behind his shoes in the scull. He took a few minutes to settle himself, breathing deeply, then used one oar to push off into the river. He began building up his pace slowly, the boat slivering through the water and leaving a ribbon trail behind. Immediately, he felt calmer, anonymous and alone, just himself testing himself against the limits of his endurance. To Seb, sculling was much harder than rowing, because of the need to keep an even pull on both oars. In a way, he preferred it, for the challenge. He thought he might always prefer the isolation of the single scull to the camaraderie of a crew boat.

He was St. Mike's star: Everyone knew he was headed for the Blue Boat—that he'd one day compete in the famous, four-and-a-quarter-mile Oxford-Cambridge race. Kevin, the club captain, granted him more leeway than most, even though Kev, whose father was career Army, had a morbid fear of the early morning marshals and stayed well within the rules. Kev reminded Sebastian, who assessed any rule in terms of whether it served his own purposes, of a dog behind an invisible electric fence, terrified of setting one paw wrong and being zapped silly. Imagine living your life that way—Sebastian couldn't. Old Kev even believed, when closer observation of his character might easily have convinced him otherwise, that Sebastian always operated within the rules. Even if he'd been so inclined, that was getting harder each day: There was so much congestion on the Cam a flurry of regulations had been issued to try to disentangle everyone and their oars. With the rules changing so often, the chances were good there was always someone out there illegally, rowing or spinning at the wrong place and time.

Still, trying to outwit the EMMs for the heck of it was one of Sebastian's favorite pastimes, although their main interest was to be on the lookout for too much early noise and too many novice boats on the river. Sebastian knew just how far to push it, and went no further. He wasn't going to risk what he already thought of as his seat in the Blue Boat.

Sebastian's thoughts kept pace with his steadily increasing speed, his powerful leg drive propelling the scull with ease: So what if the boats these days seemed to be filled with long, tall graduate students, some doing bullshit degrees just so they could row. I can compete with the best of them. I will win.

Sebastian was far from being a novice rower, even when he had been a novice. He had grown up near Cambridge, and knew the river well, from Baitsbite to Jesus. For much of his young life, he had withstood hot days in the sun and bitter cold mornings in the rain just to be on the water. He now knew the river, he thought, as well as he knew Saffron. Better than. He knew the moment boats had to cross at the Gut and Plough Reach; he knew where crews would be spinning, just upstream of Ditton Corner. He knew where the river narrowed to the point it was barely possible for two eights to squeeze past each other.

He knew that come Michaelmas term, between Chesterton footbridge and Jesus Lock, the junior and novice crews would be menacing everyone else out on the water. Uncoxed boats, rowing blind, the steerer's mind elsewhere, were a particular hazard. It didn't help that the river was increasingly crowded with rowers of all skill levels, and that long boats motoring past often had a complete disregard for the rowers, rather seeming to steer straight towards them. The "party" long boats of an evening, carrying drunken passengers, were the worst. No matter how many regulations CUCBC might pass, you couldn't regulate against stupidity. The dangerous corners of the Cam—Queen Elizabeth Way, Green Dragon, Ditton, and Grassy—each year awaited the unwary.

An uncoxed boat was bearing down on him now, all of the rowers, to Sebastian's trained eye, too quick into the catch, or splashing their blades about in a domino effect from the stern. He eased up and gave a shout—it was that collection of berks from Jesus again. This time of year, there were usually only town crews on the river; very few, if any, college crews like this lot; maybe the odd post-graduate crew. Annoyed at the interruption, Sebastian strove to regain his rhythm, his thoughts also changing course, to his parents, the famous Lexy, all the oldies who had begun arriving the day before. Some of them in their forties, from the look of them. Really old. It was a wonder they could walk. Losing their hair, wearing glasses in old-fashioned frames, flaunting their kangaroo paunches. Trying too hard, some of them, to look with it. And that was just the women. It was pathetic.

Thirty, to Sebastian, was a great age. Christ had been thirty-three when he died, hadn't he?

Thinking: Only thirteen years to go, Sebastian pulled harder and the scull shot away, skimming the glassy water like a gull.

——

Sebastian was well downriver as the old members enjoyed a celebratory meal, preceded by drinks in the SCR.

Portia, wearing her academic gown over a dark sheath, had been making her way downstairs when she ran into Lexy, coming from the other end of the corridor. Tonight Lexy had exchanged her vamp-of-the-sea look for a black one-button pantsuit that accented her whippet waist, with a filmy white blouse spilling out of the low-cut jacket. She had looped her black academic gown over one arm, along with a small and sparkly evening bag, so as not, Portia imagined, to obscure her splendid appearance just yet. Portia also imagined it was the slightly longer gown of a Master of Arts; Lexy having matriculated as an undergraduate the requisite number of years before, the "promotion" was automatic.

Portia commented on the elegance of her suit.

Lexy nodded, abstractedly acknowledging the compliment. Her manner was jumpy, which might have been explained by her next words:

"Someone broke into my room—I guess while we were at the wine tasting today," she said. "Went through my things."

"Oh, no. I am sorry. That kind of thing is rare around here, you know. The students will 'liberate' the occasional food item from one of the communal kitchens, but that's only because they're starving half the time, poor things."

"Well, it's happened now."

"We'll have to make sure the Master knows. What was taken?"

Lexy hesitated, a frown creasing her otherwise flawless complexion. "That's just it. Nothing is missing, that I can see. It's just … a bit creepy, is all. Considering."

Portia didn't have time to wonder what she was meant to consider, for Lexy had gone on to a new topic:

"You'll be at High Table, I suppose? What a bore. I was going to ask you to sit with me and Geraldo."

Portia thought this would probably be more entertaining than what went on at High Table, and said so.

"The thing is," said Lexy confidingly, peering up at Portia out of her legendarily blue eyes, "I'm rather afraid Sir James may try to sit next to me."

Portia, who had gained the impression Lexy thought that an outcome devoutly to be wished, was confused. The famous Lexy might do many things, she felt, but confide in the likes of a perfect stranger like Portia wasn't one of them. Not without an ulterior motive.

"Afraid?" she prompted.

"Oh, I don't mean afraid afraid. It's just jolly awkward. You do see?"

"You think he's carrying a torch, do you?"

"All indications are so, yes." Lexy blushed becomingly. "What do you think?"

Portia smiled. "I'm hardly in a position to know. Has he been bothering you?"

"Oh. Well, no, not exactly. James is too much the gentleman for that. It's more this hangdog look whenever he sees me. The sad eyes following me everywhere. It's obvious he wants to get me alone. I can only guess why."

Portia, who didn't really believe Lexy's answer to a request for a chat would be "no," pondered the meaning behind this extraordinary conversation. While Portia knew Lexy in the way one did know someone who was constantly in the news, Lexy could have no idea who Portia was. Portia was used to being confided in—she had that kind of face, she guessed—but this was ... different. It had, thought Portia (beginning to descend the stairs, Lexy glued to her side), all the hallmarks of a woman scorned wishing to be vindicated before the world of society, the world in which Lexy operated, the only world Lexy knew. If anything, Portia was certain Lexy would welcome Sir James' approaches, if only so she could turn around and leave him in a publicly splashy way.

Now, how to get myself out of the middle here? she wondered.

Fortunately, they had reached the SCR by this point, where the buzz of animated conversation could be heard even through the heavy wood door.

"I'm sure it will be all right," Portia, who had no such certainty, told Lexy. "Oh! I think I hear your friend Geraldo."

Geraldo Valentiano was indeed in the room, talking loudly about polo in what seemed to be his trademark predatory fashion with none other than Sir James' wife. He might have been leaning in a bit too close, but India, for her part, was openly admiring his biceps. Portia slid a glance over to Lexy to see how she was taking this, and was surprised to see a look of genuine indifference on her lovely face. Her eyes were seeking someone else. Three guesses who that might be, thought Portia.

Then Portia noticed the search operation was mutual—that is, Sir James stood near the drinks tray looking vaguely around the room, but at the sight of Lexy his gaze, anxious and worried, settled immediately on her. Portia wondered if there weren't some truth in Lexy's take on the situation. Odder things have happened, she thought, than old flames reigniting.

But Lexy headed straight for Geraldo, who had left India with the promise of fetching her a drink. He had stopped, however, to admire his profile in a gold-framed mirror, a distraction which had temporarily derailed his mission. Lexy, with a meaningful glance at Sir James, was heard to tell Geraldo and the assembly in a loud voice that someone had broken into her room.

Sir James looked about to respond, but a couple walked in just then, looking unmistakably American in a way Portia found hard to define. Perhaps it was that their clothes looked starchily brand new, as if fresh out of the boxes. The man wore a Masters' gown, also shining in its newness. The woman Portia assumed was his wife wore a dress straight from the Paris couture collections, but of an unbecoming shade of purple under her own academic status gown.

Just after the pair came Hermione Jax, Fellow of the college and one of its most stalwart supporters, financial and otherwise. Hermione in academic regalia looked to be in her element, as in fact she was. Disapprovingly, she scanned the assembled company with her protuberant, long-lashed eyes, then made her way over to the drinks tray where the Master and Bursar were now standing.

Over the growing volume of conversation, Portia heard Sir James say, "It would be jolly fun. You're quite right. A row for old times' sake." She turned and saw he was talking with the Reverend Otis and the big Texan from the bar. "Lexy was our coxswain, back in the day. I wonder if you could persuade her?"

"That's a grand idea," agreed Augie Cramb. "I used to love to row. Do we have enough to make an eight?"

"Doubtful," said Sir James. "But we could manage a four, I think. I say, Geraldo, you rowed for your college, didn't you?"

Geraldo, tearing himself away from his image, said, "Of course. I was and am a superb athlete." Clasping his hands in front of his stomach, he flexed his chest muscles by way of demonstration.

"I saw a young man decked out for rowing headed towards the river earlier," said Augie.

"That was my son," said Sir James, not looking at Augie. His voice held an odd, gruff note that might have been melancholy.

"Will he be joining us for dinner?" asked Augie.

"He's got his own friends." India had walked over to her husband. She took his arm proprietarily. Just then the gong sounded for dinner, and James led the way towards the dining hall, rather charging ahead and dragging India with him. Portia wondered:

Was he hoping to snag a seat next to Lexy? If so, he was out of luck. It was Augie Cramb, unencumbered and making an heroic sprint, who managed to gain the coveted spot.

—

A short time later, the St. Mike's alumni group sat beneath the painted bosses of the Hall's hammerbeam roof and the painted eyes of the former Masters' portraits, steadily working its way through the appetizer course (although as someone observed: "Appetizer is rather a misnomer in this case, wouldn't you say?"). The conversation gradually gathered strength and became a collection of discordant noises, like a symphony warming up on untuned instruments. Adding to the cacophony, four undergraduates, huddled in a corner, sawed away on stringed instruments until they were finally banished by the Master, well before they'd run through their repertoire.

Because of the presence of the distinguished guests, the High Table was unoccupied, the Master, Bursar, and Dean having literally come down from on high, the better to exercise the personal touch in their fundraising efforts. These were dark days indeed for the Master, who, having sacrificed much to attain his status in the college, loved his usual position above the crowd. The Bursar felt similarly. The Reverend Otis, however, was always happiest amongst what he endearingly thought of as his flock.

Portia, who was seated next to him, had trouble hearing what was said throughout the meal, and remembered little of it afterwards. Of course he, dear man, tended to waffle on about nothing in particular, but in the most soothing way. One felt positively shriven after an hour with the Dean.

The American woman (Portia had learned her name was Constance and her husband was Karl) had a voice like the crazed yapping of a caged dog. The acoustics in the room had always been terrible, and with drink the noise level became intolerable. Still, above it all could be heard the yap, yap, yapping of Constance Dunning. She seemed to be discussing triangles, which puzzled Portia, until she realized she meant relationships.

"Divorce is always such a pity. I don't care what the circumstances." Portia heard this plainly. "Don't you agree, Karl?"

Of course, Karl did agree.

Constance's yap was punctuated here and there by loud guffaws from Augie Cramb, who was clearly going all out to impress Lexy, who in her turn was probably secretly storing up the Texan's buffoonerisms to amuse her friends back in London.

Gwenn Pengelly had walked in a minute late, earning a frown of disapproval from the Master. Gwenn smiled unperturbedly and took the nearest empty seat, which happened to be on Karl's other side at the far end of the table.

Portia looked down the table, past the field of candelabra flames that flickered like gold against the polished wood, and saw that Sir James, far from Lexy, was flanked by his wife on one side and Hermione Jax on the other. How rare a sight, thought Portia: Although Hermione was always one to stand on ceremony, she had apparently happily relinquished her spot at High Table for a seat next to the illustrious Sir James.

For his part Sir James, awaiting the next course with every appearance of joyful anticipation (that smile will soon be wiped off your face, thought Portia, or I don't know the college chef), leaned over to talk with Hermione. But his eyes frequently drifted, as if by compulsion, in the direction of Lexy Laurant.

——

An hour had passed in apparent conviviality. Had the Bursar but realized it, his cost-cutting schemes usually back-fired in this regard: The inedible food led to over-consumption of wine, saving the college little and almost certainly adding to the monthly expenditures. It did, however, frequently lend a bacchanalian air to the tenor of the evening meals, featuring many a loud, impromptu toast to the founder of the college and its various benefactors. Gwennap Pengelly and Geraldo Valentiano, in particular, might have been said to have overindulged, judging by the increasing volume of their laughter. That was unfortunate on this particular evening, about which the police were going to ask numerous questions that almost none of the guests were going to be able to answer.

The conversation ranged and wandered, as conversations of the reunited will, over the fields of "Do you remember so-and-so?" and "Whatever happened to what's-his-name?" Hermione Jax, however, had other things on her mind and was emboldened to speak that mind. With Hermione, this was not uncommon.

"I realize I was probably not your first choice in dinner companions this evening," she said to Sir James, launching into one of the few conversations that would later be remembered.

While what Hermione had said was indisputably true, Sir James, true to his upbringing, demurred politely.

"See here," she continued. "May I give you some advice?"

Sir James, guessing at the topic, said quickly, coldly, "I'd much rather you didn't."

"Yes, I suppose when one can guess at the advice already, one would rather not hear it. An observation, then. You've already crossed the Rubicon with regard to Lexy, you know. Years ago. There's no going back."

Sir James arranged his silverware, which was one centimeter out of true.

"There's always a way back when it's a question of forgiveness," he said gruffly. "Otherwise we'd all be … doomed."

"A bit melodramatic that, what?"

Lowering his voice still further, although it was highly doubtful his wife could hear them over the din, he said, "I should say it depends on how many lives you think you have. I believe I have only this one, and I've made a right cock-up of … a few things. I won't have a million chances to put it right. This weekend is it."

Hermione, being in many respects an intelligent woman, forbore to ask what his wife would make of this new resolve of his. She could guess, only too well.

———

As the alumni dinner ended, Sebastian was still moving with practiced speed along the river, his sculls cutting rhythmically through the dark water, the sky as it deepened towards night making him feel both invisible and invincible. It was nearly Lighting Up, and he was reluctant to stop when his strength was nowhere near exhausted, but he didn't want to be too flagrant about bending the rules. To be selected only for the second boat, which Sebastian regarded as a fate worse than death, was one thing. To accumulate so many fines he was forbidden the river altogether was unthinkable.

Minutes later he slowed as he approached the college; leaning onto the outside scull, he turned the boat until it was parallel to the bank. As he stepped out and lifted the boat from the water, his head was filled with the future glory of winning a Blue and the imaginary applause of onlookers, which is why he never noticed the lumpen pile of black cloth to one side of the boathouse doors. He might not have seen it at all in the light ground mist but that a slight disturbance caught his ear, causing him to turn towards a rustle in the undergrowth. Some small animal making its way to shelter before total darkness fell, perhaps. It was then to the left of the boathouse he noticed a shadow, nothing more. He went to investigate. There was a scull lying on the ground, next to that lumpen pile.

If someone had forgotten to put away the college's equipment there'd be hell to pay, he thought. Was all this stuff lying there when he'd set out? He wasn't sure…he hadn't been looking in that direction.

One year, during May Bumps, a group of undergraduates had thrown a plastic dummy in the water dressed in Queens' colors. Intimidation of their chief rival was the goal. It was the kind of harmless rag that went on all year, usually in the run-up to the Bumps. So Sebastian didn't hesitate, but poked at the lumpen form with the tip of one of his oars.

That didn't feel right, he thought. He couldn't have said why it wasn't right, but the form was softer and more yielding and yet heavier than he, in his limited experience of dummies and lumpen forms, would have expected.

No. No sirree. That couldn't be right.

He stepped a foot closer, peering into the darkness. Then, dropping his oars with a loud, jumbled crash, he ran.

THE PARTY'S OVER

St. Just sat eighteen miles away in another suicidally boring meeting at Hinchingbrooke Park, Huntingdon—headquarters for the Cambridgeshire Constabulary. The meeting had convened some hours ago in a building that looked like a prison, only with larger windows, in a room that resembled a classroom in a particularly underfunded comprehensive school.

It was an unusually late meeting, even by the standards of the new Chief Constable, who would accept nothing less than the one-hundred-percent proven devotion of her team. These after-hours catered meetings had become both her stick (metaphorically) and her carrot (literally) for attaining that devotion. She was delivering herself of her usual views on Crime Management, views illustrated with colorful pie charts displaying crime trends, transgression "hot spots," and intelligence analyses. With all the fervor of the convert to the scientific method, the Chief believed that if only crime could be precisely quantified, it could be made magically to disappear.

As though, thought St. Just, anything as unpredictable and bloody-minded as the criminal element thwarted of its desires could be managed. Pacified, perhaps. 70 Bribed, certainly. Managed, never.

St. Just was sketching a caricature of the Chief in the margins of his hand-out sheet—unobtrusively, he hoped—confining himself to a very small corner of the page, trusting that his occupation and less-than-full attention to the grave matters at hand would go unnoticed. He was trying to capture the look of her hair, which she wore in a shining helmet—impenetrable, St. Just feared, to any idea that could not be summed up in a catchy slogan.

A few more of these interminable meetings, he thought, and I might develop some talent as a miniaturist. Perhaps Hilliard got his start this way.

"Citizen advisory councils are of course crucial," she was saying. Which side, he wondered idly, darkening the Chief's widely spaced eyes, was meant to be on the receiving side of whatever advice was being sent 'round? And if there was one thing that got up St. Just's nose, as his sergeant would have said, it was the kind of claptrap that made the police sound like social workers. "Multicultural Inclusiveness" he understood, but what was "Community Outreach Delivery" when it was at home, he wondered?

And was any of it adding to the number of solved crimes?

The Chief's "Reach Out!" PR campaign continued apace, the Chief wending her way through various stupefying talking points, pausing for emphasis only, it seemed, when she wished to share an insight of spectacular dullness. She remained undaunted by the fact that sending the police door to door in some of the worst neighborhoods in Cambridgeshire had netted them nothing but verbal abuse and several bites requiring stitches from a poodle of peculiarly vicious disposition in Histon. One unfortunate Constable had had the contents of a dustbin emptied on his head from the upper-story window of a rooming house. He was lucky—in another age, it would have been a chamber pot. The dustbin offender remained at large, but for every one captured, it was felt, another would soon grow to take his place. St. Just thought all the reactions perfectly justified, including the poodle's. As one community member had been heard to exclaim, nicely capturing the prevailing philosophy, the very Zeitgeist, as it were: "If we want the bloody police we'll ring for the bloody police."

Since the meeting—lecture, rather—had been planned to run even longer than usual, the Chief Constable had had catered in for the delectation of her team large trays of what he was sure she would call canapés but St. Just would call rabbit food. Thus it was that once he and the rest of her Reach Out! team had finally been freed for the night, he decided to stop on his way home at the Three Jolly Butchers for a leisurely meal and a pint. The pub wasn't crowded, and he easily secured a wooden table to himself near the Inglenook fireplace. He had already placed his order for one of his favorites, the pan-fried pork medallions with bubble and squeak. Looking about now at the low, beamed ceilings, he thought he should bring Portia here soon, as the food was as excellent as the atmosphere. That he had not done so yet was probably because he equated the place with his work, and he struggled, as did most of his colleagues, to draw a firm line between the personal and the official. Events would soon prove this was nearly impossible. He had no sooner been served than his mobile phone vibrated, the surprise jolt sending his fork flying through the air. Blast the thing. He unhooked the device from his belt and looked with apoplectic disbelief at the number. It couldn't be, but it was. The Chief herself, reaching out. Sod it. He was supposed to be off duty. He took the call outside.

"St. Mike's. Yes'm, I certainly know it. A woman. Strangulation, you think. Good God. The University Constabulary…Yes, of course. Quite outside their brief. I'll give Sergeant Fear a ring and we'll be right over."

Ringing off, he punched in the number to Fear's house, cursing the late hour. His right-hand man had taken a short furlough, but needs must. Why did murder always seem to happen after dark? But he knew the answer. "Under cloak of darkness" was a cliché for good reason. Nighttime, when the good and the just were tucked safely before the telly in their homes, no doubt watching a crime show—that was the time the predator went on the move.

———

Someone picked up the receiver on the first ring, but there was dead silence at the other end.

"Emma?" St. Just guessed. "Is that you, Emma?" Silence. Emma was Fear's four-year-old. Four going on thirty-five. What on earth could she be doing up so late?

"Emma, may I speak to your…" What would she call him? "Your daddy, please?" Silence. Thinking he just wasn't using the right vocabulary, he tried again. "Your dadda?" No. "Your Pops? Poppy?" He was running out of options, and he had a murder to investigate. "Your father, please, Emma?"

"Who is that, Emma?" St. Just heard Sergeant Fear call as if from a great height, where no doubt he was, from Emma's perspective.

"It's Inspector St. Just." Her slight lisp rendered this as, "Ith Inthpector Thaint Justh." He felt his heart melt.

"Bye-bye, Emma," said St. Just softly.

"Bye!" yelled Emma, loud enough to pierce an eardrum.

There were sounds of a minor scuffle, and Sergeant Fear came on the line.

"Sorry, Sir. Emma hasn't quite found her volume control yet."

"Just the on-and-off switch, I take it."

He filled his sergeant in on as much of the situation as he knew, concluding, "Someone called the CU Constabulary, who naturally called us in." The Cambridge University Constabulary was a small, non-Home Office force that was most often called upon to deal with crowd control and internal university matters. Murder in a college setting was rare to the point of being unheard of. Quite naturally, the University had called in the Cambridgeshire Constabulary.

St. Just quickly settled his tab with the landlord, who was getting used to these abrupt departures. He offered to package up the meal but, reluctantly, St. Just declined. As these things went, time for the next good meal was hours or days away, and he'd have to exist on the Chief's dainty offerings for a while.

Travelling at a rapid but measured pace along the A14, he arrived at St. Michael's College within minutes of Sergeant Fear, who stood waiting for him at the entrance. Already parked beside

Fear's car in a small lot at the front of the college were the SOCO van and Malenfant's red Daimler.

The two men—St. Just tall, broad, and middle-aged; his sergeant tall, with a youthful gangliness—strode towards the college, their footsteps ringing out against the cobblestones, to the massive wooden double gates, built to withstand the sieges of earlier centuries. They stepped through the inner door cut into the gate for pedestrians. After showing their warrant cards to a shaken Head Porter, who presided from within an intricately carved neo-Gothic cage at the college entrance, they were shown by his assistant the way to the Master's study.

"Frightful business, this," said the Master. He had seen their approach and walked briskly across the first court to greet them, hand out in practiced greeting. They might have been dignitaries come to plant a tree or open a new building. But releasing the handshake, the Master began wringing his own hands distractedly, betraying his anguish at having a corpse on the premises. St. Just had the distinct feeling that the corpse wasn't nearly as worrying as its location: hard by the college boathouse, according to the Chief Constable. The Master confirmed this impression with his next sentence.

"To have this happen this weekend, of all weekends," he said. "And here." He sighed deeply, adding in aggrieved tones, "Why couldn't it have been Jesus?"

St. Just felt Sergeant Fear stiffen beside him in alarm: Were they dealing with a religious mania of some sort? But St. Just, familiar with some of St. Mike's history, assumed the Master meant the nearby Jesus College. It was well known there was strong feeling between the two rivals. Something to do with one of the boat races held between the wars—allegations of sabotage resulting in wounded feelings, hurled insults, and umbrage taken—all the usual. The St. Michael's boat had sunk, if memory served, giving all aboard a good and embarrassing dunking. Such memories ran long and deep in Cambridge.

"I doubt there would be a good time, when you think about it, Sir?" said St. Just. "Or a good place?"

The Master thought for a moment and then said, "No, no, I suppose not."

But he didn't look convinced. How much better if Jesus College were going to be splashed all over the newspapers as a haven for murderers and cutthroats. Applications to St. Michael's would be down next year because of this, no question about it. The students wouldn't mind—they'd love it, in fact, the ghoulish little cretins—but their parents ... Really, it was most distressing. He voiced the last thought aloud.

"I can't begin to tell you how deeply distressing this is. It was our alumni weekend, you see. Well, that's certainly ruined, for a start," he fumed huffily. He might have been a vicar's wife complaining about low participation in the Bring and Buy.

St. Just, watching him, thought he had the kind of face designed for a periwig—the long, high-arched nose, the sullen set of the full but bloodless lips. But St. Just nodded, not without sympathy. It was definitely a sticky wicket: deuced hard to explain to the old members how standards had slipped this far since their day.

"I quite understand your distress," he said. "Now, we will need to talk with you at some length, but for the moment, if you would lead us to where the body was found ..."

This set him off again.

"Body," gasped the Master. "A body at St. Michael's." The man looked to be genuinely in a state of shock, his narrow face drained to a faint gray in the artificial light of the court.

"Sir," said St. Just firmly. "If you wouldn't mind. Time is of the essence in these matters."

The man seemed to gather his wits through an effort of will. His mouth gathered into a puckered twist, he stolidly led them across the close-cropped grass towards the river, the jaunty bounce in his step as he'd walked over to meet the policemen now completely subdued.

SOCO had already established a beachhead. The body of Lexy Laurant remained in situ, hidden by a crime scene tent that was illuminated to an unearthly glare by arc lamps. It was a scene that had all the otherworldly qualities of a low-budget outdoor film set, complete with space aliens—SOCO—pacing the area in a methodical, robot-like search for evidence, wearing booties just a shade away from being Cambridge blue. Two constables conferred to one side of the tent, their heads close together, talking quietly, as if not wishing to disturb the newly dead. The air was laden with the scents of summer and the murmurs of the men; the gentle lapping of the river could just be heard behind the muted silence. The river, regardless and apart, wended its slow, sinuous way towards the River Ouse, which in turn would travel forty miles to meet the North Sea.

A low, light mist was caught in a glimmering haze by the lamps, and lay like a light scarf on the river; no moon was visible in the night sky. As St. Just and his sergeant approached, the air was rent like intermittent lightning by the flash from the stills photographer's camera. Spectators—the staff and visiting members of the college—had long been herded back inside the college by one of the local constables sent to help secure the scene.

St. Just greeted Dr. Malenfant as he emerged from the tent and asked, "Time of death?"

Malenfant gazed laconically at his old friend for a long moment before speaking.

"Always the same with you, isn't it," he said, removing his latex gloves with a fastidious Snap! Snap! "No matter how long since we've seen each other. Just, 'Time of death?' he wants to know." Malenfant, despite his years in England, remained thoroughly French in manner and habit, the more so when agitated. "You may have observed," he continued, "that my holiday at present lacks certain…amenities. For one thing, it is not taking place in France. Puzzlingly, I remain here, in my summer holiday costume, miles from any beach."

St. Just imagined Malenfant, under his protective clothing, was wearing one of those blousy shirts the French seemed to go in for—those shirts that always made him think of old men playing a game of boules—and striped espadrilles on his feet.

"Why, you may ask?" Malenfant was now in full flow. He wore the kind of old-fashioned wire-rimmed glasses that have to be looped to one's ears. He unlooped them now, and paused to slick back his dark hair. "I appreciate your asking. My estimable colleague—my so-called replacement—has been struck down by a summer cold. I am told it is of amazing intensity, this grippe. He would have me believe it borders on pneumonia leading to an early, painful, and slow death. Pah. Between nine-sixteen and nine-fifty."

St. Just judged, correctly, that Malenfant had at last arrived at the answer to the original question.

"That's remarkable precise, even for someone of your gifts," said St. Just mildly.

"She was seen alive at around nine-fifteen. They had a formal dinner and it adjourned then. She was found at nine-fifty by some kid in a boat, so I am told." Malenfant rendered the word as keed. It was a true barometer of his distress when he allowed his flawless English to slip. He pointed to where Sebastian had abandoned the scull. "So you see, you don't really need me at all for time of death. I won't be able to get you a better estimate even after the autopsy. Now, if you'll excuse me, gentlemen. You'll have some preliminary results tomorrow and unless my colleague experiences a miraculous recovery, I will be around to answer your questions. She's been manually strangled, to answer your next question, by a right-handed killer. Stunned first, by someone wielding the scull found by her body, no doubt. No rope, no rape. Bonne nuit."

Poor Malenfant, thought St. Just. The man was a genius, but seldom was anyone so little suited by temperament to the unpredictable demands of his job. Meals, holidays, family occasions—all were sacrificed, routinely but unpredictably, on the altar of the homicide investigation. From no one else would St. Just have tolerated such curtness with equanimity, but Malenfant's written report would, he knew, be a model of over-compensating thoroughness and accuracy—once the man had gotten a grip on himself.

He also knew Malenfant had what he called a mistress in France to whom he longed to return. She would more rightly be called a girlfriend, as Malenfant was not married, but he clung to the fifties noir term as much more seductive, as having that certain je ne sais quoi with which "girlfriend" could not begin to compete. In his own way, the otherwise gloomy Malenfant was a bon vivant who happened to be a top-flight pathologist. Wine, women, song, food—these were things, St. Just knew, to which Malenfant was passionately devoted, although duty always won out. St. Just had asked him once why he continued to do the job he did. He had looked at the policeman as if he were mad. "So I am reminded to live, of course," he had replied.

"One question, Malenfant, before you go," said St. Just.

Malenfant, sighing theatrically, turned slowly back to face him. "Isn't there always?"

"Could a woman have done this?"

"Do you mean is a woman capable psychologically of choking someone to death? If you have to ask that, it is time for you to broaden your acquaintance with the fairer sex. If you mean physically, which I assume you do..." Malenfant reflected, then said, "Given the small physique of the victim, yes. A rather determined woman... but then, by definition, a strangler is determined. There are far simpler ways to kill someone. But given that the victim was almost certainly stunned, then strangled, it would be an easy enough job for anyone, man or woman. This is why accidental asphyxiation during sex games is such a recurring feature of my professional life—it doesn't take all that much time or strength and before the person realizes too much strength has been applied—poof! A minute or two's compression of the carotid arteries will do it. By the way, I'm certain we'll find your killer wore gloves."

Here Malenfant studied his own slender hands, with their long, elegant fingers—a pianist's hands. St. Just likewise looked at those hands, whose job it was to plunge into a victim's body and … well. The mind recoiled. Although both men served the same cause of bringing the guilty to justice, often in unpleasant ways, he would take his job over Malenfant's any day.

"Yes, it could have been a man or a woman. Take a little peek for yourself; just don't go inside the tent just yet. We'll let forensics do their work, shall we?—they might have more to add. Once again, I must bid you gentlemen bonne nuit."

To his retreating back, Sergeant Fear murmured, "I always think he's rather like an undertaker."

"A très chic undertaker," agreed St. Just.

They walked over to the tented entrance. The body was already in a bag, ready for transport. St. Just motioned to one of the attendants, who unzipped the bag to reveal the victim's face. A woman who had been beautiful, then. Blonde and in her thirties, maybe early forties, with regular, pretty features distorted by a mask of fear. Or was it surprise? St. Just felt he recognized her from somewhere. The artificial light caught the diamonds in her earlobes and the gold at her neck, setting them aglitter like the jewels on a pharaoh's coffin.

One of the SOCO team approached St. Just and Sergeant Fear.

"Her evening bag was found near the body, Sir. Well, we assume it was hers. We're taking it to the lab for a closer look for prints. I've written out a list of the contents—nothing out of the ordinary though." He handed him the list.

St. Just asked Fear, "At what distance are we from the college proper, would you say? A five-minute walk?"

"Less. It took us about three minutes, but we were in no particular hurry."

St. Just nodded. He looked up and about him, taking in the scene. Across the river, the lights of one of St. Mike's oldest and largest foes, Jesus College, glared balefully, as if in retaliation for the SOCO lamps. There once had been a bridge joining the colleges but an early Master of St. Mike's, goaded beyond the limits of his patience, had literally had it burned down during an ongoing feud over access rights. There was also, St. Just noted, no footpath.

"Have someone find this young man who discovered her body—let him know he's to remain available to us. We'll need to decide the batting order for talking to everyone."

The Master had been hovering some distance away from the crime scene. As the two men approached, having overheard them he said, "You mean Sebastian Burrows. The young man. He's inside with the others. I've asked them all to wait up for you in the Senior Combination Room. Was that all right?"

"That was precisely fine. Let me have a further word with you first, Master. In your study, perhaps?"

GETTING TO KNOW YOU

HE SENT THE MASTER on ahead, having arranged that they would meet him in his study in a few minutes. St. Just exchanged a few words with one of the constables, then he and Sergeant Fear headed towards the college proper. They ran into Portia at the foot of the main staircase. She looked as if she'd been waiting for St. Just, as no doubt she had.

St. Just nodded to Sergeant Fear, indicating he should wait for him with the Master, then turned to her. She was wearing what he knew was her standard summer work outfit: cropped black yoga pants and a matching sleeveless top. She was looking even more delectable than in his imaginings. But first things first.

"So, what do you know about all this?" he asked her.

"I just wish I knew more," she said. "I wasn't part of the group. This really has little to do with me, this weekend, so I paid little attention, and I've been wracking my brains since I heard what happened tonight. Actually, the Master let it be known that he preferred it if the 'loose ends' hanging about—the summer people—laid low until the old members had left. If we absolutely felt we had to emerge from our rooms for sustenance, we were to strive to look dignified, intelligent, and sober. What he thinks we look like on usual occasions one can scarcely imagine. In any event, it hardly mattered. The honored (read: wealthy) guests were all housed in the Brooke Wing, separate from the revolting masses. I just met people in passing, really—a chat here and there. I've been up to my ears in The Paper Without End."

Even with St. Just, Portia could not bring herself to reveal how often she abandoned the dratted thesis to turn to the almost visceral pleasure—the sights, sounds, smells—of the world inhabited by her fictional detective. Of working out the puzzling dynamics of his latest case.

"It's all right," St. Just said. "Just tell me whatever you remember of what's happened tonight. Start with after the dinner."

"Well..." she began. "I went up to my room after dinner to freshen up. This was a bit after nine-fifteen. Then I came straight back downstairs and headed into the SCR for a glass of port. The Master had invited me to join the group. I gather he felt I wouldn't let the side down too badly. Some of the Fellows—Professor Puckle, for example—might start droning on about Lacanian theory, or Freudian analysis, or something, which is pretty much everyone's cue to run for cover. So it was quite an honor to be asked, if you knew the way the Master's mind works. Frightful snob."

"Did you have much to do with Lexy Laurant?"

"Hardly anything," Portia replied, her lips curved in a little moue of disappointment. "She was lovely to look at, is nearly all I can tell you. My impression, for what it's worth, was that she was massively insecure, the type to cling for ballast to any-one who came along. I think she was flirting with the Argentine she brought along in order to make Sir James jealous—they were married once, did you know that? He's here this weekend, cur-rent wife in tow. That was my sense of what was going on—Lexy was playing the jealousy card. But the whole thing looked rather a game. Harmless, too, I would have said. Well, before she was killed, I'd have said that."

"The Argentine?"

"Sorry. His name is Geraldo Valentiano."

"Sounds like a silent film star."

She smiled. "Not far wrong. Just wait until you meet him. You are in for a treat."

"Where did they meet, he and Lexy? Any idea?"

"Dunno," she said. "I doubt it was at a Mensa convention."

"Anything else you can think of?"

A shrug. "Lexy was very wealthy. But then, I gather they all are, so as a motive, money would seem to be a wash. She did tell me on the way down to dinner that her room had been broken into, but that nothing had been taken."

"Really?" St. Just mused on that for a moment, then said, "This Geraldo—did he seem possessive of her … jealous?"

"Not exactly," she replied, drawing out the words as she con-sidered the question. "But he seems the type to own people, rather. Especially women. I guess you could call it a form of jeal-ousy."

St. Just sighed. The investigation had just begun and he was already weary. Suspects galore and probably motives to match. But if it weren't a complicated case, and a high-profile one, the

Chief wouldn't have landed him with it. He almost longed to be out with the Reach Out! team, being eaten alive by household pets.

Portia was looking up at him worriedly, seeing his exhaustion clearly in the unforgiving light of the overhead chandelier. His was a handsome face, candid and open, with a beaked nose that jutted from the strong planes of his face like a promontory of his native Cornish coast. His thick dark hair fell more or less in a center part, but the white hair that had begun to fringe around his ears was becoming pronounced. That and the small scar under his chin gave him a slight air of a battle-scarred tomcat.

They stood close together for a moment and a small surge of mutual reassurance seemed to pass between them. St. Just could feel the skin around his eyes soften and relax as he returned her gaze.

"I'll want to talk with you further, of course," he told her, and smiled. "Meanwhile, think back for me over everything that's happened. Oh, and I don't have to tell you, do I? No investigating on your own."

"Who, me?"

"You. I mean it, Portia."

She all but stuck out her tongue at him, but she subsided—willingly enough, to all appearances. Why upset him, when all she really intended was to keep her eyes wide open from now on? With a promise to see her when he could, St. Just left to find Sergeant Fear and the Master.

The Master was looking slightly improved by being returned to his natural habitat, like an otter released into a pond, but he was not improved by much. His manner as he waved the policemen to two chairs in front of his desk was distracted, his mind clearly elsewhere. Sergeant Fear, having first discreetly moved his chair to a far corner of the room, pulled out his policeman's notebook and riffled through it to a clean page. He was restless; called out from a rare night at home with the wife and family, half his mind was still with them. Furthermore, with two small children, the sergeant had only recently come to appreciate the value of an unbroken night's sleep. Unconsciously, he snapped the elastic band of the notebook until St. Just turned and silenced him with a "Would you mind?" gaze.

"Put us quickly in the picture, would you please?" St. Just asked the Master. "When was the last time the victim was seen alive?"

At the word "victim" the Master gave another little shudder of distaste.

"Lexy Laurant," he replied with emphasis, "was last seen by me and I should think several others in the Fellows' Garden, talking with Sir James. This was following the dinner. We were all on our way to the SCR for port."

"You saw this yourself? You're certain? Excellent. Tell me: What was her manner? Was she nervous? Upset?"

"They seemed to be having a normal enough conversation, given the circumstances."

"Would you elaborate on the circumstances?"

The Master sighed. "As you will no doubt hear from all and sundry, they were once married. Lexy and Sir James, as he was later to become. Both the marriage and the rapid breakup of it occurred when they were both students here. There was a great deal of un-pleasantness. A very great deal. Still, things of that nature have a way of sorting themselves out with the passage of years, don't you find?"

St. Just's experience was that the passage of years could also lead to regret, pent-up anger, and lingering recrimination, but he nodded as if to accept the Master's halcyon view of all things marital.

"Sir James is a writer, you know. Knighted for his contributions. He has had some great success in particular with—now, I want to make sure I get this right: Cygnus and the Northern Cross. I believe that's the title."

St. Just said, "We'll need you to fill us in on the security arrangements at the college. This is why I wanted to speak with you first."

Did he imagine it, or did the Master's shoulders relax slightly at those words? His nervousness was understandable—no one really wanted to be first up in a murder investigation. But his relief at the change of subject, towards mechanics and away from personalities, seemed a tad obvious.

"I see," said the Master. "As to the security arrangements— well, such as they are, I will gladly tell you about them. We have a CCTV system that's a combination of dummy and real cameras." St. Just nodded. He had noticed the bare-bones arrangement at the boathouse. "Anyone could get to the boathouse, although the building itself is kept locked and the keys strictly accounted for. And before curfew, anyone could get into the grounds at the back. It's part of the Porters' duties to patrol, but of course they can't be everywhere. The Fellows' Garden has an outer gate kept locked after curfew following an unfortunate incident in which we found a donkey drinking from the commemorative pond. He wore a Magdalene scarf and a straw boater, as I recall. The under-graduate population, sadly, is not what it was."

There was a moment of silence as St. Just and the Master appeared internally to review the changes wrought by the passage of time, and by the influx of scholarship students. Fear, sitting in his corner like a spider with a notebook, recognized this as one of his superior's techniques: He was good at getting the nobs to let down their hair. Fear tested the point of his Biro against his notebook and waited.

St. Just said at last, "Things are not what they were in my day, I can tell you." Silently he added: Thank God. "Well, I'm sure you will appreciate that we'll need to talk with the Porters, especially whoever was on duty tonight. And I will need a list from you of everyone present in the college this night, including staff, of course. Those in the kitchen, the bedders, and so forth."

"The college servants. Yes, yes, of course. But you can't think—some of them have been here years, since I've been here. Anyway, there's a reduced staff, because of the time of year. We shut up entire areas of the college. It empties out except for the 'orphans' who can't afford to fly home. Even when we're at full capacity, there's often not enough to go around to operate as we'd like," the Master finished sadly.

St. Just said in a commiserating tone, "Not quite what it was in the day?"

"My, no. Not that St. Michael's ever had much of a day, really. But now, we're running this place on a veritable shoestring. You get half what you used to get out of the servants, too."

I'll bet.

"I do hate to trouble you," said St. Just, "but we'll need a room set aside, somewhere where we can conduct our interviews. I think that's much preferable to asking everyone to come to the station, don't you?"

The Master, who had turned several shades paler at the mention of the station, agreed wholeheartedly that holding the interviews at the college would be much the better course.

"I think it would be easiest if you use my study, at least until other arrangements can be made," he added. "You'll have complete privacy here. I hope you won't mind my asking, but how was she killed?"

St. Just told him.

"Oh, dear. Oh, my, oh my. My goodness me." He began wringing his hands again. It was a little like holding a conversation with the White Rabbit. "There's been nothing like this since—well, I shall have to check the archives. Possibly that gambling dispute in the early eighteen hundreds. That ended badly. One dead, but no one sent down for it, thank God. They were able to hush it up rather quickly. Anyway, I'll go and see what I can arrange for you."

"One question before you leave: Who else representing the college was at tonight's dinner?"

"Apart from myself, the Bursar, and the Dean: Portia De'Ath. Also Hermione Jax—she's a Fellow of the college, but she was also here as part of the alumni group."

"We'll need a word with all of them."

"All?" Again, the Master blanched. "The Reverend Otis, as well?"

"I gather he is the Dean? Yes. Is there any reason not to speak with him?"

The Master, as has been noted, regarded the Reverend as a moron at the height of his powers, but thought better of saying so.

"I'm sure it will be all right," he said weakly. This was all spinning far too far out of his control for the Master's liking. The Dean would warble on, saying God knew what, with no one to contain him.

Once the Master had rabbited off, St. Just said to Fear, "Any member of the college would have easy access. And of course there is no limit to the number of old members who might be running around with keys or duplicated keys to heaven knows what—the Master doesn't seem to have taken that into account. It makes it all the more trying, this sort of monk-medieval atmosphere. Not like a murder in a modern block of flats, for example, where one could at least hope for decent video camera surveillance." In fact, many of the colleges had reluctantly gone in for these modern protuberances attached to their stone walls, the unsightliness being the lesser of two evils—the other evil being robbed blind. But St. Mike's clung steadfastly to appearance and tradition, St. Just had noticed; although there were static cameras at the boathouse, which was a relatively modern building, he hadn't noticed them otherwise.

This murder, he thought, would undoubtedly change things. Or would it? This was Cambridge, after all.

NARCISSUS

St. Just was a fair man, and he struggled to meet all suspects, however suspect they might be, with an open mind and on an even footing. But he did not like Geraldo Valentiano on sight and that was a fact. The man reeked of wealth, in addition to an overpowering men's cologne. Wealth and entitlement and having far too much time on his hands to, oh, say, cruise about the world on his yacht. His idea of hard labor would be taking the helm of this yacht for a few thrilling moments before going below decks to order up more champagne.

He was extraordinarily handsome in his movie-star way, with more than a hint of the voluptuary in the full mouth, the languor in the large, long-lashed, slightly downturned eyes. Like Bambi fallen into a vat of cologne. Perhaps in his upper thirties. St. Just did not doubt he was attractive to women. The thought of this man under the same roof as Portia made his stomach clench with anxiety. There she was, innocently toiling away night and day on her thesis, oblivious to the danger. He trusted Portia absolutely, but he was also absolutely certain this man would not be able to stay away from her loveliness. St. Just could not bear the thought of Portia anywhere near this ... this rogue.

With an effort, St. Just pulled himself together, plastering an amiable expression on his face.

"How did you come to know Lexy Laurant?" he asked him now, rather more bluntly than he intended. "And for how long did you know her?"

The man shot his cuffs, arranging the fall of his sleeves just so, before answering.

"We met in London, a few months ago. At Boujis."

Sergeant Fear looked up from his notebook. "Please spell that, Sir."

"B-O-O ... " he began. "I don't remember. It's a nightclub."

"How old was she, by the way?"

"She said she was thirty-two, but you know how women lie about their ages."

"No matter, we'll of course have access to documentation regarding her age. Now: Did she have any enemies?"

"How should I know?"

The amiable expression was starting to hurt. "Tell us what happened tonight," St. Just said evenly.

"Again, how should I know? We all went to dinner, we came out, this kid came running into the SCR screaming bloody murder. Oh, sorry. He was yelling, I meant to say. It was only then I realized Lexy had not joined the gathering. Sir James ran out to see what was the matter. A few of the men followed him."

"Had anything been troubling her? Had anything happened out of the ordinary, either tonight or earlier?"

"Hmm?" A chip in his manicure had diverted Geraldo, occupying his full attention.

"I asked you," said St. Just with stilted patience, "if anything had been troubling Lexy."

"Oh. Well, there was this situation with her ex being at the reunion."

"How was she taking that?"

As anything that did not directly concern the man seemed to bore him stiff, he looked for a moment as if he might not answer. Having Lexy's affections sidetracked away from himself seemed to strike him as either an impossibility or, at worst, some minor social embarrassment, like losing one's date for the May Ball to a rival. Annoying, but nothing to worry about. She'd come crawling back—they always did. The man exuded a sexual self-confidence that would have been commendable in a Darwinian sense, had St. Just not found it so maddening.

"What caused the pair of you to come here this weekend?"

"It was Lexy's idea. I thought it might be fun, so I came down from London with her."

"And what did you do once you arrived in Cambridge?"

"After we unpacked? The usual. Had a late lunch, rented a punt, wandered about. Came back here, had sex, changed for dinner."

The casual mention of sex was jolting. It may have been intended to provoke, or it may have been simple braggadocio. St. Just suspected it was in the man's character to make the nature of his conquests clear. He heard Sergeant Fear stir uneasily behind him.

"Did she talk about Sir James to you?"

94

"She may have done. I tuned most of it out. She liked to relive the moment when he ran off with India. Mostly, she was over it. I helped."

I just bet you did. St. Just wondered how much the man's ego might be shielding him. He might be telling the truth to the fullest extent of which he was capable. His belief that no woman would want anyone else, having met the divine Geraldo Valentiano, was no doubt solid and sincere. Whether it had anything to do with present reality was anyone's guess.

"How were you and she getting along?"

"Just fine." Noticing the weighted silence, he managed to tear his eyes away from examining his manicured nails to look at the policeman directly. "Really great."

"That's wonderful, Sir. No quarrels, no misunderstandings then?"

"I just told you, we were getting along fine."

"She could be a little … clingy, is my understanding."

"She was a very feminine woman. That didn't bother me. I am used to dealing with all kinds of women."

"How very splendid for you, I'm sure. Now, you say she was feminine. What else? What kind of woman was she?"

He shrugged. "Good looking. Desirable. Amusing at times."

Like any good possession. A good hunting dog, perhaps. "Yes, yes, quite. What I meant was her personality. Was she a kind person? A selfish one?"

Geraldo thought, which seemed to require a great deal of effort on his part. He probably found such unusual activity rather stressful. Finally he said, "She wouldn't compromise."

"Can you expand on that?"

"She always had to do things her way. Like coming here. I was growing tired of it."

"How tired?"

"Don't try that on me. I didn't mean it that way."

St. Just, who would have been within his rights to come down hard on the man, decided to leave it for now.

"What did you do when dinner had ended? Please be precise as you can."

"I went to the gents. Then I headed for the SCR."

"No detours?"

"None."

"Did you see Lexy on your way to the SCR?"

"No."

"You didn't escort her from the hall?"

"What on earth for? She could walk."

Off St. Just's thunderous look, he decided it wise to add:

"She was one of the first to leave. Jumped up and ran out. Probably crying again. You can't blame a man—I was growing tired ... but not that tired. No way. I have an alibi: I was surrounded by people all evening. Except when I was in the gents, but that was no time at all. Oh ... "

"Oh?" asked St. Just helpfully.

"I did step out for a breath of fresh air. Just for a moment."

"Where did you go?"

"I strolled over to the tennis courts, on the grounds to the far side of the college."

"Tennis, anyone?"

"What?"

"That's some distance from the buildings, and it was growing late. Why did you go there?"

"Why not?" Geraldo shot back truculently.

St. Just weighed the chances he'd do more than repeat this assertion as to his whereabouts, whether true or not.

"Did anyone see you?"

"No. No one needed to. I didn't kill her, it is impossible that you will find evidence that I did, and that is the end of that. If you wish to pursue this line, I shall have to summon my solicitor."

"Lexy was quite a wealthy woman, was she not?"

"So am I, a wealthy man. I am not interested in women for their money. I am not what you English would call a gigolo."

"That would be the French, Sir. We probably would call such a man a bounder. We often use the words cad or parasite, in point of fact."

St. Just stood back and watched disinterestedly as Geraldo's mulish face turned red beneath the perpetual tan.

"I'll have you on report for that," he said at last.

"Fine. Here's my card, Sir. It has the main number for the station, as well as my extension. But you will want to ask to be connected to the man who is ultimately in charge." Of course, the Chief Constable was a woman, but he doubted such an eventuality would occur to Geraldo Valentiano, and it would undoubtedly have him stepping off on the wrong foot if he did bother to call the station. The man was all bluster, of that St. Just was sure. Most bullies were.

He dismissed him, warning him not to leave the college grounds until further notice. He left, St. Just noticed, with some alacrity.

"You really think money might be a motive here, Sir?" asked Sergeant Fear when they were alone.

"She was wealthy, and according to Portia, a vulnerable type. The perfect pigeon for a man like that. Let's have a rundown on his financials and find out where he got the cash to live as he apparently does ... or if he's living above his means now. And yes, the fact that she was wealthy might be a factor overall. Someone as famous as Lexy may also have been the object of envy."

Sergeant Fear nodded.

"We need to get someone talking with the college servants, but I would be amazed if they're involved. There was a little money found in her purse, so robbery isn't looking like a motive."

"Still, Sir. Money isn't the only motive, if it was someone from the staff. Some of them have been here years, according to the Master. And some people leave a long trail of memory. Like a snail."

St. Just smiled. "You're quite right, of course. An ancient grudge cannot be overlooked. Her wealth and beauty could have aroused all kinds of feelings, especially in someone who felt like one of the 'have nots.' The outsider looking in at all this privilege."

He swept out a hand to encompass the room's sumptuous if somewhat worn furnishings—the carved, stained oak; the fireplace surround of antique tiles depicting the nine Muses, the leather chairs and leather-bound books.

"And there is always the crime of passion, of sexual jealousy," he went on, "although I can see the Argentine jealous of no one but himself. No one else could hold his attention for long. That does not discount the possibility that Lexy impugned his manhood, somehow. Some slight, however silly, that he would feel would have to be avenged. Even so..." he trailed off. St. Just's inclination was to discount no one too soon, but the Argentine was so blithe, so carefree, so indifferent and unconcerned. Most people involved in a murder spared at least a moment's thought for the victim.

If Geraldo Valentiano did commit this crime, they were indeed dealing with a cold-blooded monster.

EXPERT WITNESS

St. Just said to his sergeant, "Let me take a look at that list the Master left with us—the list that was mailed to all the participants of this weekend." He ran an eye over two pages of typescript. "Just names and addresses, mostly London addresses, excluding the Americans." He read aloud: "There's a Karl and Constance Dunning, no doubt a married couple, of New York; an Augie Cramb of Texas; Gwennap Pengelly—now, how is it I know that name?"

"She's on the telly, Sir."

"Of course, that's right, the news announcer. God help us. All right. Then there's Sir James and Lady Bassett of London—may God continue to come to our aid. Hermione Jax, with an address just outside Cambridge, so she doesn't live in college despite the fact she's a Fellow. No doubt she took rooms here for the weekend to avoid having to drive after the revels of High Table. Very sensible. Next listed: Geraldo Valentiano, who maintains a London residence, a home in Argentina, and one in France. He has been careful to list them all. I suppose we are meant to be impressed."

Sergeant Fear, who had been taking notes, asked, "Is that the lot?"

"That's the lot as far as the visitors are concerned. Then of course there's the boy, Sebastian. I say…" thoughtfully he tapped the paper against the Master's desk. "Let's get Portia in here first. I want you to hear her impressions of everyone. It will help to have someone as observant as she give us the lay of the land before we start the interviews."

He had passed the stage with Portia where at the sight of her he could do little more than make an inarticulate, guttural noise in the back of his throat, followed by what he was convinced were some of the most inane comments in the history of recorded or unrecorded speech. Still the sight of her lifted his heart, and it was a moment before he could speak.

"I've organized some tea to be sent in," she told them. "You look famished. I should avoid the biscuits if I were you, however. I think the Bursar's found a bakery that sells week-old goods."

St. Just got her settled in a chair and handed her the list. He knew Portia would be able to give him not just her impressions as to character, but a sense of whatever undertow may have been in motion throughout the weekend. She read through the list and then, looking up, began to speak.

"Constance Dunning, the New Yorker, is the most hideous, non-stop whinger you'll ever meet. She has already earned the sobriquet 'Constant Complainer' from the bedders, and she only arrived yesterday. Her husband bears it well, to quite a remarkable degree, in fact. He's rather a poppet. She's … well, you'll see. What their ties might be to Lexy, if any, I don't know."

She returned to the list.

"India—that's Lady Bassett to you—I'd say she has brains, and she's enormously attractive, if in rather an equine way. Good, English-rose skin with a high color. She always looks like she's just come in after a particularly vitalizing ride on a sunny day. Her son looks a great deal like her—Sebastian, I mean."

"The boy who found the body?"

She nodded. "Her husband, Sir James. Not Sebastian's natural father, by the way—stepfather, rather. I commented to someone how much Sebastian resembled India and that's when I was told—by the Reverend Otis, it was—that Sir James is Sebastian's parent only by marriage. Anyway, he's quite a famous author, did you know? I mean famous in terms of winning acclaim and literary awards, not famous as in best-selling, necessarily. Two entirely different things, of course. Yes, he and India are quite the team. He seems devoted. I'd say it's quite an intellectual bond, and it's a good match in that regard—as I say, she has brains, so does he. Plus he fancies her silly."

St. Just said slowly, "A match that required his leaving a first wife. Do you think Lexy was still carrying a torch for him?"

"I've thought about this, and I can only tell you her eyes would follow him absolutely everywhere." She paused to adjust a side comb in her hair. "I mean, she literally couldn't seem to take her eyes off of him. At moments it appeared mutual, all this gazing about. Then she'd get this wistful, sad, pained look. Hard to say what was in her mind, but she certainly looked lovelorn."

"And what was his response? It would rather have given me the creeps to be stared at like that. How did he respond?"

"He was gallant. He has rather a poker face, all stiff upper lip, so it is hard to know what he may really have felt, but he covered any discomfiture nicely. He strikes me as a bit buttoned up, wanting to do the right thing for King and Country. You know the type. India noticed all this, by the way, and she's easier to read. She didn't much like it, but she wasn't going to throw a scene over it. At least, not until the pair of them got safely back home. I overheard them talking together—the college is like living in a fishbowl, you know—and she was trying to persuade him to leave. He agreed, but basically asked her to wait and see."

Again, she referred to the list.

"Ah. Next up: the Texan. Big, tall, nice-looking man, friendly almost to a fault. He's had some adventures, but he manages to make every one sound incredibly boring before he's done. Given to providing extraneous detail in answer to questions one has not asked. Not the sharpest knife in the drawer, despite his evident success in business. Maybe he's only thick in some ways. Some people are like that. Genius, but only in one or two areas.

"Gwennap Pengelly—surely you must know Gwenn Pengelly, as she's more commonly known. The woman with 'the nose for news.' What I wouldn't have given to have her job at one point in my life, when I was hankering after glamour." She smiled at him. Portia had one of those smiles that caught the observer unaware—how he loved surprising or goading that smile into action. Not the easy smile of the seductress, the charmer, the con artist. One felt, thought St. Just, that one had to earn the privilege of seeing that smile transform her face.

"This was before I gave it all up to sit in dusty libraries, no doubt developing life-long allergies to dust mites. Anyway, she and Geraldo Valentiano go back some way. Oh, I see you didn't know that? Yes, well. His reputation precedes him. It would be hard to find an attractive woman within miles who had not succumbed, or was not planning to succumb. The two of them seemed quite friendly this weekend, as well. I overhead a little of their conversation. She was definitely being romanced, and not for the first time."

St. Just, looking rather alarmed lest Portia also find the Argentine charming, asked, "And Lexy? How did Lexy feel about all that?"

Portia considered. "Irritated. I'm not sure she minded all that much, not really, but it looked bad. Made a bad impression, and I think impressions were rather important to Lexy. She seemed to have other fish to fry—Sir James was her focus, as I've said—so she wasn't positively seething over it. Anyway, Gwennap is very high profile, and a better match for the Argentine, really. Maybe he was getting ready to dump Lexy for her—is that your thinking? It could have provoked a quarrel? Yes . . . Geraldo is what we call a bad boy, no question. I imagine trouble with women is a recurring theme of his life."

St. Just cleared this throat before saying, "But you were immune, of course?"

Portia smiled. "That's rather the point. No woman is immune. But any sensible woman wanting a quiet life would definitely stay clear of him. No good saying to oneself that a casual fling couldn't hurt. It would hurt like mad, before it was over. He's rather poisonous, I think."

Good, thought St. Just. Keep thinking that. Sensible girl. As for Geraldo, he'd talk with him about the relationship with Gwenn, but first he'd let him hang about a bit longer, beating his chest, or having it waxed, or whatever.

"Very wise," he said aloud.

Sergeant Fear nodded in unison. He knew Portia only slightly, but already held her in the highest regard. She'd done St. Just a world of good—nothing and no one must be allowed to interfere with that. Already his dislike of the Argentine was beginning to harden. Unlike St. Just, he felt no compunction about needing to keep an open mind. The man was a good old-fashioned rotter, and that was that.

"Who do we have next?" asked St. Just. "Let's see. Hermione Jax. Wonderful, Empire-like ring to that name, don't you think? What's your impression of her?"

Portia replied slowly, "Decent enough sort, but I find her rather a type, I'm afraid. All tweeds and twinsets and long brisk walks by the river. No pearls, however—much more likely to wear a necklace that looks made of dried seaweed and barbed wire. Earrings to match. You know the sort of thing. Often seen wheeling about on her bicycle, with the basket full of her shopping and odd snippings of plants. She seems to have a formidable intellect, or she does a good imitation of having one, although I can't recall a brilliant remark I've heard her say. She can be rather frightening in her bluestockinged way. She's a botanist or something of the sort, but I suppose these days she'd be called an ecologist—she's written several famous tomes on the topic. Much given to ranting about the destruction of the planet by Mankind. That would be with a capital M—women are generally absolved of blame in her canon. You would be wise not to invite her views on the role of peat diggings with respect to existing British waterways, unless that is a topic of great and fathomless interest to you.

"That leaves … let's see, apart from the odd stray student: the Master, the Bursar, and the Dean. The Master you've met, and I'll leave you to draw your own conclusions. As to the Bursar, well."

And Portia gave them a quick rundown on what, from her viewpoint, were the Bursar's crimes (Portia, the gourmet, was of course appalled at being subjected to what came out of the college kitchen, "Although the rumors he's come to an arrangement with the zoology department are complete slander, but it is Cambridge and whenever an obscure and appalling cut of meat appears on the table one can't help but wonder"), concluding, "And then there's the Dean. What you see is what you get with the Reverend Otis. He is such a sweet man. We have to keep a constant eye on him or he'd be swindled every time he set foot outside the college, or put all his money in the first charity box he came across."

"An innocent."

"To quite an alarming degree. Sometimes that type can cause havoc unknowingly. He somehow knows everything that goes on and will repeat things in all innocence that should not be said. For example: The sous-chef and the gardener were having quite a pash and he kept repeating how much fresher the vegetables had been in recent months. Everyone knew, of course, but the Reverend Otis, why we had such a sudden uptick in the quality of the Brussels sprouts. I would think someone in his position would be more worldly, wouldn't you?"

"One would think. All right. Now, tonight in the SCR, after dinner. Tell us—whatever. Your impressions."

She closed her eyes a moment, thinking back.

"James comes to mind first. He was a bit distracted looking. I had the impression he was watching the door ... for Lexy? Anyway, he stood talking with India and the others, but kept rather a wary eye on the Argentine as well, I thought."

"My God. Not yet another conquest for Mr. Valentiano?"

"Could be. James seemed to think so. He was guarding her like a pit bull."

"If Geraldo Valentiano did this," said St. Just determinedly, "it will be a pleasure having him up for it. I find him rather a useless person, don't you?"

How thrillingly macho, she thought, deducing the reason behind St. Just's evident dislike. She returned the list to him, and watched as his eyes again scanned the list of names. Suspects all. His face held the puzzled, fretful look of a man examining a computer-generated letter from the Inland Revenue. She knew he would worry at this case until he solved it, at least to his own satisfaction, and she loved him for that tenacity. She knew already he would not entirely be hers again until the case was over. But it was what made Arthur, Arthur. She had long since accepted she could not envision life without him, and if these terrible working hours came with the territory, she'd just have to cope.

"Did anything happen during dinner tonight that struck you?" he asked her now. "Anything at all?"

She thought back to the meal, and what she had been able to hear of the conversation. As usual when people reminisced about events to which others had not been witness, the conversation

struck her as a trifle dull, although the others had seemed engrossed—happy, even. They had been talking at some point about
Pennying, she remembered, the drinking game they had used to
play during Formal Hall using Smarties, with, apparently, disas-
trous effect. As she had looked up from her meal, they had all been
laughing. Someone had slipped a penny in someone else's drink,
making the pennied person obliged to drink up. No wonder the
results could be ruinous. Had anyone struck her as being melancholy or distracted? Maybe the Bursar, but that was his default position. No doubt he was worrying about how much the meal was
costing. And if a look of any significance passed between Lexy and
another of the diners, probably no one could have said.

She related all this to St. Just.

"Sorry not to be of more help. They just seemed to be en-
joying themselves. I was a bit distracted myself. The writing, you
know—it makes me preoccupied and oblivious to my surroundings, sometimes."

"It's all right—you're doing fine, in fact. Now, everyone was
in the SCR when you got there after dinner?"

She said slowly, "I think so. There may have been one or two
missing but offhand I can only say there were more there than
were not there, if you know what I mean. Excepting Lexy—I did
notice, for some reason, she wasn't there. Well, people did notice
Lexy. I saw her sitting in the Fellows' Garden earlier, just after dinner."

"Was she alone?"

"No. Sir James was with her."

"Do you recall in what order everyone left Hall after the
meal?"

"Sorry, no, as I was among the first to leave. I wasn't really part of the group, as I've said, so I'm afraid I rather bolted at the first opportunity. Tried to bolt, I should say. I was waylaid by Gwenn Pengelly, and then the Master wanted a word. Anyway, as you pass through the gallery from the dining hall, headed towards the SCR, you overlook the Fellows' Garden. She was there—Lexy, I mean. As I told you, I went up to my rooms to freshen up, then I came straight down. I imagine others did the same, or visited one of the ground-floor facilities. They all drifted in to the SCR after dinner fairly quickly, is all I can tell you."

"But by—what—say, nine-thirty? You'd all gathered together? All except Lexy."

She nodded.

"When you saw Lexy in the Garden, what was her manner?"

Portia shrugged. "She was just sitting quietly. She was with James, as I've said."

"He sat with her?"

"No, he was standing."

"And he was definitely one of those you saw shortly afterwards in the SCR?" St. Just could not keep the tension from his voice. Sir James would probably have been the last person but one to have spoken with Lexy.

"Yes. Guarding India."

"And what was his manner with Lexy?"

She considered. "Placating. He seemed to be—oh, I don't know. Calling on all his reserves of patience. Not angry, but maybe trying to convince her of something, was my impression. Placate her, perhaps. Of course, one couldn't hear what was said. The windows in the gallery overlooking the Fellows' Garden are sealed closed. Anyway, he was definitely in the SCR dogging India when I arrived, which was fairly quickly. So he can't have stayed long with Lexy. Not long enough for ... you know. Which in any event he wouldn't have done in such a public spot."

"Try to remember who else was definitely there in the SCR." The leather chair creaked like a wooden ship under St. Just's weight as he sat forward.

She sighed. "One wishes one weren't so distracted by that blasted thesis—and whatnot—all the time. Let's see, the Reverend Otis was there, of course. I was talking to him, you see, and I had my back to the room ... I was rather trying to dodge the Texan, if and when he came in."

Fear thought St. Just looked inordinately pleased to hear it.

Portia went on, "Let me think about it some more—maybe there was a voice or two I heard and could recognize. I'll try to make a list, give you the approximate times I think they came in, or at least—and this is very different, isn't it?—when they were in the room talking. But I wasn't wearing my watch and I was facing away from the clock on the mantelpiece, so even times will be very rough estimates. At some point Geraldo joined us—the Reverend Otis and myself—for a moment. I'm sorry, that's all I can recall."

St. Just said, "So, what do we have? At some point after dinner—"

"It ended at nine-fifteen, but some people hung about in Hall, talking."

"Right. Let's say you saw Lexy and James in the garden at nine-twenty—would that be roughly accurate?"

She nodded. "Perhaps a minute or so later."

St. Just folded his arms across his chest, and she noticed the elbow was giving out on the light sweater he wore. Typical. St. Just was always scrupulously clean in meticulously pressed clothing, but some of his wardrobe was so worn Oxfam would have rejected it.

"So, some time after that," he said, "Lexy left the garden, we assume for the boathouse. We'll need to ask Sir James if she left him or if he left her sitting there, and find out if any other witness saw her leave. We'll also need to look for signs that she was dragged from where she'd been killed—say, the garden. The killer had plenty of time, as it turns out, before she was found, but dragging her about would run the risk of exposure—as you point out, the garden is much too public a spot for that to be a likely scenario. Much more likely she was killed at the boathouse. But—why was she there? Just wanting to be near the river? Sergeant Fear, I'll need a diagram of the grounds. Get someone to clock the distance from the garden to the river. She could have been carried, of course. She was a little thing, and we have at least one strapping candidate who could have lifted her, even dead, as easily as carrying a large toddler. Your Argentine, for example," he said, with an amused glance at Portia.

"He is hardly my Argentine," she said firmly.

St. Just grinned happily and went on. "So, she was meeting someone, or someone found her. She met up with someone, by accident or design." He sighed. "We're not getting very far yet. But thank you, Portia. That was invaluable. We'd better have a word now with the young man who found her."

GOLDEN LADS AND GIRLS

THE YOUNG MAN WHO answered the summons to the Master's study also fit the profile of someone strapping enough to carry Lexy Laurant's body without effort. He was perhaps twenty years of age, tall and blonde in a way that recalled the genetic legacy of Norse invaders of the medieval British Isles. He wore his hair long in front, razored in the back, and he had a coltish habit of tossing the thick strands off his forehead with a shake of his head. He sported the British white-man's tan, a darkening of the fair, rosy complexion already reddened by the icy blasts of winter.

He was trying, St. Just thought, to look man-of-the-world-ish, as if discovering corpses were pretty much a monthly experience in his adventurous and full young life. St. Just felt sorry for him—the first corpse is always the hardest.

He anticipated St. Just's first question by denying any real knowledge of Lexy, and spent most of the interview painting her as a figure lurking on the periphery of his vision. This would be normal for one of his youth. She was not that much older, but perhaps just old enough to hold little fascination for a young man barely in his twenties. Still, by Hollywood standards, she wasn't too old for him by a long shot. Realistically, however, Sebastian struck St. Just as too immature for the role just yet, barely out of the pram. Lexy may have been immature in her own way, but still: Sebastian belonged to a different young world entirely, and it was hard to imagine what common ground these two might have found. St. Just hoped he wasn't giving in to some creeping old fogey-ism: He could be wrong, completely out of touch with the current mores.

"As I say," Sebastian Burrows reiterated, "I barely knew her."

"Even though she was once married to your stepfather?"

"Precisely. She was once married to my stepfather, that's all." Again, he shook back the golden locks. St. Just wondered if it were a nervous affectation, or an indicator he was lying. "No blood tie."

"How often had you met her?"

Sebastian answered indirectly.

"I know her mainly through the tabloids and magazines, and a few chance sightings in London."

"Where, precisely?"

He named several nightclubs, including Boujis, that St. Just knew were all the latest rage. Sebastian could be lying about how often he met her, thought St. Just. They might frequent the same nightclubs very often. Run into each other, get to know each other. It wasn't impossible ...

"When you saw her, on these extremely rare occasions then," said St. Just, "it would help us awfully to get your impressions. Of her character."

Sebastian shrugged. "I don't know, I tell you."

"Do try."

"All right, my impressions, however fleeting: She was kind of neurotic, you know? She liked excitement, noise, people around her. She liked to be the center of attention. This is only my impression from her look, the way she dressed. I didn't really notice her, it's just that she seemed to be everywhere I was for a while."

As he didn't seem to want to budge from the "hardly knew her" line, St. Just moved on to ask him about the events of the evening. Immediately, he sensed a shift in Sebastian's tone. The reminder of the murder sobered him. In response to his request that Sebastian outline his movements, Sebastian said, "That's easy. I have a schedule I rarely stray from."

Why was he here during the summer? St. Just wondered. Did he have nowhere else to go? But Sebastian was speaking:

"I'm in training," he said, with a little glow of pride. "I stick to rather a rigid daily schedule so I can be sure to get my time in. This night I went into the water at about nine, after my workout. Later than I liked—you don't want to be caught out there after Lighting Up. Penalties and so forth. I really do try to play by the rules. I want to compete at a very high level one day, you see."

"And Lighting Up on this particular night was when?"

"21:51 hours."

Sergeant Fear's head came up from his notebook. "So precise?" he asked.

"It's the time at which the sun sets to ninety-four degrees below the zenith, if you want the official definition," Sebastian informed him. "But God help you if you ignore Lighting Up or

Down. Not a good idea, in any event. You're liable to row straight into the bank on a dark night."

"And so you finished your practice and arrived at the boat-house...?"

"Just before. Say nine-fifty. May I go now?"

"How do you keep track of the time so precisely as you're sculling? You'd have to stop to look at your watch, wouldn't you?"

Sebastian shook his head.

"The curfew warning still chimes at nine forty-five, although it's mainly a holdover from the very old days. There's a warning chime, as I say, followed in fifteen minutes by the final chime—curfew."

"Tell us what happened. You finished your practice, returned to the boathouse, and..."

"And I was carrying the boat and equipment from the river when I saw her, sort of crumpled there. Well, you know. I went over, took one look, dropped everything, and ran for help."

"You didn't have a mobile phone with you?"

"Funnily enough, I did have it in my pocket, but I don't usually. I mean, I'm out there working, not taking calls, and if the worst should happen I wouldn't want to see the mobile end up in the water. That's why I didn't think of it, I suppose—I don't normally have it with me on these occasions. I just ran for help, which was less than two or three minutes away, in any event."

"Did you see anyone about? At any time?"

He shook his head. "No."

St. Just sighed. Not much help there. "We'll need a signed statement from you to this effect, of course," he told Sebastian.

"Now, you say you didn't know Lexy too well, but the same must not be true of your stepfather, her ex-husband?"

"How would I know what was true of him?" said Sebastian, staring down peevishly at the Persian carpet. "I barely saw him as I was growing up. I was sent away to school, and he was not really interested in 'bonding,' to use that hideous expression, when I was at home. No more was I. Frankly, I was grateful that he didn't come over all fatherly, trying to teach me how to fish or shoot or whatnot."

"He didn't try to be your friend, or anything."

"God, no—not really. That would have been worse, wouldn't it, by far?"

A fate worse than death. St. Just supposed he could see the boy's point of view.

"And your relationship with your mother?"

"What about it?" asked Sebastian, still addressing the carpet. St. Just noticed his hands as they rested on the arms of the chair—gripped the arms, rather. They were a rower's hands, large and capable, to match his rower's physique. Strong shoulders, arms, and legs.

He also had the hard narrow waist of a rower; St. Just could see the muscles of the boy's flat stomach clearly outlined against the thin material of his shirt. St. Just remembered from his own rowing days that it was the best exercise of all, as it worked every muscle in the body. Sebastian, he thought, could practically have choked Lexy one-handed without breaking a sweat.

"Did your mother's marriage to Sir James affect your relationship with her in any way?"

It didn't seem to occur to Sebastian to wonder what this had to do with Lexy's murder. St. Just didn't really know himself, but was trying to get a better sense of this young man.

"Not really. I was at school, as I've told you."

"Was their marriage a success, did you think?"

Sebastian looked genuinely baffled at this question. It surprised him so that he dragged his gaze away from the carpet at last and looked quizzically at St. Just.

"I've really no idea at all. I think so."

St. Just thought, after some reflection, that was probably true. The doings of these two oldies was probably too far outside the boy's realm of interest. St. Just may as well ask Sebastian for his views on the comings and goings of the Hapsburgs.

"But, you must have formed some opinion of James, at least insofar as his appropriateness as a mate for your mother?"

Sergeant Fear also wondered at the direction of St. Just's questions. Did it matter what the boy thought of the parents? He shrugged and continued to jot down notes in case it did.

"I've told you. I rarely saw him or my mother. He's a nice enough chap, I suppose. I got along with him well enough. He was clever, as I said, never to try to play the heavy-handed father bit. You know, come over as all in charge or giving unwanted advice or interfering or anything. Well, he did once try to give me advice on women and that was quite an awful moment, but we shouldered through even that somehow. He talked about how they had to be wooed and courted, for God's sake, like he was reading from some eighteenth-century guide for the gentry. I just let him get it off his chest and then I thanked him kindly. I think he realized it was a failed experiment and it was never repeated."

"So, your love of rowing—not something you got from James, then?"

This was greeted with a snort of derision. "God, no," he said again. "If it doesn't have hooves and a saddle, James is not terribly interested anymore."

Sergeant Fear began to interject a question.

"When you were out in the rowboat, did—"

Sebastian turned to him and said, through gritted teeth, "It is not a rowboat. It is called a scull." A sudden alertness came over the boy as he was turning back around. He cocked his head and said to St. Just, "If that's all, I have to go." He pulled a mobile from a pocket of his jacket and began fiddling with the keys. For this we grew opposable thumbs, thought St. Just, watching him.

"Put that away," he said mildly. "We're not done here."

With elaborate reluctance, Sebastian obeyed. St. Just could almost see the scales in the boy's mind, weighing the pros of getting out and away quickly with the cons of making an enemy of the police. Still, he apparently couldn't resist muttering, "The law has nothing to do with me. Laws were invented by old white men."

St. Just, who had heard many a criminal espouse much the same philosophy, said nothing, refusing to be drawn into this sophomoric debate.

They talked awhile longer with Sebastian but elicited little of note: The young man again insisted that he scarcely knew Lexy. St. Just suddenly wondering where the scull that lay next to Lexy's body had come from, Sebastian reluctantly admitted he always left the boathouse unlocked while he sculled, but locked away the equipment on his return.

"Except this time, of course. I just ran for help."

"Surely that's inviting theft," said St. Just. "To leave the place open while you're on the water."

Sebastian, admitting as much, said it was "too much hassle and besides, I'm not gone all that long." St. Just gathered that as the property wasn't his, Sebastian wasn't overly concerned what happened to it.

As Sebastian was leaving, he stopped and turned back into the room, his tall frame dwarfed by the ancient panel door.

"When will I be able to get back into the boathouse?" he asked. "I'm in training, as I told you. That's why I'm staying over this summer."

"Oh, not the chance to catch up with the parents that's the big draw then?"

Sebastian rolled his eyes and screwed up his face in the time-honored tradition of youthful contempt for the company of elders.

"No," he said flatly.

"A murder investigation takes precedence," St. Just said mildly.

Sebastian had the grace to look abashed. "Of course. Sorry. That came out the wrong way."

Once the door closed behind him, Fear asked, "Why all the questions about James?"

"I'm just trying to get a feel for the dynamics of the family formed when James threw over Lexy for India. There's usually some sort of feeling, you know. Lots and lots of emotion to go 'round, especially among the offspring who are affected by the new arrangements. And yet Sebastian seems to be handling it all with some maturity—or indifference. Assuming he's telling the truth."

"Do you like him for this murder?"

St. Just shrugged.

"It's difficult to say. With that athlete's build, he's more than physically capable. And he is still at an age to waver on the fence between maturity and immaturity. A sudden passion, a flare of hatred, and he might strike out, maybe without the intent to kill … maybe with just the intent to quieten her … maybe she was taunting him somehow … Yes, I can see any and all of that happening with someone like Sebastian. The why is the puzzle."

"Isn't it always."

"He doesn't have an alibi, did you notice?" asked St. Just.

"I did, Sir. He's vouching for himself, him with his fitness routine and his sculling schedule. Lights up or down or whatever it is. There was nothing to prevent him coming back early, at any time, really, and killing her. Certainly, as you say, he has the hands for it."

"Let's have his stepfather in here next."

GOLDEN LADS AND GIRLS: PART II

SIR JAMES WAS A man dark haired and dark eyed, a complete contrast to his stepson's fairness. He wore glasses with thick, black frames that might have been selected from a manufacturer's "Serious Writer" catalog. He looked shaken, but composed. St. Just had a feeling Sir James would look composed if the college suddenly came under mortar attack. He had the air of a man not only raised up to deal with that sort of thing, but one who might live for the chance to display a little derring-do. A chance to throw on some armor, save England, and rescue his lady fair.

St. Just put these fanciful chivalric ideas aside, invited Sir James to take the chair just vacated by Sebastian, and said, "We've just spoken with your stepson."

"I know. Poor kid. I saw him just now, looking completely gored. This must be a nightmare for him."

"I think you'll find youth is a great restorative in and of itself. He's shaken and trying to hide it, but by tomorrow it may all be a fading memory."

"I'll have a word with my wife. Perhaps we should get him away from here."

"Not anytime very soon, Sir. We'll need everyone to stay around until we're satisfied they have no more to tell us about these tragic events."

"Oh, I see. Yes, quite. Of course. Anything … anything at all …"

"I've heard from other sources a bit about the … somewhat unusual arrangements of this weekend. The fact that Lexy Laurant was your ex-wife. I'd like to hear the circumstances from you."

"I thought you might. But it was years ago, you know, and I can absolutely assure you it could have nothing to do with this … this appalling tragedy."

"You and Lexy were married how long?"

"Three years. We met at the college. Married in haste, as they say."

"I see. And you and your present wife have been together how long?"

"It will soon be seventeen years."

"You also met her while you were here at St. Mike's?"

"Yes. I was here as a visiting scholar. I was here for some time working on a book, you see."

"That all seems clear. Now, as to this weekend get-together: Was this in any way pre-arranged?"

"Did I know Lexy would be here, do you mean?"

"Yes."

"Not until it was too late to prevent her coming. Not that I could have prevented it," he added quickly. "Lexy could be rather headstrong." Seeming to fear that last sentence might be misconstrued, he rushed on, "But only in some ways. Basically, she had a gentle nature." He shook his head reminiscently. "That's what makes this all the more inexplicable to me, that she should … should die like this."

"In what ways was she not headstrong, Sir?"

James just looked at him. This was indeed a poser.

"Never mind, Sir. So you didn't know she would be here, until, presumably, you received the list of attendees from the college." He held out the copy of the list in his own hands.

"That is correct. Well, to be precise, I didn't know until I saw her here. She was quite capable of changing her mind."

"Still, since the invitation went out to all the old members connected with a certain time frame, you knew she would receive an invitation, along with your wife?"

"If I'd thought about it, yes."

"And did you, Sir? Think about it?"

"Fleetingly, perhaps. I must tell you, Lexy was always heard to say, and loudly, that she detested this place, so my thinking about it would consist of cataloguing all the reasons she would almost certainly not be here."

"But, as it turns out, you were wrong."

He smiled bleakly; the skin under his eyes was smudged with dark shadows. "Yes."

"And your wife's reaction to finding out that Lexy was going to be here?"

"She wasn't exactly pleased, of course. What woman would be? But India is a sensible soul. She soon decided she would simply rise to the occasion. Meaning, ignore it. She could afford to."

"No jealousy, then?"

"Good lord, no. India—Lady Bassett—is too level-headed for that, I tell you. Plus, she has no reason whatsoever to doubt me, no reason for jealousy—over Lexy or anyone else, for that matter."

St. Just allowed a long pause. When James did not elaborate further on his complete devotion to his present wife, St. Just went on:

"You had no residual feeling for Lexy, then."

The man heaved an enormous sigh, as if he'd been expecting—and dreading?—this very question.

"I was fond of her, of course. I suppose one always retains a vestige of fondness for someone who reminds one of one's youth. We were young together, and happy, and in love—for a time. One can't pretend those years never existed. But I had 'moved on,' as the parlance goes. I'm afraid I thought seldom of Lexy these days, if at all. Awful thing to say now, I know, but it is the truth."

"Now, this evening, when you heard of her death, what did you do?"

"I simply could not believe it. I thought Seb must be mistaken."

"But you went to investigate."

"It was rather a reflex action. But really, the situation couldn't be ignored while we stood about sipping our port, could it? Although I did gather others were inclined to do just that. Some things about Cambridge never change, you know. Anyway, just to calm Seb I went to have a look. I thought it likely he'd stumbled across a tramp sleeping it off ... it was bloody dark out, you know. The moon was hidden behind clouds, and the Bursar has never been one to 'waste' money on electricity." He broke off. "This is just ghastly. There was ... a certain amount of talk when I left Lexy for India, you know. It wasn't universally received as joyous news ... a lot of jealous old cats here, rather. This will just rake up all the old scandal. The media will have a field day. I can just see the headlines now: 'Killing at Cambridge College.'"

Sergeant Fear looked up. "'Murder at St. Michael's,'" he offered. This earned him a cautioning look from St. Just, tempted as he himself was to enter into the headline game. He and Sergeant Fear often had private bets on how far into bad taste the press might wander over a particular case. More often than not, the pair of them could not begin to anticipate the worst efforts put forth by the members of the media.

"Good God," said James. "I don't suppose you can prevent that in any way?"

"It's doubtful, Sir. It's their job."

"Just imagine, doing that to earn a living."

"Now, Sir, your divorce from Lexy. I'm afraid I'll have to ask."

"It's not germane, I tell you. Ancient history." Off St. Just's look, he subsided. "Oh, very well. What?"

"It was an amicable parting, was it?"

Sir James observed the ceiling, as if the answer might be written there. "I'll be truthful. It was not amicable. I never believe people who say their divorce was, do you? By its definition, divorce means something has gone horribly wrong in a marriage and both sides can barely stand to be in the same room together.

In our case ... well, I suppose I behaved like a cad. I did behave like a cad—all right, I'll admit it. But I met India and that was it. It was really the most astonishing, life-changing thing. I was mesmerized. Bewitched by her, I suppose some would say. If I could have helped myself, stopped myself, believe me I would have done so. But I don't think it ever occurred to me that that was an option."

"Do you still feel that way, Sir? No regrets?"

"Utterly and completely. I couldn't bear to be parted from India for a day. So, no—no regrets whatsoever, except that I know it all hurt Lexy. But I simply can't imagine my life without India."

India's motive was looking weaker by the minute, if Sir James was telling the truth. St. Just could sympathize with any man who felt bewitched, since James had well described his own reaction on meeting Portia, not too long ago. Good to know that kind of coup de foudre could lead to lasting love.

"I did wonder," James was saying, "when she turned up with that Argentine fellow."

"Geraldo Valentiano. Yes?"

"I just mean to say, I can't really see him wanting to harm Lexy, can you? I gathered the impression they didn't know each other that well, or for that long. You had to know Lexy to—"

"To what, Sir? Hate her?"

Back-pedaling madly, Sir James said, "She was highly strung, Inspector. Anyone can tell you that. Even so, it is impossible to imagine her doing anything that could provoke him to that extent. A lover's quarrel? Well, the hot-tempered Latino is rather a cliché, is it not? And quite undeserved, in my experience. Anyway, in this case, he doesn't strike me as showing much interest outside himself."

St. Just thought that a fair and accurate assessment of the Argentine's baseline character, but was less willing to give Geraldo a free pass in the hot-tempered department.

Sergeant Fear looked up from his notebook.

"What was Lexy's attitude towards him? Valentiano, I mean?"

James looked first to St. Just before answering:

"That's rather a good question. I'm not sure I can say. She seemed—my impression only, you understand—but she seemed to regard him as decorative more than anything else. Of course, that may be a bit of prejudice on my part: He was a damnably good-looking man. Always did get my back up, that type."

Amen to that, thought St. Just. Aloud he said, "You think she was using him to make you jealous?"

"Well, I wouldn't say that... I don't really know. It does rather sound like something she'd do, I suppose..." His voice trailed off. His gaze rested on the fireplace, its hearth filled with summer flowers. Sir James seemed to be lost in the past—the past of his marriage to Lexy, presumably.

"You were seen talking with her. After dinner."

Sir James seemed slightly taken aback at this. He blinked several times. "Was I? Yes, I rather suppose I would be."

"What was the topic?"

Sir James said nothing.

"I'm going to have to insist that you answer, Sir. Was she hoping for reconciliation between you two?"

He shook his head ruefully. "She knew that was out of the question."

"Hope is different from knowing, though, isn't it? Did she have hope?"

Reluctantly, Sir James said, "She may have done. I did nothing whatsoever to encourage her thinking along those lines. Nothing. That you must believe absolutely."

"Your meeting with her in the Fellows' Garden—was that by pre-arrangement?"

Looking taken aback by the question, Sir James didn't respond immediately. Finally he said, "No. I stepped out for a cigarette, and there she was. I allow myself one cigarette after each meal, you see."

"She knew your habits, did she? So she might have hoped to run into you."

"That is possible. Of course, I could have gone 'round to the front of the college."

"What did you talk about?"

"She said something about how the memories were flooding back, and didn't I feel it, too? The past revisited. 'I feel such melancholy,' she said. She asked me—" Here he paused, as if needing to collect himself. And when he spoke again moments later, his voice was husky and raw. "She asked me if I'd ever loved her. Now, in retrospect, that seems so incredibly sad, knowing she had such a short time to live."

"And how did you answer, Sir?"

"I told her the truth. I told her that of course I had loved her. Thank God. If it gave her any peace to hear that, I am quite glad we had the conversation we had."

"Did Lexy smoke?"

The question seemed to surprise him. "Not to my knowledge. Never. Why do you ask?"

"Just wondering what drew her outside, if not to meet you."

"A breath of air, I'd imagine. These college dinners can be stuffy in more ways than one."

"Did she have her evening bag with her?"

Again, that look of mild, puzzled surprise. "Yes, I believe she did. I didn't really notice."

"Did she know many people still living in Cambridge?"

"Probably a few. Perhaps people connected with her old department. I don't really know whom she's kept up with."

"What did she read at Cambridge?"

"Law."

"Really?"

"Yes. But she barely scraped through her final exams and never practiced the law, to my knowledge." He paused to inspect an immaculate cuff. "Probably just as well," he continued. "Lexy was very bright, don't misunderstand. But she could also be rather … undisciplined. Not everything you'd want in a solicitor. Law was her father's idea."

"Her parents? Can you help us get in touch?"

"Both long dead, I'm afraid. Motoring accident. That's what makes it rather sad. Apart from her nightclubbing friends—and the less said about them the better—she was quite alone. She never remarried, had no children."

"Sir James, who do you think did this?"

"A passing madman, of course. It must be. Really, who else could it have been?"

"That's what I'm asking you, Sir."

"You think one of us—the group that's here for the week-end?"

St. Just let the silence stretch out, an artful pause, then asked, "You say your wife was not given to jealousy?"

This seemed to galvanize Sir James.

"Not in the least. It's preposterous to suggest otherwise, to imply—"

"But, she must have disliked Lexy, rather. Lexy who wouldn't let go, who hung on, making things uncomfortable for the pair of you, especially this weekend. Making both of you feel guilty, perhaps."

"Don't be absurd, man. Besides, aren't you forgetting, India was in the SCR, with many others to attest to that?"

"There's that, of course," said St. Just mildly. "Well, thank you. You've been most helpful."

After Sir James left, having reiterated his pleasure in doing any-thing he could to help, Fear said, "If you ask me, Sir, that was a man choosing his words carefully. It was as if he was trying to avoid giv-ing offense—do you follow?"

"Nil nisi bonum. Speaking no evil of the dead. An ex-wife, just brutally murdered—possibly that is not the best time to get the truth out of an ex-husband."

"We really are limited to the people here at the college, do you think?" asked Sergeant Fear.

"The only other access was by river," St. Just replied. "And that is the one area the wretched security cameras would have picked up—they are all trained, did you notice, on the access points from the river? Of course we'll be viewing the tapes closely—but I doubt we'll see more than a clear shot of Sebastian's departure and arrival back at the boathouse. It definitely makes one think this crime was committed by someone who knew the college, knew exactly where the security cameras were targeted and knew how to avoid them. Knew that some of the cameras were dummy cameras. Knew, in other words, the security was pathetic, and rather relied on that fact. That doesn't speak of a random passer-by. As I say, we'll look at the video, but I promise you, if it shows anyone in any kind of river conveyance, it shows them going straight past the college, not turning in to hop off and kill Lexy. Who just happened to be standing there. And there's another question—if she was standing there, why? Whom did she hope to meet?"

"Our friend Geraldo?" asked Sergeant Fear.

"Perhaps. He has rather the same alibi as all the others. They didn't all head straight for the SCR en masse, but rather slowly drifted in. We need to get a handle on who was late in showing up. Let's have Lady Bassett in here next."

India Bassett strode athletically into the room, as if about to leap on a horse and ride off. St. Just politely indicated a chair opposite him instead. She looked at the item of furniture a moment as if unsure of its purpose before finally sitting down.

St. Just took a moment to survey India, as she asked to be called, as she settled herself in. She was in fact rather a horsey looking woman, her face long and mobile, but she also possessed a homey quality that didn't quite go with being a member of the riding-to-hounds set. She seemed a comfortable person to be around, St. Just thought, an impression that was reinforced as they talked. Her tanned complexion drew attention to rather startlingly blue eyes, the whites of which shone with apparent good health. Crow's feet were just beginning to etch their way permanently into her skin. The blonde hair, sun-bleached beyond all hope of resuscitation, could have used a spot of conditioner or whatever it was women used.

She'd taken off her academic gown, which she carried slung over one arm; under the somber gown she had worn a dress in a bold summer print of red and yellow. It recalled to St. Just the dresses women wore in the summers of his childhood. He would have put her age at forty-five, but he thought her weather-beaten appearance was probably misleading him.

Sergeant Fear, for his part, liked her as well. A sturdy, earthy, no-nonsense sort, as her husband had implied.

St. Just began by asking her where she was from the time she came down to dinner. She gave them a brief summary, ending with:

"Dinner ended at nine-fifteen, but then I stayed a bit to talk with the Master. He is a dear but he does tend to wander on. Of course, he's on a mission this weekend. We walked together to the SCR."

"You were with each other the whole time?"

"That is correct."

"Now, I realize this is awkward, given your situation, but I will need your impressions of Lexy Laurant."

She nodded understandingly as he spoke. "I can only feel pity for her now, of course," she said, "but in life she could be … difficult." A heavy note of irony had entered her voice: She might as well have come out and said she had found her impossible to deal with. "The divorce hit her hard, no doubt of it, but it was all ages ago." There seemed to be an unspoken "These things happen" subtext to her words.

"Did she seem to be over it?"

"Not entirely, no. But we were spared the hysterics and scenes of previous years. Her new angle seemed to be to wave Geraldo under my husband's nose at every opportunity. It was the sort of behavior that is much easier to ignore."

"So. Let's back up for a bit. You walked with the Master to the SCR. That took how long?"

"It's rather a large college and so a bit of a walk, with the gallery and then the long corridor leading to the SCR. I'd say a few minutes, walking slowly, yes."

"And you went straight to the SCR. You didn't stop at the cloak room, for example."

"Oh! Well, I did, of course, but only for a moment. Really, I was just trying to shake off the Master, if you want the truth."

"That's why we're here, yes," said St. Just, with just a tinge of exasperation. "To get at the truth. I understand at some point while you were in the SCR the curfew warning bell rang. You all could hear it?"

"Yes. Quite clearly; it's a most annoying sound, like a flock of geese calling for help from inside in a large tin. And then shortly after that, Seb came running in. Poor child." She shook her head. "Seb and his precious rowing. Do you know, he is so disciplined in that regard—I can't tell you what a relief it's been since he discovered this talent. He's not terribly disciplined in any other way."

"Who was in the SCR when you entered?" asked St. Just.

"That's rather difficult. The Master had reattached himself and was bending my ear again by then. Let's see, I believe the Americans were there—they're always frightfully hard to miss, aren't they? At least, she is—Constance. And dear old Hermione was gassing away about the polar ice caps."

"When did your husband arrive?"

"Oh, didn't I say? He was already there. I tell you, I was rather waylaid by the Master. They are quite desperate for donations, poor lambs."

Fear, pen flying, found he was a bit in awe of this woman who could speak so offhandedly about the Master. He thought: She's the real thing; not given to show. Upper crust—not flashy, though. Real upper crust.

"So, you weren't entirely fond of Lexy, would it be true to say?"

She answered coolly, "Some women make rather a success of divorce. Lexy was not one of those women. I'm afraid that instead she continued to carry a torch for my husband. Writing him letters and so on. 'Asking his advice' on this, that, or the other. Just 'happening' to be where she knew he would be. To be completely frank, she never stopped thinking of him as her husband, I don't think."

"Do you have any of those letters?"

"Oh, I'm sure not. They used to aggravate James no end. I'm certain they went straight into the fire, as he told me they did. But you should ask him."

"Her view of things was rather 'finders, keepers,' was it?"

"Something like that. Exactly like that, now you mention it. Her head, I think, was rather filled with romantic nonsense, and she always had an inability to deal with reality. In the real world, relationships dissolve, lose their—I suppose one must say—their usefulness. Hard as that sounds, it is the way of the world, and Lexy never came to grips with it. She was, in many ways, a born victim, you know. The manner of her death was, while a shock, not completely out of character, if one can put it what way. Lexy would always manage to create, and to cultivate, chaos around her person."

Sergeant Fear, hearing this opinion voiced with such confidence, felt somehow this assessment was spot on—even without his ever having met the victim.

"I mean, here she was," India went on, "intelligent in her own way—although crafty might be a better word, and educated—" here she threw wide one arm rather as St. Just had done earlier to encompass the paneled walls, the Carolean bookcases, the seals and crests and other emblems of prestigious learning, "and beautiful to boot. But what did she do but throw herself at someone like—well, forgive me, but that boyfriend of hers, whatever his name is, is so obviously a scamp. What on earth could she have been thinking? You don't suppose..."

"Suppose?" prompted St. Just, responding to her look of confusion.

"Well, that he had anything to do with this? Some heat of passion type of crime? I overheard them quarreling you know."

She nodded emphatically, gratified by the effect this had on her listeners.

"Indeed. I heard them quarreling, and quite violently."

OVERHEARD

"THAT'S RIGHT. YOU MAY well look shocked." India rearranged the diamond bracelets on each arm, creating a show of twinkling lights against the wall and ceiling as table lamps caught the sparkles and made them dance. Seeing she had the full attention of her audience, she went on:

"It was our first night here … just last night, in fact. The windows in my room were open, as they were in most rooms, I'd wager—apart from Mrs. Dunning's. She's done nothing but complain about the cold since she got here. Hermione, although rather mad in her way, is quite right about global warming, you know. The college used to be freezing year-round. It's been quite warm since we got here, even in the dungeon-like rooms along that corridor, and we've had to keep the windows open all night. No air conditioning in the old part of the college, of course, and—"

"Anyway," St. Just cut in. She smiled charmingly, not in the least offended.

"Sorry, I do go on. Anyway, I was unpacking—James was down the corridor, trying to coax hot water out of the college's rusty old pipes for a shower. This was before the big kerfuffle about Lexy's room being broken into, which was also impossible not to overhear. Oh, I see you do know about that? Well, I'll get back to that in a minute, shall I? Anyway, I was unpacking when Lexy and her friend started a real argy-bargy."

"What was said?"

"I could really only hear half the conversation without actually hanging out of the window, you know. Her little girl voice didn't carry, somehow, and it sounded anyway as if he were nearer the window, she on the other side of the room. I did hear her say—she got rather shrill at moments, which is when I could hear her well—I heard her say, 'I didn't bring you here to make a fool of me.' To which Geraldo replied, 'No, you don't need anyone's help for that.' I thought that was rather good, frankly. But he mainly kept saying, 'Don't be absurd!' or 'I did nothing of the sort!' and so on. Denials. I remember particularly when he said, 'You'll get your money back and more, don't worry.'"

"You're quite certain, money was mentioned?"

"Quite certain."

"Do you recall anything else you may have overheard?"

She shook her head. She wore a little diamante headband—not quite a tiara—and the movement dislodged it. Her hand flew up to catch it before it fell. She placed it in what looked like an antique jet-beaded handbag.

"I'll try to remember, but I think that was it."

"As to her room being broken into . . . ?"

"Yes, wasn't that another tempest? Honestly, being next door to that room was like trying to fall asleep in King's Cross. Again, because it was so stuffy in the room, we heard more than perhaps we were meant to, through the open windows."

"Your husband was with you, then?"

"Yes."

"Go on."

"We heard Lexy raise the alarm. This was Saturday afternoon. Complaining that the lock on her room had been forced. I guess the Porter and several members of staff were called in to investigate—we could hear various voices, all talking at once, asking her if anything had been stolen. 'No, I don't think so'—I heard her say that plainly enough. 'That's what's so very odd,' she said. 'All my jewelry is right here'—presumably, still in her jewelry case or whatever she travels with."

St. Just sat for a moment, lost in thought. Sergeant Fear took advantage of the lull to extract another Biro from his pocket, having run the first one nearly dry. At last, St. Just said, "You are certain it was Geraldo Valentiano she quarreled with?"

"Positive. I mean, there can't be too many others running about the college with that Rubirosa-type accent."

"I'm sorry," put in Sergeant Fear. "Would you spell that, please?"

She spelled it out for him, and seeing the Sergeant's continued look of puzzlement, said kindly, "He was a bit before your time. Mine, too, come to that. He was a famously louche playboy of the '40s and '50s. Worked his way through the list of any heiress or actress of the day worth knowing. A legendary Lothario. I only know who he was because my mother used to speak of him with great fondness—she was suspiciously fond, if you know what I mean. Anyway, our Argentine is much the same type of egg. All melting glances under the moonlight. Then, poof! Next day, gone. Lexy was rather a fool, you know."

"Well, this has been most helpful, Lady Bassett," said St. Just.

"India, please! We shall all get to know each other rather well before this is over, I should imagine."

"I imagine so. Please let us know if you can add anything to what you've already told us."

She merely shook her head, looking, for the first time, rather helpless. When she had left, Sergeant Fear turned to St. Just and said, "Funny Geraldo didn't mention any quarrel over money while we had him in here."

"Yes," said St. Just faintly. "Of course, if Lady Bassett is the only one who overheard this altercation ... "

"You think she was lying, Sir?"

"I think she might have a motive to protect her husband if she thinks he might be implicated. Not quite the same thing, is it, Sergeant, as proof she's lying?"

Sergeant Fear allowed that it was not.

"As to the break-in, if that's what it was, it sounds as if there were plenty of witnesses to the conversation about that. We'll have to talk to the Porter and find out what he knows about it. We'd better have a look in Lexy's room. Make sure Geraldo kips somewhere else tonight, if he thinks he's staying there." First pulling back his cuff to look at his watch, St. Just drew the list of names towards him again and said, "Who's next? ... Mr. and Mrs. Dunning of New York, USA. We'll have the wife first, I think."

Constance Dunning was a formidable-looking woman of militaristic bearing whose counterpart in Great Britain would no doubt be the mainstay of the Women's Institute; the heart and soul, not to mention the veritable backbone, of the village fete; the bastion of the Bring-and-Buy table. What equivalent role she might perform in the United States, St. Just could not imagine, but surely the entire world needed someone such as she to keep it whipped into shape. Stepping with thunderous intensity into the room, she seized the reins of the conversation immediately, settling into an armchair and proclaiming in ringing tones, "This is a shocking thing to have happened. Positively shocking. We come to England to get away from this kind of thing."

"Yes, I do realize—"

"First, we endure the most endless flight from New York, during which we are served five small, broken pretzels as an appetizer—five—only to arrive at Heathrow, which is an absolute madhouse—a madhouse, I tell you. Talk about your melting pots! Where are they all going? Where can they be traveling to? And the whole time we're being gouged left and right, nickled and dimed to death, the exchange rate being what it is. I bought a T-shirt yesterday—a T-shirt, mind, and not of a very good quality cotton—that must have set us back thirty-five dollars. Highway robbery, I told the clerk. I lay the blame at the door of the European Union—such a bad idea that was. And then to come here and suffer the outrage of a police investigation, well, I never—"

Sergeant Fear wondered when St. Just was going to make Constance Dunning put a sock in it. He looked over to his superior, who seemed to be listening with every sign of attention and sympathy. Fear had to hand it to him. They'd interviewed witnesses together that Fear would cheerfully have shot, given a gun, while St. Just managed, for the most part, to maintain an interested and encouraging air about him. Most suspects loved him, and if the feeling weren't reciprocated, they seldom came to know of it.

"—and her so young. What is the country coming to?"

She was giving little signs of slowing down, of exhausting her little store of clichés if not her enormous backlog of grievances. St. Just skillfully made his move.

"I ask myself that twice a day, Mrs. Dunning. The police, well, we have our work cut out for us, what? Now, you can be of the most enormous assistance to us, a woman of your caliber—"

And what would that be? A twenty-two? wondered Sergeant Fear.

"—and obvious gift of insight into the human condition. We need to know exactly where everyone was this evening, and what you observed. Your observations could be absolutely crucial to the success of our investigation."

Mrs. Dunning visibly expanded under this treatment. She wore a purple dress of a shiny fabric stretched taut as shrink-wrap across a massive chest. The serried strands of a pearl neck-lace nearly disappeared into her thick, fleshy neck; ankles bulged from the tops of black court shoes.

It didn't hurt that St. Just was handsome as the devil, but the sergeant had met many good-looking policeman who seemed to spend all day running about poking sticks in people's eyes. Now he watched as Constance Dunning, tittering slightly, patted her dark hair against her round head and said, "Of course, I'd do anything to help the British bobbies." And then, miraculously, she shut it and waited for St. Just's first question. Sergeant Fear drew a little smiley face in his policeman's notebook and then took down her particulars as they were offered.

"Now, Mrs. Dunning," said St. Just. "Let us start with why you came on this trip. As you say, it is frightfully expensive, and air travel is not the pleasure it once was."

"Well, my husband was keen to see the old place after so many years. We keep getting these things in the mail from the college, these brochures, and this year was our year, you know. Twenty-two years since Karl matriculated here. I said to him, 'It won't come around twice, this anniversary, and we may not be here for the thirty-year mark.' You never know, do you? So I said, 'Let's go.' And we did. Went."

She seemed to want to expand on the theme of the shortness of life and the fleetingness of time but, making a super-human effort, she subsided, again waiting expectantly to see how next she could help her British Bobby.

"And how did things, well, strike you once you were here? Any nuances or frictions, open quarrels? Especially any surrounding the person of Lexy Laurant?"

Sergeant Fear felt his superior was making a huge mistake here, asking such open-ended questions. Constance Dunning was the type of witness who could easily keep them here until doomsday talking about rubbishy nuances rather than cold hard facts. But she surprised him again by coming in at under sixty seconds.

"She had eyes only for that ex-husband of hers. The wife didn't like it much, but was trying not to let it show. The Argentine fellow didn't give a tinker's damn what she did—Lexy, I mean. But as to open quarrels, no. They're all British, except for that Cramb fellow and the Argentine, who lives here. That kind of thing rubs off. Stiff upper lip and tally ho, you know what I mean?"

"Yes, indeed I do. Would you mind telling us about your own movements, and what you know of your husband's, from the time you came downstairs this evening for dinner?" In case she might cut up at this suspect-type questioning—generally a signal for any red-blooded American to call the nearest embassy—St. Just added smoothly, "It's essential that we know where everyone was, at exactly what times, and an impartial witness such as yourself is always used as the benchmark in a police investigation on British soil. It's SOP at Interpol, too, of course. We'll issue countrywide bulletins, should that become necessary. BOLOs and so on. You do understand how crucial your testimony might become."

"BOLOs," she repeated breathlessly.

"Yes."

She lifted her large head, which sat like a bison's atop her bulky shoulders, without apparent recourse to the intervention of a neck, with keen interest. Sergeant Fear, who had never heard such a load of codswallop in all his years, did not dare meet St. Just's eyes, but desperately fixed his own eyes on his notebook, fighting back the maniacal laugh threatening to erupt.

"Of course, Chief Inspector," she said. "I quite understand." Another pat of her hair, and she leaned in conspiratorially—in case MI5 were listening in, presumably—before launching into a more or less cogent summary of her evening. Down to drinks at seven-thirty on the dot. Dinner at eight. Dinner finished at nine-fifteen or maybe a little later, she wasn't sure. She headed straight for the SCR. Her husband used the facilities and joined her shortly thereafter.

"And you, Mrs. Dunning," St. Just asked delicately. "You yourself had no need of, erm, the facilities?"

"I have the constitution of an ox, and I don't see any point in layering on powder and lipstick like some I could mention here—that television woman for a start. No. I came straight in."

"Did you see anything unusual, anything at all that might help us?"

"No. Coming out of Hall, through that overhead passage window, I saw Lexy talking with James in the Fellows' Garden. It was the last time I saw her—alive." She allowed herself a little waver of melodrama on the last word, then sank back in her chair, her mental survey of the hollowness and futility of all life's endeavors reflected sadly on her face. Apparently satisfied with her performance, she added, "That strapping young yellow-haired fellow came dashing in at five minutes before ten o'clock. I know. I checked my watch."

St. Just beamed at her. It was apparently all and more than she could have hoped for in the way of reward. They talked a few more minutes to no further purpose and then she left the room, meek as a lamb.

"A police investigation on British soil, Sir?" said Sergeant Fear as soon as the door had safely shut behind her broad back. "Interpol? Benchmarking? And, BOLOs? Be on the lookout for what?" St. Just was, Fear supposed, his mentor. But St. Just's quick ability to read a person's character and play to it ... Fear suspected St. Just possessed a gift that couldn't be taught. "Why didn't you mention the Flying Squad while you were about it?"

St. Just grinned widely. "The Chief Constable would be pleased," he said. "You see, I have picked up some of her jargon, after all. I guess we'll have the husband next, God bless him."

———

Mr. Dunning looked to be a pleasant man in his mid-forties. He was nearly bald, with just a small fringe of salt-and-pepper hair left to encircle his head. He sported gold-rimmed glasses and a little goatee that brought his round face to a Lenin-like point. This all contributed to his looking rather older than his true age, which he stated for the record to be forty.

"Your wife has given us a summary of your movements this evening, but of course we have to verify—and sometimes, re-ver-ify—every statement for accuracy. You do understand. So if you wouldn't mind, Sir ... "

And Mr. Dunning proceeded to give them a summary that matched his wife's, although his grasp of exact times seemed to be more tenuous than hers.

"I think everyone was back in the SCR by half past. Maybe sooner," he told them.

"I see. That's all fairly clear. Now, I would like your impressions of the atmosphere this weekend."

"Oh, my," said Mr. Dunning mildly. "My wife is much better at this sort of thing—atmospherics, you know—but I'll do my best." His eyes blinked thoughtfully for several seconds behind the glasses. At last he said, "Well, she wasn't happy, anyone could see that. The victim, I mean. Lexy. It was a shame, really. She was just as pretty as a peach, that girl. Woman, really, of course, but she had a girlish quality to her."

"But you knew her when she was a girl, isn't that correct? When you were here at St. Michael's as students together?"

"Well. Hmm. No. No, that wouldn't be accurate to say we were together, and I certainly wouldn't want Constance—Mrs. Dunning—to get any ideas in her head like that. Lexy was, if you want to know the truth, simply not in my league. I doubt she even noticed I was alive. She pretended to recognize me this weekend but I could tell she really didn't. You have to realize, there were hundreds of kids running around back then—you're not getting a true picture of the college out of term, as you must be aware. Those of us here this weekend—well, little pretense is made that we've not been cherry-picked because we've reached a certain, shall we say, financial threshold in our lives. That's why there are so few of us here. I don't mind. I love St. Mike's and they'll get plenty of moola out of me before all's said and done."

"What was Lexy like at that age?"

"Oh, I don't know. An angel with a temper? But that makes her sound angry, or violent. Not that. Just very emotional. Very fragile. Prone to scenes."

"Rather a difficult person to have around?"

"Oh, I don't know," he said again. "It never bothered me. But as I've said, our paths didn't cross much."

Anyone married to Constance Dunning might require or acquire the ability to let things slide off his back, reflected St. Just. The thought gave birth to his next question.

"Did you meet your wife here at St. Mike's?"

"No, indeed. We met on my return to the States, a few years later. Been married ever since."

"Did you notice anything unusual about this weekend? Any unusual alliances or feuds forming, perhaps?"

"You want to hear anything, however minor, I take it? Well, Augie Cramb is here this weekend, as I suppose you know or will learn. He comes across as buffoonish, but I wouldn't be too taken in by that if I were you. He comes from oil money and made more of his own in the tech world. We were in the same boat together, literally, back in the day. Rowing, that is. He seemed to go out of his way this weekend to befriend Sebastian, the boy who found the body. I saw them talking together on several occasions—probably about his rowing. I did tell you it was a minor thing. Just something I noticed."

St. Just could think of no further questions to ask him. With the traditional request that he make himself available for further questioning by himself or one of his men, he told Karl Dunning he could leave. He left.

UNQUIET AMERICAN

AUGIE WAS THEIR THIRD American of the night, but he was of a much different cut from the Dunnings of New York. Slow of speech, relaxed in attitude, he sprawled in the armchair vacated by Karl Dunning, but unlike Dunning with his rather precise, buttoned-down, yet helpful manner, Augie filled the room with his large body and his booming drawl. He spoke at such a leisurely pace Sergeant Fear had no trouble keeping up with him in his notebook, although a few words gave him trouble. He'd have to look them up later, back at the station. What, for example, was a pawdnuh?

Now Augie Cramb was saying something about calling his gopher back home.

"I'll ask him to email y'all a few photos from that time. You'll see. Lexy could make a dead man walk, if she felt like it. Trouble was, she didn't much feel like it, mostly. Wouldn't put out for no one, excepting, I reckon, that husband of her'n."

"I see," said St. Just. "Now, w—"

"Cold as charity, our Lexy," Augie warmed to his theme. "Cold as a nun's—say, you boys ain't Catholic, are you?"

St. Just shook his head. "C of E."

Augie Cramb looked puzzled. Was this one of those wacky cults? Plenty of those where he came from, but what would these two policemen be doing as members?

"Go on, Sir. You're saying Lexy lacked … a passionate nature?"

"Oh, she was passionate in that arty-farty way she had. Everything was 'too, too' and 'simply mah-velous, don't you know.' But there was no beef in that taco, no siree. No huevos in that ranchero. For that, a man needed to look elsewhere. Damn waste, it was. A cry and shame, as my daddy would have said."

"Are you trying to say she was frigid, Sir?" asked St. Just.

"Ain't that what I been a-tellin' you?"

No, you sidewinder. Sergeant Fear, exasperated by trying to translate the man's accent and vocabulary, was beginning to show the strain. The page of his notebook reserved for Augie Cramb was smeared and blotted with crossings-out and corrections. Here and there he'd added a few stars by the man's statements—Sergeant Fear's own system for ranking the truthfulness of a witness. St. Just call it his Torquemada Michelin Guide. One star meant truthful; five meant the sergeant believed the witness was almost certainly lying.

"Are you speaking from personal experience, Sir, or are these your impressions? Perhaps you're repeating a rumor you heard elsewhere?"

"Well …" and there came over Cramb's features a worldly-wise, man-to-man smirk: James Bond letting his hair down. "Normally, I would defend a lady's honor to the death, but since this is her death we're talking about—yes, we took it for a test drive once, after a spectacularly drunken night in the college bar. It was not a success, and the experiment was never repeated."

St. Just, wondering if the failure might not have been more on his side than hers after a night's drinking, asked mildly, "And that was the end of it?"

"Tell you the truth, Inspector, she gave me a wide berth after that. Ashamed, I reckon, of her performance. Next thing I knew, she'd taken up with Sir Whatsis—James Bassett—and that took care of the problem nicely. Still, for all the coldness, all the men were half in love with her."

"And you?"

"Oh, I have to admit, if I'm honest: She was way out of my league."

St. Just and Sergeant Fear surreptitiously exchanged glances. The phrase was becoming a little too familiar.

"Hmm." St. Just reckoned Lexy might have a different story to tell about the drunken night, had she been there to tell it.

"She was our cox, did you know? Yep. Me, James, and Karl were all in the college eight boat. Happiest time of my life. You wouldn't think it would be such a turn-on to have a purty little gal like that screaming bloody murder in your ear first thing on a freezing cold morning, but let me tell you—"

He paused to lick his lips before continuing his reminiscences.

"Moving right along, Mr. Cramb, I wonder if—"

"A'course, that didn't work out in the long haul, the business with James. Man'd have to be blind not to see India was the one for him. Well, they say the course of true love is a rocky road and I reckon it's true. Anything else I can do for you gentlemen?"

"I'd like your general impression of the events of the weekend, anything you may have noticed, anything at all," said St. Just.

"I really couldn't say. I kept to myself, mostly. Had a few conversations with that young Sebastian feller. Nice kid. Needs someone payin' attention to him, is all. Don't we all need that? Or we'd all go to the bad ... Anyway, as I say, I knew why I was invited here and apart from a private conversation with the Bursar I was pleased to keep myself to myself. We're a self-selecting group at this weekend hootenanny, you know. It is well understood that we'll be hit up for money at some point, and hit up hard. Or we would have been, before all this happened. Anyway, those who don't want to be held upside down until the last penny drops, so to speak, stay well away from these events. The weekend after this is for what I think you guys call the punters—the ones who think a five-hundred dollar donation is a big deal. A'course, they ain't invited, that type, to this weekend."

"So, I gather you've donated generously in the past, which is why your name turned up on ... shall we call it the A-list?"

"Thas right. An old barn of a place like this takes serious cash to keep it going. I've been happy to oblige. More where that came from, anyhoo. Well, gentlemen"—and here he slapped his knees preparatory to rising—"if there's nothin' else, I'll be—"

"Actually, Sir, we were just getting to the interesting part."

"Inerestin'?" He hesitated, then slowly settled back in his chair. "Okay. Shoot."

Don't tempt me. Sergeant Fear, who generally liked Americans, couldn't quite pinpoint why this one kept getting up his nose. But he had a feeling something was being left out of the man's testimony, and deliberately. A shift of the eyes, nearly imperceptible, made Fear think Cramb was hiding something, or at least avoiding it. Whether it was something important or not, Fear couldn't say. His daughter Emma sometimes had that evasive look, and she was only four. Just to be on the safe side, he placed an extra star next to Augie Cramb's comments about Lexy.

St. Just said, "You say James and India were meant for each other. What went on back in the day when James left Lexy for India?"

"What didn't go on. Doors slamming, boo-hooing, weeping into the pond at midnight. And that was just the bedders—only kidding, but it upset everyone within range. When I said Lexy was passionate, I reckon I should have flat-out told you she was a drama queen. There was more of that on view this weekend, but much milder than what we were used to seeing. Damned awkward for a man when a gal cuts up like that. Spent half her time moping about on that bench by the fountain in First Court, sighing over a poetry book or whatever, or simply looking bereft. I used to think all that was needed to complete the picture was a reflecting pool."

"How did India take all this—what was going on this weekend?"

Cramb let out a little bark of pleasure. "India's what you'd call a man's woman—the kinda woman that men both trust and lust after. She's got balls on her, that one. She might not have liked what she saw, but I think she knew James well enough to know Lexy was no threat. Sexy gal, India, always was, though she looks like a prairie dog after a hailstorm half the time. James took one look—back in the day, as you say—and acted like sex had just been invented. As far as James was concerned, that was probably the case, especially after his time with Lexy. These boarding schools you fellers have over here—take all the stuffing out of a man. India runs that show, unless I miss my guess. If anything, the shoe might be on the other foot, if you know what I mean."

"Sir?"

"India and that Geraldo looked mighty friendly to me. Friendly, that's all I'm sayin'. But I don't reckon Lexy liked India running all over that property any more than she appreciated India poaching her husband some-odd years ago. That's all I'm sayin'," he repeated.

That was quite a lot, thought St. Just. Cramb was the first person to mention this. Karl Dunning may have been right: It might be a mistake to dismiss Augie Cramb as a complete buffoon. Maybe Lexy, "passionate" Lexy, had confronted her old rival India. Worth looking into.

"And your movements after dinner, Sir?"

"Skipped to the loo. Hah! That's what you'd call a trans-Atlantic joke. Heard it on the Queen Mary II coming over one year. Anyway, I popped in and out—stepped out front for some air. Had to make a phone call, too, on my cell. Porter saw me. I strolled the grounds a bit, then came to the SCR. Wasn't long after, Sebastian came in to fetch help. Poor kid looked like he'd seen a ghost. I stayed with him and sent James as advance scout to see what was up."

He pushed back the sleeve on his left arm to reveal a thick gold wristwatch. It had several small windows on its face to display things like the tides and the phases of the moon. If it also read out horoscopes in six foreign languages, St. Just thought, he would not have been surprised.

"Why didn't Geraldo Valentiano go?" he asked. "After all, he was Lexy's escort, was he not?"

"You have got to be kidding me," Cramb replied. "That pantywaist? Last man you'd want in an emergency. No, James said he'd go see what was wrong and I for one was pleased to let him do it. Sound enough man, James, but Geraldo I wouldn't trust an inch. He uses pomade on that hair of his, you know. I wouldn't be surprised if his hair were dyed, too. And his hands are manicured." He glanced at his own rough hands that looked as if they were often employed in ripping trees from the ground. He shook his head. "Can't be trusted."

He sat back, arms folded, having delivered this string of conclusive evidence. "And that's that."

"How long were you on your mobile, Sir?"

"My cell? Dunno. Ten minutes? Five? You can check the records, fine by me. I got me one of them phones that works internationally. Had to make a call home."

"You're married, Sir?"

He shook his head.

"Never met the right lady. And the divorce rate being what it is, a man's gotta be cautious these days. Thar's golddiggers in them thar hills. That all?"

"Yes, for now. Thank you."

Cramb stood and hitched up his pants. Despite themselves the two policemen stared, fascinated, at the belt buckle he wore in place of a cummerbund. Highly polished and intricately carved, it depicted an enormous steer's head, its eyes represented by two large turquoise stones. It and the wide belt would have been suitable for securing the college gates, let alone holding up Cramb's trousers. His feet were shod in tooled-leather cowboy boots.

"Good luck catching whoever did this," he said. "Lynching's too good for him. She was a nice little lady, and purty as a daisy. Damned shame."

After he left, St. Just said, "We'll need to take him up on his suggestion of checking the phone records. It might help us pinpoint these times. Still, a ten-minute call on the records doesn't mean he was talking to anyone for ten minutes. He could have been put on hold the whole time, or have reached an answering machine. The mobile could have been in his pocket, engaged, as he strangled Lexy."

"I didn't much care for him, Sir."

"I noticed the chill. Any particular reason?"

"Dunno. What kind of man wears clothes like that?"

"It's his culture. It's how people dress where he comes from. Think of him as a Maori tribesman and it will come easier. Let's see…" and he consulted the list again. "Time for a word with Hermione Jax."

———

With Hermione Jax, they were firmly back on British soil after their adventures in the Wild West. She proved to be a woman in her early fifties, with iron-gray spectacles and a steely spine to match, St. Just would warrant. Her thick gray hair was coiled atop her head like an intricately braided laundry basket.

Within a very few minutes, she impressed St. Just as being the rugged type of British intellectual of whom legends were repeated, by whom astonishing discoveries were made, and after whom girls' schools and colleges were named.

She sat across from the policemen, her feet in their sturdy brogues planted squarely on the carpet, tweed skirt draped between her knees, and hands clasped firmly on top of her walking stick. Despite her apparent physical robustness, her camel-like visage held the gaunt, zealous imprint of the fanatic. It was the kind of face one would expect to have found amongst the crowd that stormed the Bastille. St. Just noticed she had a small plastic bottle of hand sanitizer looped over her belt. Her eyes drawn as if instinctively to the senior officer, she began by demanding to know what the police had learned so far.

"Early days yet. Is it Miss or Mrs. Jax?" asked St. Just.

She folded her lips into a straight, disapproving crease. "It is Ms. Jax, Inspector, and I am astonished that I should have to enlighten you on that score. Women fought and died for the respect signified by that title. They were force-fed in your prisons, and trampled by your horses. I insist upon its use."

Whatever Lola wants. Sergeant Fear, flipping to a fresh page in his notebook, sat up a bit straighter in his chair. Ms. Jax had that effect. St. Just, meanwhile, wondered why the horses were suddenly his.

"I do apologize, Ms. Jax," he said. "Now, I just have a few questions. I need you to tell me what you know of this matter."

"Nothing whatsoever. I only wish I did. This sort of thing's bad for the image of the college. Silly woman—and she was silly,

I have to say—to bring herself here of all places to be killed. It doesn't bear thinking about."

"Inconsiderate, one could say."

She pierced St. Just with a lancet glare.

"Don't coddle me, Inspector. Of course I realize the poor girl can't be blamed. But it's nothing to do with the college, of that you can be certain. It is unfortunate it happened here and now, is all that I am saying. It could ruin the fund-raising drive. People don't like it when other people are murdered. Puts them off."

"Quite. Now, Ms. Jax, how well did you know the participants of this weekend?"

"Remember 'em all, of course," she said gruffly. "Of course, I was older than most of them by about ten years, and I didn't waste my time, like most of them did, on foolishness, but I remember them well enough. What do you want to know?"

As often with St. Just, what he wanted to know probably had nothing to do with the case, but he was curious to learn more about Ms. Hermione Jax.

"Why don't you start by telling me how you came to be here at St. Mike's? What made you choose this college? Choose Cambridge, for that matter?"

"You mean, what took me so long to get here?"

That hadn't actually been the question, but he let her answer it anyway.

"Simply put: my father," she went on. "I cared for him all his life, and throughout his final illness, which lasted all through my young adulthood. He was of the old school that didn't believe in education for women—there was never any question of my going to any college, anywhere. He made his decision and I abided by it.

At least, I pretended to. When he died, he left me his fortune—he'd never have done that if he knew how I'd spend it, you can be certain. Anyway, I had the freedom at last to do what I'd always most wanted, and I applied straightaway as a mature student. As to why St. Mike's: In the day, they had a tutor here who was one of the world's leading experts in botany, my chosen field." As if to clarify an impenetrably dense point, she added, "That is the study of plants."

St. Just nodded, not greatly offended. The Great British Public seemed to view policemen, despite having been entrusted with its own personal safety, as barbaric numbskulls. He was, to some extent, used to it.

"As a mature student," he said, "perhaps you had a different vantage point that could be helpful. You say you remember them all, the people here this weekend. Tell me what you remember."

"Strange to tell, what struck me right away was that nothing had changed. Lexy was always at the eye of some storm or other. Spoiled silly, of course. Wasted her time and opportunities here. When I think of the deserving girls who could have had her place! But Lexy—with her it was men, men, men. Man mad, she was. It always comes to a bad end, that kind of thing. You can't hitch your wagon to some man's star. A woman has to be independent."

She stomped her cane on the carpet for emphasis and then sat, smoldering, awaiting the next question.

"Quite," said St. Just again. It seemed the wiser, not to say, the safer course, to simply agree with her. She looked more than capable of wielding that stick to good effect if aroused. "And the others? What about them?"

"Well, of course, having snared James as quickly as possible—I blame the family; they have been allowed to breed too closely for generations; even Lexy and Sir James are cousins, you know, although quite distant ones—as I say, having made a career of snagging James and then succeeding in her neurotic fashion, well, we were all subjected to the absolutely shameful goings on when India next got her claws into him. It was a veritable soap opera, and of course it went on for months. Positive months. Now that I am being forced to relive it all, it puts me in mind of the Cambridge don who married his bedder some years ago. She managed it in the usual way. There's nothing new under the sun, my good man."

Sergeant Fear, curiosity piqued, asked, "And what way is that, ma'am?"

Hermione turned her head and, aiming more or less in Fear's direction, replied, "She ignored him. Treated him like dirt under her feet." Thump. "Men can never resist that."

"I see. Right you are," Sergeant Fear said, thinking: If she thumps that cane of hers again I may have to go over there and snap it in two for her.

"Fortunately, Lexy moved out of college completely once the divorce was underway, and James and India set up housekeeping elsewhere, so we were spared much of what went on when Sebastian was discovered."

He might have been found under a tree. "So James wasn't aware of his existence, this stepson?"

"Course he was. And any man worth his salt would have dropped India on the spot once she turned up pregnant, but not James. Poor chump. He had it bad."

"Please. Let's back up a bit. You're saying James and India were together when Sebastian was born but that James was not the father?"

"Didn't I just say that? And, it nearly sent Lexy over the edge. She always was unstable, but for James to leave her for a woman who was pregnant by another man—well, you can imagine. Can't say I blame her entirely. Rumor was she couldn't have children of her own. A rum situation all 'round. Well, at least, as I say, we were spared much of that. The situation got so complicated, not to say noisy, that the Master and Bursar stepped in, had a word, and everyone was found other accommodation."

St. Just had to admit it had to have been a delicate situation for all.

"Do you have some theory of your own as to why Lexy was killed, Ms. Jax?" he asked.

"I should have thought that was your job, Chief Inspector."

Clearly, the kind of flattery that worked a treat on Mrs. Dunning was going to cut no ice here.

"What was the state of her relationship with Sir James and Lady Bassett?"

"I don't know. I paid no attention."

"Lexy's relationship with Geraldo—was it serious, would you say?"

"I would say a relationship with that bullfighter or whatever he is would be as enriching as a relationship with a peacock. As to serious, I couldn't say. He's not quite one of us, is he? NOC, most definitely. Not Our Class—no indeed. I felt altogether that he was here for show. Lexy was up to her usual tricks—trying to ignite the jealousy of Sir James."

"Did she succeed?"

An eloquent shrug.

"No idea."

"And your own movements during and after dinner, Ms. Jax? Did you notice, for example, when Lexy left the table?"

"Same time as we all did. Quarter past the hour. She may have been first out—she was near one end of the table and didn't have to crawl out from the bench as the rest of us did."

"And that's the last you saw of her?"

"Yes."

"You didn't notice her in the Fellows' Garden?"

"I've just said, haven't I? I was busy having a word with the Reverend Otis. Well, I may have just noticed her in conversation with Sir James. She seemed to be trembling, upset, so I looked away. It doesn't do, that kind of thing. Then I went up to my rooms to throw some water on my face—it's been devilishly hot, as you know. Then I went down to the SCR."

"At what time?"

"I've no idea. There was nothing special about my going there. I do so most evenings when I'm in college."

"Who was there?"

"I didn't notice," she said, her voice tinged with exasperation. "It was getting crowded. I headed straight for the drinks tray. Then I engaged the Bursar in conversation."

Ignoring the guests, it sounded like. She would be like that, St. Just thought. Insular, regarding the college as "hers," fiercely protective, a self-appointed guardian of St. Michael's past and future. A guardian of morals as well, no doubt. He felt he'd met the type before. The extreme of her type could be quite, quite potty. And dangerous, given the right circumstances. He dared a direct look into her eyes. She glared back, pop-eyed—outraged, perhaps, by his insolence. He was strongly reminded of Winston Churchill in the later years, when he had grown to resemble a cigar-chomping bulldog.

"Will that be all, Chief Inspector?" she said at last, rising to her feet as she said it. The cane seemed to be only for appearance's sake, as she rose with great alacrity, not putting any weight on the prop. She probably kept it to hand as a weapon, ready to incapacitate any thief foolhardy enough to think of having a grab at her purse or her bicycle. She would remain independent and eccentric to her dying day, frugal (her clothes showed no signs of the wealth she had inherited, but looked like Oxfam finds), fiercely dedicated to her chosen field of study, and a slave to the college where she had first tasted freedom. Both physically and psychologically suited to the crime, then.

But that description fit most of the others, of course.

"Good night, Chief Inspector," she said, and sturdily marched out of the room as if to engage the hidden enemy. Sergeant Fear might not even have been there.

"She's a right old trout," he told St. Just. "And batting for the other side, I'd wager."

"If you mean gay, Sergeant: No, I think you're mistaken there. But I would wager that wherever she loved, she'd love with a fierce devotion, regardless of whether the devotion were returned or even deserved."

"Do you think she could have done it?"

"Oh, certainly. Without turning a hair. The way she waited out her father so she could get her way in the end speaks of rather a cunning if not a devious nature, does it not? And she doesn't really account for her time well. But as to motive ... if she had some noble cause driving her, I guarantee it will be something that would strike any modern juror as preposterous. I thought her kind had long since died out, and she's not really that old. Who's next?"

THIS JUST IN

GWENNAP PENGELLY BREEZED IN, introduced herself—"Puh-leeze call me Gwenn, not Gwennap"—shook hands with both men, sat down, and gave them her London home and office addresses and no fewer than three phone numbers where she could be reached—all without being asked.

St. Just sized her up as she chirped on. She had a broad, angled face with an almost Asiatic cast to the eyes, and a head that appeared to be too large for her body. But that may have been an illusion caused by her fashionably emaciated frame. Her hair was parted in the center and fell to her shoulders in artfully cascading curves and twists. She had freshened her makeup: the lips of her pouty mouth glistened pinkly, and her eyes were heavily ringed in black. These enhancements didn't appear to be repairs to hide her grief, for the whites of her panda eyes shone with health and vitality. Rather, so might an actress prepare for her debut performance. In common with other media personalities he had met, and in the course of his career he had necessarily met a few, she was shorter than she appeared on television.

"My mobile is best, of course," she was saying now. "It's never turned off and I travel with three spare batteries. 'Breaking News Never Sleeps.' That's our motto at the station. Complete marketing bollocks, of course, but it sounds good, doesn't it?" She beamed brightly at both men in turn then, seeming to remember the gravity of the situation at hand, composed her features into a scowl of concern. It was a trick she'd picked up as a broadcaster, no doubt—that ability to organize facial features and tone of voice to suit the story. Much like an actress, thought St. Just. She wasn't particularly good at it but then, given her nightly recital of atrocities around the globe, she didn't have to be. The words spoke for themselves ... so to speak.

"You'll want to know where I was—where everyone was, of course—and anything that happened leading up to the crime, especially anything of a suspicious nature. We-l-l-l, I spent the day mostly on my computer researching a story. I took a break for lunch at Fitzbillies. Then I came back and worked until six. Took a shower in one of those ghastly, germ-breeding, mold-infested stalls they subject us to here—I suppose to show the dire need for donations to renovate. The Master is no one's fool, let me tell you, and his sidekick the Bursar is twice as cunning. Anyway, down to dinner. The Master rolled out, I swear, the same speech he gave years ago in welcoming us to the college, only this time with a thicker overlay of the sense of the History of it all. And how we must preserve our great traditions, whatever the cost. Honestly, he might have lifted the whole thing from the Queen's Speech. Hermione Jax sat there lapping it up, of course. She's had a pash for the Master for years. Unrequited, needless to say. But that hasn't stopped him from cashing her cheques left and right. Fortunately, she's rolling in it, so little harm done, I would imagine. Her father was one of the Hanover-Forspeths, you know, on his mother's side. They're all barking, of course. Old Hermie escaped from a dreadful, doomed existence when her father died. Oh, I see you know about that?

"Anyway, we got through the dinner somehow—I think the main course was yak, I swear it, and a very elderly yak, at that. Some things never change—and the Master instructed us to reconvene in the SCR, where no doubt we were to be treated to yet more toasts and speeches and heavy-handed hints about the need for more funding. Imagine the crush to get in first—not! Anyway, I went to my room and fixed my face and wandered ever so slowly down. I wasn't in the room a minute when that tall young blonde came roaring in, blubbering."

Here, much to St. Just's relief, and Fear's, who was getting writer's cramp, she paused to draw breath and beam at them again. Before she could resume, St. Just cut in:

"Tell us about your time at St. Michael's, when you were a student here."

"Certainly. Well, to be frank, I loathed the place when I was here. Talk about a hotbed of misogyny. Any reasonably attractive woman"—and here she paused, eyelashes fluttering, clearly waiting for the requisite protest as to her remarkable beauty. None forthcoming, she went on rather sulkily, "Well, any attractive woman simply was not taken seriously. And even the Ms. Jaxes of this world had a difficult row to hoe. I just kept my head down and got through it, somehow. Finished with a decent second, before you ask. I never claimed to be a genius."

"Did you know Lexy at all well from that time?"

"I did at first—we hung about a bit together. We were much the same age, with some interests in common. We played tennis a few times, doubles. But she quickly took up with James and it was the usual story—no time for old girlfriends when a man comes on the scene. And I—well, I had my own fish to fry about then. Rather a dashing young man reading Renaissance Lit. He broke my heart, of course, but at least he did it poetically." She grinned again, that famous grin admired by viewers the width and breadth of Great Britain. She really was a good-looking woman, thought St. Just. Perhaps there had been some rivalry between Gwenn and Lexy?

She went on, "The whole place was a petri dish for this type of love affair thing, come to think of it."

"How did anyone get enough work done to finish their degree?" wondered St. Just.

"That's quite a good question, actually."

"You say Lexy quickly got caught up with James. Was it your impression she was the pursuer, then, and not the pursued?"

She laughed. It was a squeaky laugh, like a pencil eraser rubbed across a glass window. Coquettishly, she gave her head what St. Just was certain she thought of as a saucy toss, setting the curls abounce. Twinkle. Smile. "Golly, yes," she said.

St. Just felt he'd had quite enough of this sort of thing. He was reminded why he seldom watched the news on telly. He preferred to get his information from people who had not first been coiffed and shellacked to within an inch of their lives, as if they were going to a dinner party. Radio had much to recommend it; print still more.

"Are you all right, Ms. Pengelly?"

"Whatever do you mean?" Toss, bounce. Smile. "Of course I'm all right."

"Sometimes neck pain can take people that way. A sharp spasm, following by twitching."

Coldly. "I said I'm all right."

"Good. Then, you were saying . . . "

"Yes. Well. James couldn't make a move, inside or outside the college, where he didn't run into Lexy, 'by accident.' She positively threw herself at him." Gwenn flexed her wrist in a dismissive motion. "He joined the chess club; she joined the chess club—just try to imagine Lexy, of all people, in a chess club. But of course, I'm forgetting, you didn't know her. Anyway, he joined the Student Union; she joined the Student Union. It's a wonder she didn't follow him into the men's loo. Lexy lived in a positive bubble of denial, you see—he was never all that keen, I don't think. Of course, he had reasonable looks and some old family money. One couldn't blame her. Is there a Type A–B personality? Then Lexy was it. All over the place. She still lives—lived—a somewhat rackety life in London, so I've heard. Never quite settled down."

"Did you? Blame her, I mean. Feel any resentment?"

The automatic smile froze, although the eyelashes continued to flutter.

"How do you mean?" she said at last.

"I mean, did you feel any resentment at their relationship?"

"Over a dried-up stick like James? Certainly not. James was an old man before he turned six years of age. Far too serious for my taste. Besides, as I told you, I had other fish to fry. Lexy was—I've just realized, I made her sound like some kind of man-eater. It wasn't like that at all. She was insecure, is all—one of the most insecure women I've met in my life. She loved James; rather, she seemed to need him rather desperately, which can be the same thing, can't it? Thank God, or maybe not, he reciprocated, at least for awhile. Then he met India and—pow.

"India had—what was it? A life force that Lexy lacked somehow. Like Lexy, if India wanted something, India went after it. But there was more—" and here, the eyelashes went into overdrive, "and it was this: India's presence somehow held the promise of unbridled sexuality, no strings attached. Have you ever met anyone like that?"

The two policemen, wide-eyed, remained diplomatically silent.

"But there are always strings—strings that entangle not one or two but several lives, even threatening to destroy everyone caught in the net. Still, what man could resist India, or even want to? Lexy, by way of contrast, was an ice princess. Lovely, seemingly untouchable."

Again she tossed her head in the coquettish manner that was apparently hard-wired into her character.

"There was a time I worried about Lexy's stability, during all that," she said. "We all did. She seemed headed for the loony bin. Then the Master got them all separated and that seemed to help. She was seeing a rower by the time we graduated. But she never gave up her pash for James."

"Even as late as this weekend?"

She nodded. "You only had to see her—her eyes, following him wherever he walked. That dishy Argentine was—what do you call it? A beard? Anyway, he was here just for show. That much was obvious."

"They seemed to get along, did they? Lexy and Geraldo?"

"Yes, I suppose. But again, it was all for show. He certainly wasn't along to provide thought-provoking commentary on the global economy, that's for certain. Now, Chief Inspector, you will be giving me an exclusive on this story, won't you?" She flashed her best, professionally whitened smile. Through some trick of genetic inheritance each of her front teeth was slightly and evenly gapped, in a not unattractive way, like a row of vertical fence slats.

"There will of course be a statement issued from communications at some point," he told her, knowing full well that wasn't what she wanted to hear. Too bad. "One further question: Did you see much of Lexy once both of you had left University?"

A shrug. "Here and there. She held down a few Sloane-y jobs, wrote a society column for a while. Our professional paths sometimes intersected over that—she had fantastic access to after-party tidbits of gossip. You know: who went home with whom, who was leaving whom. Then she retired from working to become, well, Lexy Laurant."

There seeming to be little more she could tell them, he bid her a good night. Sulkily, cheated of her "scoop," and leaving her audience less than dazzled, she left the room.

And DCI St. Just and Sergeant Fear called it a night soon after that.

NEEDLES AND HAYSTACKS

ST. JUST LET HIMSELF into his flat, where the air was stale from his brief absence, and as he stood, taking in the uncluttered space, he felt himself begin to relax. The hallway of the flat led directly into the sitting area, a cozy spot that encouraged reading by the fireside, or gazing into space, and generally offloading the cares of the day. His sister had seen to all of it, employing a man named Jim and his entourage one year as a surprise birthday present. St. Just had endured a surreal four weeks of being grilled as to his preferences, quizzed about his tastes, and gently interrogated with regard to the colors to which he was drawn. It was as close to being professionally psychoanalyzed as he would ever come, St. Just imagined, and probably far more beneficial.

He flipped the switch that managed the room's recessed lighting. Deerstalker was still at the neighbors' being fed and worshipped while St. Just was away, a common arrangement given St. Just's erratic schedule. He'd have to collect the cat later; everyone, perhaps including Deerstalker, would be well asleep now.

He wondered anew why he kept a pet, although "kept" was never the operative word with cats. Nor was "pet." Often, days or even weeks would go by without his setting eyes on Deerstalker, only to be met on his return with that cat-patented *You again?* look, followed by a dismissive turn of that regal little skull. It wasn't as if Deerstalker were angry with him about these absences. That would imply a personal rather than a business relationship, and the business they were in together required simply that Deerstalker be housed and fed according to his own exacting standards.

Deerstalker was one of the few emissaries from the animal world that did not immediately fall under St. Just's spell, or at least, pretended not to. Although he would on occasion allow St. Just to pet him, their "together time" was strictly rationed. Apparently lulled to sleep, he would suddenly leap from St. Just's lap and run from the room as if remembering an urgent engagement, only to reappear when he chose, hours later, without apology or explanation, or even a passing glance.

Shrugging off his jacket, St. Just scanned the headlines in the days-old newspaper on the sofa. Another screed of paranoiac vitriol from the Middle East, and more double-speak from Russia. Another child gone missing—thank God, on someone else's watch, but weren't they all on our watch? Another august British institution gone bankrupt. The newspapers lately had been full of photos of stockbrokers shouting across trading room floors, or with eyes cast heavenward, hands clasped on foreheads. For all St. Just knew, these were old photos trotted out for every bounce in the markets, although recent news had been unusually bad.

His eyes retreated from these tales of mayhem and carnage to his artist's pad, opened to a half-finished pastel drawing of Portia.

He couldn't quite capture the light in her blue eyes; he'd made a mess of it with repeated attempts and would have to start over. Something about being too close to one's subject, he thought, grinning. He was tied to her like a hawk tethered by mews jesses, a fact he accepted not with resentment but gratitude and not a little fear, for his love for Portia was bittersweet—to him, the risk of loss would always be the flip side of the happiness coin.

He started to tear up his poor effort, but found himself reluctant to actually destroy the page that held her image. He flipped instead to the page where a picture was emerging of the Chief Constable, who was a beautiful woman of strong facial structure, he had to admit, despite her off-puttingly trendy social beliefs. There, he felt he'd caught the light of fervor in her eyes, almost exactly. It was a look not unlike Hermione Jax's.

He stopped to reheat some soup and bread, and after this small meal, he poured out a brandy to sip while he worked. An hour later he started to pour out a second brandy, then decided that might be a brandy too far. Still wide awake, he picked up his copy of Baudolino from the side table. He was starting to believe the book was cursed. He could never get past chapter three because a case always interrupted him at right about that point, as Baudolino was telling his story to Niketas. By the time St. Just got back to the book, he'd have forgotten some of the salient details; he felt he had to take a good running start at it by beginning again at the first chapter. Maybe if he just kept reading … Dutifully, as clouds scudded by outside his window, he sat in his easy chair and began reading again. At chapter three, his mind began to wander, wishing himself with Portia. And his eyes closed in sleep.

The next day, early, he returned to St. Michael's College and went up to Portia's rooms. She was in the second court where they kept the Fellows who chose to live in college (stored them, Portia insisted was a better term). But her set of rooms was large and featured an Oriel window. When away from her, he pictured her sitting there like a princess in a tower.

Ordinarily, she might have stayed with him in his flat the night before, but as she was involved in a murder investigation—again—there was no question of that: She was, in theory and officially, at least, a suspect. The few times he had stayed in her rooms in college had not been a success—she had a single bed, for a start. He had long before, and with unseemly haste, asked her to move in with him, but that trial balloon hadn't flown.

"We'll live together when we're married," she'd said.

"And when will that be?" he'd asked, suddenly stung with hope.

"I don't know. When I've finished my thesis?"

Seeing the look on his face, she'd quickly and penitently added, "I'm going to be married to you for the rest of my life. Since I plan to live a very, very long time, I want to enjoy, to savor, if you will, my last time as a single woman. I've been single for thirty-five years, you know. Hard to give that up. Not that I'm planning any wild adventures. But if I want to stay in bed 'til noon writing my novel, that's what I'll do. If I want to go up to London on the spur of the moment, I will do that. I may have a private film festival one weekend, watching old movies like Rebecca, and weeping over How Green Was My Valley, and analyzing old episodes of Inspector Morse. All of that will change once we're married"—and here she held up a hand to still his protest—"no, it's changed already, and you know it has. I can't make a move but that I want you in my plans, as a key part of my plans. Once I'm one half of Mr. and Mrs. Arthur St. Just, it will be 'worse.' Wonderful, but worse. This is nothing to do with you, and everything to do with the fact that we met and my world changed overnight. Give me time. Just a little."

It wasn't that he didn't understand—he understood too well, and so reluctantly accepted what she told him. They'd be together soon enough. This day he drank her excellent coffee and, after a brief chat, left her to resume the investigation. Sergeant Fear was waiting for him downstairs.

"We've told them to stay clear of their rooms so we can have a proper search," he informed St. Just. "And the Master's given us a diagram of who was in what room. Shall we start with the victim's room?"

But they soon found themselves lost in one of the labyrinthine passages of the college. After ten fruitless minutes, they were forced to ask the way of one of the few students they came upon. She introduced herself as Saffron.

Even though it was edging on High Summer, Saffron wore large, suede, fur-lined boots, suitable for competing in the Iditarod, offset by a pair of shorts so tiny St. Just had to closely husband his eyes, fixing them firmly on her face as he asked her the way back to the rooms being used by the guests. Fear blushed a deep red and stared at the ceiling.

She'd done something strange to her hair, which, fortunately, gave St. Just something to stare at. It was pinned, twisted, and spun into random coils, finally falling down about her neck in pink-and-blue-tipped tendrils that matched her eye shadow. Her lips were painted a matching blue.

She nodded. "They'll be in the Rupert Brooke."

"Interesting choice of name. Had he some connection with the college?"

"None whatsoever. A former Master was an admirer: 'The damned ship lurched and slithered. Quiet and quick / My cold gorge rose; the long sea rolled; I knew / I must think hard of something, or be sick…' From 'A Channel Passage.' Quite the worst subject for a poem one can imagine, is it not? We had it in the sixth form. It was the boys' favorite."

She led them through a corridor of Harry-Potterish aspect, past strange and fusty exhibits of rocks and shells and stuffed creatures—likely donated cast-offs of former members—to what had been Lexy's room during her short stay at the college. The multi-colored young woman named Saffron left them there.

Lexy's room was much as St. Just had expected, an explosion of frilly, expensive clothing, including no fewer than five pairs of shoes. The room itself featured a large bay window overlooking First Court, with a view across the court to the staircases leading up to the sets of rooms opposite.

"Five pairs of shoes for a weekend visit?" asked Sergeant Fear.

"Either she liked to be prepared for anything or she couldn't make up her mind."

The air in the room held the smell of her flowery perfume mixed with the lighter scent of her cosmetics—the face powders and rouges and the various unguents no doubt meant to keep her forever young. Death had beat these elixirs to it: She would forever be thirty-eight; she would forever escape the dreaded Four-Oh birthday.

St. Just turned to face the mystifying display of containers and jars on top of a makeshift dressing-table—it appeared she had commandeered the nighttable for this purpose, propping up a handheld mirror to apply her makeup. The two policemen stood stolidly surveying the wide-ranging tools of artifice. St. Just crossed the room to open the door of the cupboard. It seemed she had only bothered to hang one or two items; the rest spilled in ripples and foams of satin and lace from an expensive set of luggage left open in the middle of the room. A magazine of the glossy gossip-and-fashion variety lay open to an advertisement for shoes—someone, presumably Lexy, had used an eye crayon to circle three styles of interest. On the page opposite the ad was a photo of a young blonde woman, evidently inebriated, being lifted out of the gutter outside a London nightclub. Today's role model.

"SOCO's been through all this, of course, but I wanted a look for myself," St. Just told Fear. "They found traces of drugs in her suitcase, were you aware? Traces, but no drugs. They think prescription, not street, but we'll know more later. Let's have a closer look at that door."

The door into the corridor bore the clear marks of having been jimmied from the outside. The lock still functioned, but barely.

"So she was telling the truth about that, unless for some unfathomable reason she staged the break-in herself," said St. Just.

He turned and stared about him at the room, willing it to give up its secrets. But it seemed to be no more than what it was: a room temporarily and briefly occupied by a woman whose real life was lived elsewhere. He remarked as much to Sergeant Fear.

"We'll need someone in London to have a look at her home, talk to her neighbors."

"On it," said Sergeant Fear.

Geraldo's room, next door, was the masculine equivalent to Lexy's—the yang to her yin: flashy, expensive clothing tossed casually about, as if a manservant would appear any moment to deal with it all. Similar to Lexy's room, there was no reading material to speak of, not even a men's fashion magazine. The room itself was smaller, but otherwise identical. Geraldo possessed, if anything, more jars and bottles of unguents than Lexy. Sergeant Fear picked up a jar, read the label, and snorted.

"It's a 'facial regenerator,'" he reported. "That's aftershave, to you and me. Complete with Vitamin B5 and antioxidants. Whatever next?"

"I wouldn't scoff too quickly, Sergeant. What you're holding there may be the very secret to his reported success with the ladies."

They tackled India's room—Lady Bassett's—next. While as messy as Lexy's and Geraldo's, the frilly, lacy, demimonde aspect was missing. Here were sensible clothes, tweedily expensive and made to last, whereas Lexy's had every appearance of being expensive and made to be replaced each season. The few pieces of jewelry in a small travel case were of heirloom quality. Here a magazine was left open to an article on gardening, much marked and annotated by the reader. A tennis racket, perhaps forgotten by the room's usual occupant, leaned against the back of the wardrobe. She was evidently a diabetic; a packet of low-dosage insulin and needles were tucked hidden in the wardrobe.

"It's a much larger room than Lexy's or Geraldo's," noted St. Just. "You can see where the college was hoping most of the money was going to come from."

"Sir James' title probably helped turn the Master's head."

Their survey of the next rooms produced nothing of interest, at least from a police standpoint. Gwennap Pengelly's room, in addition to being surprisingly neat, was a fortress of IT equipment and wires. Augie Cramb's room also reflected a passion for gadgets, camera equipment, and the like. Hermione Jax's room was as sparse as a nun's, explainable perhaps in part by the fact she had had less far to travel than the others. The separate rooms of the Dunnings reflected the differences in their characters: his toiletries and clothing were laid out neatly, while hers had been flung about with abandon. Her room was saturated by a perfume St. Just didn't recognize, but found profoundly disagreeable in such large doses.

"Phew," said Sergeant Fear.

On the desk by the window, a stack of postcards lay ready for mailing. St. Just picked one up at random—a beautiful scene of the Backs—and turning it over read the commentary. It was, as he expected, a litany of complaints to someone back home, a litany that ignored the beauty of both the card and her surroundings. Again he remarked at the attraction that could hold together two people of seemingly polar-opposite temperaments and inclinations like Karl and Constance Dunning. He didn't think he himself could stand to have Constance Dunning in his house.

Sergeant Fear looked up from the Master's diagram and said, "Only Sir James' room to go."

St. Just, recalled from his reflections, said something that sounded like, "Humph?" Then he said, "Go ahead and have a look 'round, will you? I doubt you'll find anything."

"What exactly is it we're looking for, Sir?"

St. Just shrugged.

"The personality of the occupant. They've all left us some clues, even in the short time they've been here."

Sergeant Fear returned in a few minutes.

"Neat as a pin, everything he owns is hand-tailored, expensive looking. You know," and here he adopted a fruitily upper-class voice: "'Spare no expense, my good man! And don't spare the horses!' He's reading," and here the sergeant referred to his notes, "something called Baudolino."

St. Just barked out a laugh. "Please tell me you're joking. How far along is he in it?"

Puzzled, Sergeant Fear replied, "He's bookmarked it about halfway through."

"He must have more leisure time than I." St. Just carefully replaced the postcard on the desk. "Anyway, I think it's time we sloped off for a word with the Porter and a few others. Come along."

They got no further than the foot of the main staircase before running into Hermione Jax. St. Just had the distinct impression that, like Portia the night before, she had positioned herself there to wait for them. It turned out he was right.

"There you are at last," she said accusingly, as if they had missed a pre-arranged appointment. She gave a resounding thump! with her walking stick. "I have something to tell you. Something I've just remembered. It's about the Master."

"Really?" St. Just arranged his expression into one of polite attention.

"Yes. You see, I had completely forgotten this in all the excitement. I didn't go straight into the SCR from my room but I decided to pop in on the Master in his study. This was right after dinner—immediately after. There was something I forgot to tell him, you see."

"And what was that?"

"Hmm?"

"What was it you had forgotten to tell the Master?"

She continued to stare blankly at him for a moment, then said testily, "You can't expect me to remember that, not after all that's happened."

"Well, then, perhaps you can tell us how you knew where to find him. Wouldn't the SCR have been a more likely place to look?"

"Not at all. He's always in his study."

"I see."

She seemed to change subjects, although later St. Just wondered if her thoughts weren't all on the same train. The mess must be cleaned up quickly, and the college, in the form of the Master, must not be dragged through any mud.

"Really, Inspector, this kind of thing can't be allowed, you know," she said. "Murder is of course a shocking thing, but in this case we must take the long view."

"How so?"

"We moderns like to think of ourselves as superior but if I could do away with my enemies as tidily as did Henry VIII, would I not? Of course I would. So would you—I dare say it. No doubt something of the kind has transpired here."

St. Just struggled to keep up with her reasoning. She seemed to be saying there was no need for this fuss—murder was a commonplace of the human condition. "You mean," he said, "like that tedious person at the next carrel in the library, snapping away at his chewing gum? If only we could just get out a writ or whatever they had in those days and have him done away with?"

"Precisely. Especially people who snap their chewing gum."

"It is a tempting thought, I must say."

"There you are. I rest my case."

"But one leading to civil chaos," he concluded.

Her umbrage wrapped around her like a cloak, Hermione Jax, with a valedictory thump of her cane, turned and stalked out of the main hall. She disappeared into one of the doorways leading into the bowels of the college. St. Just remarked to Sergeant Fear, "Is she covering for the Master, or is she trying to shorten the length of time she was away from the group, and thus without an alibi? And I wonder: Does her dog-like devotion to the Master cut both ways?"

She had left open the door through which she had disappeared, allowing in a distant gush of baroque organ music. The two men peered through the opening. A sign pointed them the way to the college chapel, where the service had evidently just ended. St. Just had forgotten it was Sunday. The Master had petitioned to allow the service to go on as planned, with the choir singing a much-rehearsed "Coronation Mass" by Mozart. St. Just had seen no reason to refuse, although he sent in a team to search the chapel before he released it to college use once more. A grateful Master was overheard to say later, "So reasonable. It's hard to believe he's a policeman. Peterhouse man, though. Pity, that."

A figure robed in vestments—almost certainly the Reverend Otis—stood talking, his back to them, with Sir James and Lady Bassett, their tones low and sorrowful. The policemen saw the back of what looked like a tonsured head, the hairstyle owing to genetics rather than religious practice. The Dean's shiny skull had an unusually pronounced ridge of bones. St. Just, always captivated by the variety of the human form, realized that the prominent bones formed an upside-down "Y"—precisely like a peace symbol. It reminded him of T. S. Eliot's "skull beneath the skin," and of Sebastian in his scull, and from there led him to thinking how inconvenient for the murderer had been Sebastian's slavish devotion to his schedule. The finding of the body might otherwise have happened hours later than it had.

Sergeant Fear raised his eyebrows inquiringly—Should we interrupt?—and St. Just shook his head. Time enough to talk with the Reverend Otis, and given the Master's anxiety on the subject, St. Just felt it might be more useful to catch the man when he was quite alone.

With the Master they were in luck—and the Bursar, with whom they'd not yet spoken, was with him. Both men looked up rather guiltily as Sergeant Fear knocked on the door and immediately pulled it open for St. Just.

The Master made the introductions. It transpired that the Bursar's "civilian" name was Mr. Bowles, and he seemed to have joined the Master in a state of shock.

"The press have got wind of this, you see," the Bursar explained. In fact, the press could be heard faintly beyond the crinkle-crankle college wall, yipping like starving sans culottes in search of a bread line.

To St. Just, the Bursar looked like a particularly alert, newly hatched bird, his eyes large behind his glasses, his beak sharp, his attention avid. "Well, we knew it couldn't be kept from them forever, but you'd think they'd have the decency to wait."

"Not high on their list of priorities, I'm afraid, at the best of times. Decency. Nor patience," said St. Just. "In fairness, it is going to be a big story for them. None of them will want to miss out. They have editors to answer to."

"Fairness," said the Master, scoffing at the word. "It's that Gwenn Pengelly behind this, you mark my words. She had the absolute gall to ask if I would allow her television crew in so she could interview the guests for her show. Just imagine!"

"That would probably be accurate, Sir—the story would have leaked through Ms. Pengelly almost immediately. Can't be helped." St. Just added, "Now, we'll eventually have to question all the staff who were on duty last night."

The Master puffed out his thin cheeks in a blustery outrage, "Oh, surely not. There are no windows in the kitchen overlooking the grounds. It's highly doubtful any of them saw anything, let alone did anything."

"But during dinner, they were best placed of all to observe," countered St. Just. "No one, in my experience, really notices the staff. Which leaves them a world of time to notice the guests."

BOATHOUSE

"Did I ever tell you I used to row, Sergeant?" St. Just and Sergeant Fear were strolling through the grounds that led to the boathouse. "In my college days?"

He hadn't, but Sergeant Fear wasn't surprised. St. Just was built for the sport, with his long muscular legs, solid as tree trunks. They would act as pistons propelling the boat, with his long arms getting the maximum reach out of the oars.

"You've the build for it, Sir."

"Thank you, Sergeant, that's very flattering, but that's really not why I brought the subject up. This college is uniquely set up for rowing, with the boathouse being right here. Most colleges have to convene elsewhere. Makes it handy."

"For what?"

St. Just turned his head to look at Fear.

"I'm not sure yet."

They reached the scene of the crime. A fresh collection of constables stood guarding the area as a modified search team continued to see by daylight what, if anything, had been missed the night before. A woman uniformed in a sleeveless yellow Day-Glo jerkin stood to one side, quietly observing. St. Just remembered an exchange he'd once overheard between a similarly clad young woman and an inquiring member of the public:

"You're a copper, right?"

"No, the jacket was on sale. It's a difficult color to wear for some people, irradiated yellow. Of course, I'm a ruddy copper. What do you want?"

Lexy's body had long since been removed, along with the SOCO tent and other paraphernalia required to investigate the doing away of one human being by another.

St. Just conferred with the others on his team, who reported no new findings.

"They keep these college grounds as clean as the Queen's stables, Sir," said Constable Brummond. "If there was anything left behind by your killer, it would stick out like a tart in church. We've practically found nothing worth bagging. No helpful cigarette butts with traces of DNA on the filters. All the villains seem to have packed it in, anyway. Bad for their health."

Brummond was a twenty-year man, with all the grace and instincts of an alley cat on the prowl. More than once, he'd been put on gardening leave for one infraction or another, but he always came back. He'd never risen beyond the rank of Constable, but whether from inclination or temperament, St. Just never asked. He just requisitioned him whenever he could. Brummond had the sharpest pair of eyes in the force. Sergeant Fear, on the other hand, had more restful qualities. St. Just swore having Fear with him helped him think.

"There's nothing here, Sir," Brummond went on, "except a bit of gravel disturbance over there nearest the boathouse, where she was found."

They walked over to the point where their careful footsteps began making crunching noises against the small stones.

Brummond pointed some feet away. "Since this is the kind of place that practically has the gravel counted each day," he said, "the slightest trace of disorder shows. Could have been the scene of the struggle, likely it was. He left her where he'd killed her."

St. Just looked up at the building. Brummond followed the path of his gaze.

"We're out of luck there, as you know, Sir. They're using a mixture of dummy cameras and live ones. But they've got the lot trained on the river. After all, they're thinking in terms of protecting the contents of the boathouse. Some of these boats are worth many thousands of pounds—in fact, they all are. Anyone coming by water to steal would be captured. But it's an outdated CCTV system, which relies on an old time-lapse system linked to analog cameras. The intended use was never, I'll warrant, to capture a killer lurking on the grounds. It wouldn't have occurred to them. These college blokes are all living in the sixteenth century, seems to me."

"If they were, they might be better prepared to deal with violent death, as well as theft. Cambridge in the sixteenth century was not for the faint of heart."

Brummond nodded. "I see your point, Sir. Anyway, that kid—Sebastian—was apparently trusted with the keys, along with a few others. You want to have a look inside? By the way, inside we found what is probably the twin of the scull that was used to attack the victim. Forensics bagged it."

The men walked through the large doorway into the capacious lower level of the wide, two-story building. The room was stacked with racks holding different types of racing boats; rowing blades and sculls, riggers, and related equipment filled the rest of the available space. They squeezed past this equipment to reach a set of stairs in the rear that led up to a gym filled with rowing machines, weights, and other fitness equipment. At the back were showers and a changing area; to one side, a well-equipped bar and meeting room.

St. Just whistled.

"In my day we were lucky to have access to a couple of eights that hadn't had their riggers bent all to hell."

"It's an expensive sport, Sir, and increasingly popular," said Brummond. "It looks like St. Michael's is rolling in it."

That wasn't the impression St. Just had gotten from Portia. The Bursar may have pinched his pennies elsewhere, but not here, evidently.

They spent a few minutes admiring the bar room with its flat-screen television and its sumptuous chairs and sofas, then walked downstairs and out of the boathouse. A movement caught St. Just's eye; Sebastian was standing several yards away. Hovering anxiously, was St. Just's impression. When he saw St. Just looking at him, Sebastian quickly turned and walked away.

St. Just turned to the other two policemen and said, "I suppose we might have a look through all those lockers in the changing area. Organize it with the Porter or whoever would be in charge of that, would you? Better yet, I'll have a word with him now."

So St. Just and Sergeant Fear next headed towards the elaborate, fan-vaulted cage that housed the Porter. An ex-Army man like many of his kind, William Trinity readily agreed to organize the locker search, but could throw little light on the overall situation. He had today regained some of his usual unflappable manner, honed over years of dealing with hordes of anxious first-year students. But he had little information to share with the detectives. Yes, it was unusual that he would have been here the night before in addition to today, he agreed in reply to questioning, but they were down one man this week. He also replied that there had been a great fuss over nothing when the lady had reported her room broken into. She herself admitted nothing was taken.

"How long have you been working here?" St. Just asked him.

"Twenty year now."

"Was the lady known to you from her time as a student here?"

"She may have been. I've seen thousands pass through here though, Sir. Can't expect me to remember them all. In fact, I only tend to remember the troublemakers."

"It's always difficult, patrolling an environment like this, with so many nooks and crannies to it," St. Just observed. "It's what makes both Cambridge and Oxford hard to police."

"Too right."

"I imagine you've seen it all."

"I have indeed."

"Drugs and so forth?"

The Porter seemed to take this as a personal affront. He carefully adjusted his bowler before replying, patting it squarely atop his head.

"No indeed. Not at St. Michael's."

St. Just doubted very much that St. Mike's had a special dispensation in that regard when every other college was fighting a running battle against the noxious stuff, but he decided not to risk further losing the goodwill of this particular witness. Just then another constable approached to tell them someone in the college kitchen wanted a word.

"All right," said St. Just. "Tell them we'll be right there." He left his card with William Trinity with instructions on how to get in touch.

The college kitchen looked as if a factory from the time of the industrial revolution had been dropped into the center of an old monastery. The stone floor had worn smooth as glass over the centuries by the continual tread of feet going from the walk-in fireplace—big enough to roast an ox, to which use it probably had been put—to the enormous central refectory-style table. It was otherwise typical, St. Just supposed, of any kitchen attached to a large restaurant or school; the need to feed hundreds of rapacious students and their instructors several times a day necessitated a ruthless efficiency. Several young men and women were engaged in food preparation. As he watched, they all looked up from their chores simultaneously, as if harkening to the same bell.

"What is that?" St. Just heard one of them say.

His eye was caught just then by an enormous, fierce-looking tom. Evidently the mouser trade was booming. He sat in the dead center of the room, an Oberbürgermeister of a cat, sleek, fat, and complacent as a robber baron, concentrating now on his post-meal wash. It was a meticulous, demanding job, every claw requiring equal, specialized attention. St. Just would not have been surprised if the cat had next begun cleaning his teeth with a silver toothpick. He wore his mantle of power lightly, but it was clear a successful mouser answered to no one.

"Tom Jones," said a sharp voice. "You know you're not allowed in here."

A short, squat woman approached, drying her hands on an apron that nearly reached the floor. The cat, looking over his shoulder, gave her a glancing once-over before resuming his ablutions.

St. Just said, "Someone wanted a word?"

"That would be me." She was nearly as wide as she was tall, and she had arms like a stevedore's, the muscles rippling as she kneaded the white cloth. St. Just reflected that Philip Marlowe might have described her as a woman built like a refrigerator and twice as cold. "I'm the chef here," she said, squinting at the men in turn, taking their measure from under thatched eyebrows. Seemingly satisfied, she extended one ropy arm to shake hands and said:

"Mary Goose—and I've heard all the jokes already, ta very much." She paused to ruffle the salt-and-pepper hair she wore in a choppy no-frills cut. "Anyway, I saw her, you see. The blonde that was done in. In the garden that night. I was there. I wasn't supposed to be, and I'd appreciate your keeping that information under your hat."

She suddenly turned and shouted, "Fuck away from that!" St. Just saw the cat, a large fish in its mouth, moving with swift feline grace towards the exit.

"Bugger it." She rolled her eyes in a display of colossal annoyance, then informed St. Just, "I'll be finding the bones all over the garden now. Bloody hell. As if I don't have enough to do. Where was I? Oh, right, in the garden."

"How did you happen to be there?" he asked.

"Stepped out for a smoke, see. The Master frowns on that. It was in the middle of the shift, see. But the meal was finished, there was nothing that needed doing right then, so I stepped out into a corner of the cloister walk. The members had all left the Hall by the gallery at that point. That's when I saw them. A blonde woman sitting on the bench in the Fellows' Garden, talking with this dark-haired man."

"Did you know either of them?"

"Never saw either of them before. I've not been at St. Mike's as long as all that."

"Could you hear what they were saying?"

She nodded emphatically. "Yes, I could. Clear as day. He said, 'We were happy together, Lexy. Cling to that memory. I do. Those were wonderful times.' Something like that—it wouldn't half have made you sick to listen to him. He was sweet-talking her, you see, but really, trying to get away from her."

This was a break, thought St. Just. Mary Goose was the only witness so far who could have overheard the conversation, the gallery used by the others being glassed in.

"And what did she say?"

"Nothing. She just gave a little shudder, like she was crying, stricken with grief, you know." Stricken with grief. It sounded like a line she'd heard on the telly. "Or maybe it was foreboding, given what happened to her next, poor lady."

"And then?"

"Then what? That was about it. I came in on the tail end. He said something like, 'Well, perhaps you'd like to be alone. I'll leave you now. See you in the SCR in a bit, right?' And he walked off. I heard him take the stairs, those stairs that are at one end of the cloister—the opposite end of the cloister to where I was standing, lucky thing. And from there I would guess he headed down the corridor to the SCR."

"She didn't follow him?"

She shook her head.

"I left myself then. She was still sitting there."

"And the time for this would be when?"

"Nine twenty. No, I tell a lie. Maybe nine twenty-five."

"I see. Thank you for coming forward. I don't see any reason why the Master has to know about the cigarette."

"Thanks, mate. You're a real gent."

"Just for my notes," said Sergeant Fear, "how long have you been the college cook?"

Mary Goose, in the process of leaving, spun around, making the starched white apron billow out from around her hips like a ship's sail.

"I'm the chef, young man, not the cook. The chef, got that? And I've been here near fifteen years."

A chastened St. Just and Fear left via a door that led to the kitchen garden, which was surrounded by dry stone walls. There was no sign of the cat nor the fish, but no doubt Tom Jones was wise enough to put a safe distance between himself and the chef. From there, the policemen walked out onto the broad green expanse of lawn leading to the river. Beyond a screen of trees they heard the repetitive thwump of a tennis ball being struck. They followed the sound: Geraldo Valentiano was hitting balls against a tennis backboard. He had apparently had the foresight to pack a white tennis outfit, or perhaps that was just part of his standard travel gear as he jetted from world hotspot to world hotspot.

He paused to watch the policemen approach.

"How long are you going to hold me here?" he demanded to know, when they were within hearing range. "I have to get up to London."

"What exactly is your business there, Sir?"

Geraldo gave a silky shrug.

"This and that. Look, it's too bad, what happened to Lexy, but that was going nowhere. She asked me here to be her escort for the weekend. I thought it would be what you call a lark—was I wrong!—so I came along. I have nothing to do with this, I tell you." His voice ended on an unattractive whine. "I'm just an innocent bystander."

St. Just looked at him a long moment.

"When you can leave, I'll be sure to let you know. In person."

STIRRED AND SHAKEN

JAMES AND INDIA SAT in the beer garden of the Green Dragon, having asked for and received police permission to leave the college grounds for a few hours. They had walked as close as possible to the river, having first debated whether they could somehow annex one of the college's double sculls to make their escape.

"It would be a neat way to dodge the media. We could just float right by them, traveling at great speed," James had said. "Imagine the publicity for the new book. At least Lexy wouldn't have died completely in vain."

"James!"

"Sorry." He had the grace to look abashed. "I suppose that was in rather bad taste."

"Rather. Besides, are old members allowed to take out a scull?" she asked.

"Are you joking? They have a murder investigation on their hands. Who is likely to care?" He laughed. "A couple of scofflaws, that we are."

But in the end James and India took their chances, leaving via a tradesmen's gate, judging correctly that the members of the media (who tended to travel in packs) would be gathered at the front gates, hoping for a sighting of any of the suspects. The removal of Lexy's body the night before had been all they could have hoped for in the way of drama. Perhaps lightning would strike twice.

Now James, his hands wrapped tightly around a pint as they sat at one of the pub's outdoor tables, looked across at his wife.

"Do you remember when we used to come here? It wasn't that long ago, was it, but it seems almost as if we were children then."

"We were children. Life is never again as simple. Just getting through exams was all that mattered. That, and having a dress for the May Ball."

They paused to watch a pair of ducks float by, male and female, the female gliding in the wake.

James said, "I've always wondered, do they mate for life? Or is that only true for mallards?"

India shrugged: Don't know. Don't care right now.

"I just don't see who could have done this," he said then, picking up on her distraction. It was the third time he'd spoken some version of those words that day.

"You must be joking, James. Surely the police are spoiled for choice. My money's on Geraldo, however."

James shook his head firmly. "There's not really a lot of choice, on the face of it. Lexy could be a pain, we all know that. But ... it was as if I always knew that her anger was directed at me, not the world. I guess I'm trying to say, she wasn't really a pain in a generalized way. It was tightly focused, her anger, and I understood that. I treated her badly. Her feelings were justified."

"I think this is guilt talking again. It's time to let go of that, James. You can't help her now."

But he didn't seem to have heard.

"It's abominable. She simply did not deserve this."

India was silent, tilting her glass, watching the sunlight play along the rim. Her linen shirt, so full of starched promise an hour ago, now hung in limp, wrinkled folds. It was the kind of day so unseasonably hot people standing by the river no doubt thought lingeringly of throwing themselves in. She took a sip of her Orangina. Tempting as it had been to order a martini, it seemed a time to keep her wits about her.

She asked: "What did you talk about? In the garden with her?" she asked her husband.

"Oh, that."

She paused to look at him thoughtfully. That guilty look...

"Is there a subtext here?" she said at last. But she knew the answer already.

He remained silent, his features haggard and drawn, offering a preview of the man he would be at sixty.

"Yes, that," she prodded. "You spent most of your time dodging her up until that point, or so you say."

"Surely you're not jealous, India."

He smiled, the gentle, indulgent smile he reserved just for her. Some things, he thought, were better forgotten. Sunk to the bottom of the deep blue sea and forgotten. "Of all people," he said, "you know how I feel about you. It's as I told the police: I stepped out for a cigarette, and there she was. I couldn't exactly turn tail and run. And when I think that was my last memory of her ... I'm glad I stayed. But, well ... she had some idea I'd have tired of you by now—as if I could! As if any man ever could!—and she hoped there might be some way she and I could reconstruct the past. Resurrect it."

"I see," India said coldly. James looked at her, a plea for her understanding in his eyes.

"I'm sorry, darling. I never meant for you to hear of this. It was all nonsense. But now that this has happened ... Anyway, the short story is, she had some idea we might start up again. I told her as gently as I could that it was impossible. The result was predictable. Tears and drama, muffled sobs, the whole bit. I left her, but as I walked away, heading for the corridor to the SCR, I saw her flounce away in the direction of the river. It was the last I saw of her. The last anyone saw of her, except her killer, of course." He sighed, and took a long pull on his drink, draining the glass. His hand trembled as he set it back down on the table. "She was always such a flighty sort, and too trusting at times. I still think it likely a tramp came upon her somehow, or she ran into some addict who thought she was carrying money ... something ... something purely evil—" He broke off.

"James." India held out her hand, and grasped his arm tightly. "Don't. You must stop this. Please don't distress yourself. You're right, it was some freak ... accident ... She was in the wrong place at the wrong time. And doesn't that sound just like her? Some people are born unlucky. I always thought she was one of them. Born under an unlucky star. Isn't that strange? When so many people thought of her as the golden girl. I never did. But then I had a closer view of her over the years." She sat quietly, following some related train of thought. After a while she said, "Sebastian..."

James looked up sharply. "We have to keep him well out of this."

"How can we? He discovered the body," she said. "Don't the police always think that makes you a suspect? I've never really understood why, but it's always that way on the telly."

"If that happens, if they start applying pressure, we'll get our solicitor—just like on the telly. I'll have a word with Sebastian, and with the solicitor. Just to make sure we're prepared for the worst."

She sighed, nodded.

"Now, don't you start worrying." He smiled. "One worrier in the family is bad enough."

"You don't think..."

Reading her thoughts, he said, "That Sebastian had anything to do with this?"

They looked at each other, neither willing to answer the question.

———

St. Just felt as little like someone who might appear in a detective show on the telly as could be imagined. It was early days in the investigation yet, but it was right about now he always felt the first stirrings of a mild panic. No more than a fluttering at the edges of his heart, a small riot quickly quelled, but there nonetheless. The early hours were crucial to solving a crime, before evidence and memory faded, and he was never more aware of the swift passage of time than at the start of an investigation.

James and India's surmise was correct: Sebastian was a suspect in St. Just's mind, although an unlikely one, unless and until St. Just could establish some prior connection between Sebastian and Lexy. Sebastian's arrogance was not a point in his favor. And St. Just thought it likely that under pressure, Sebastian, for all his breeding and posh background, could snap, just like anyone else. Perhaps a pampered background had made him even more vulnerable. It was thinking these thoughts that found him heading down yet another interminable corridor in search of what he knew now from witnesses was Sebastian's girlfriend, the exotic young woman who had shown them the way to the Rupert Brooke wing. Sergeant Fear was away helping set up the library room the Master had lent the police to use as a temporary incident room.

The Porter had given St. Just directions to Saffron's room, but not a supply of breadcrumbs, which might have come in handy. Finally, rounding a corner, he recognized one of the exhibits he'd seen that morning—a buffalo or bison skull, at a guess—and knew he was in the area from which Saffron had come.

He came at last to a door labeled with her name; he imagined there couldn't be two people named Saffron Sellers in the college. She was sporting the oak: The massive, outer door to her room was closed, indicating she was not to be disturbed. Fat chance, he thought, pounding his fist against the wood.

"Open up! Police!" He felt foolish using the stock phrase, but she had to be made to know the rules had changed, and these charming college traditions could be damned. Her dissertation or whatever she was doing in there would have to wait.

He put his ear to the door. He could hear someone stirring. He pounded again, and was rewarded with the sound of the inner door being opened.

"All right. All right!" came an exasperated female voice. The same rainbow-colored hair he remembered appeared around the edge of the door. The hair was more disheveled than before, however, which he wouldn't have thought possible. She'd made some haphazard attempt to pin it back with jeweled barrettes in the shape of butterflies.

"Some people have to sleep, you know," she informed him. She pulled a quilted white robe tighter around her slim waist.

St. Just looked at his watch.

"It's nearly noon."

"Yes. I know that. I have to work tonight."

"On your studies. I understand."

"No, I mean work work. I pull pints in a pub in town. I'm at Cambridge on a bursary scheme. Unlike some. It includes a monthly stipend but you couldn't keep a small dog alive on what they give you. That's why I need my sleep. I'm working again tonight."

She pushed back her hair. He could see the exhaustion in her eyes, enhanced by her smudged black-and-blue makeup.

"Must be tough, to tend bar and try to keep up with your studies."

She shrugged. "I try to be philosophical about it."

"What subject are you reading?"

"Philosophy." A small grin. "Now, if there's nothing else?"

Oh, my. And probably reading Nietzsche. Weren't they all? Cambridge was rife with students embracing nihilism and the death of God, if only to annoy the hell out of their parents. Did they really believe what they spouted? Despite the evidence St. Just witnessed daily in his job (a clear rebuttal, if ever there were one, to the idea of a superman), the stark aloneness of such a philosophy had never held any appeal. The thought that existence was pointless both repelled and frightened him. There must be a point.

"This won't take long," he assured her. "If you'd like to put on some clothes, I'll wait outside."

She looked down at her robe. It was frayed around the hem. Signs of a long-ago spill of coffee or tea, unsuccessfully washed, splattered the front. But with it all, the wild hair and makeup and the cheap polyester robe, Saffron didn't look slatternly. She looked poor.

"These are clothes, aren't they?" she asked. "If it will get this over sooner, come on in."

It wasn't the most encouraging invitation, but she did step back and allow him to pass through. She headed for the single bed in the room and wrapped herself in the white duvet before sitting on the edge of the bed. Like her robe, the duvet was threadbare, but it was spotless.

"You'll want to know what I know about Seb, is that right?"

"Oh, I suppose I'd like to know more about you and Seb. Like, how long you've been dating."

"Dating?" She emitted a little snort. "Dating. How quaint. Well, we've been dating since I got here. A little more than a year now."

"Sorry, I'm not up on the expressions young people might use these days. I should say, you've been in an exclusive relationship—for one year, is that right?"

She shrugged, an attempt at insouciance that did not quite come off. St. Just, watching the slow creep of blush onto her already English-rose complexion, realized he'd accidentally hit bone. "Exclusive on my side," she said. "I don't have time to play around. I don't know about Seb, but he doesn't seem to have a lot of free time, either."

Tempted as he was to ask, he didn't see how Seb's fidelity or lack of it could play into the investigation. Instead he asked, "Give me an idea of what you did, where you were, last night. From about six on."

"I was with Seb. Here, in my room. He left about eight to work out. He did that most nights—spend a little time in the gym, then he'd take the scull out until Lighting Up."

"This was his set routine?"

She nodded. "Almost invariable. He wants to get in the Blue Boat. If not this year, next. Eventually. Seb can be a bit driven, but that's the only way you win. So he tells me."

Actually, he was right, as St. Just remembered from his own time spent around rowers set on competing one day against Oxford. For months on end, rowing would come first in Seb's priorities, behind his degree, behind Saffron.

"So, he left you about eight. Is that the last you saw of him, until perhaps after we questioned him last night?"

"Ye-e-e-s. Yes."

"You don't seem sure."

She drew the duvet tighter around her, only her face and feet protruding. Even on a summer morning, it was cold in the room, the damp kind of cold that could seep into Cambridge stone and lodge there for centuries.

On the wall behind her bed, she'd nailed several dozen necklaces and bracelets—bright, gaudy beads in reds and blues and yellows that caught the light, and ropes of plastic pearls. She looked like part of an exhibit of religious artifacts, or a fortune teller. Perhaps a fertility goddess from an ancient Northern tribe.

He thought the display of costume jewelry a resourceful, not to say colorful, solution to the lack of storage space in the room, which was sparsely furnished with fittings that were antique without being valuable. He wondered if Seb's room would be this threadbare, or if the stepson of Sir James rated better lodgings? He thought he knew the answer to that.

"We-e-ll..." said the duvet.

"What is it?" asked St. Just, treading softly.

"It depends on what you mean by 'saw.'"

St. Just folded his hands and looked at her, hoping this was not going to devolve into one of those "what is the meaning of 'is'?" discussions.

She sighed, and allowed her head to emerge slightly from its duvet shell. "I saw him from the window of my room. Just there"— she indicated the large mullioned window above her desk, which stood next to the bed. St. Just walked over. Her room overlooked the back of the college, and she had a view, slightly distorted by the old glass, between the branches of a tree near the window—a view to the boathouse and the path that ran towards it.

"What exactly did you see?"

"I saw him setting out in the scull. Before you ask, I don't know the exact time. But it's about when I expected to see him setting out, if you follow. He hardly deviates from the program he's set for himself."

"You saw nothing else?"

Again, the hesitation.

"I was reading quite a good book, and I just happened to glance up. I went back to the book and thought no more about it."

He picked up a book that lay open on the desk.

"Insanity and Criminal Responsibility?"

"Yeah. You should read it. Fascinating stuff."

Leafing through the pages, he felt he could read it, but understanding it would be another thing.

"And this held you spellbound, did it?" he asked. "For how long?"

Again that hesitation.

"Actually, if you really have to know, I was reading P. D. James." She indicated a shelf next to the desk. Most of the books there were crime novels. "I needed a rest from all the rubbishy academic papers. Next thing I knew, I heard all the hullaballoo, I don't know, around ten."

He looked at her closely. Her small face again retreated into the duvet.

"If there's anything you know you aren't telling me"—and he was sure there was—"now would be a good time, Miss Sellers."

"I've told you." Again the small, muffled voice.

He made as if to leave, then turned and said:

"I'd take care if I were you. I can protect you if I have all the facts. Without them, you're on your own in what has already proven to be a deadly game. Do you understand me?"

The duvet nodded.

"The girl's lying, of course," St. Just told Sergeant Fear. "But I don't know that it has anything to do with the murder."

They were in a reference room just off the main library. It was a handsome, closed area stacked high with what looked to be old ledgers, some dating back to the eighteenth century, and with two oriel windows looking out either side to the grounds of the college. The Master had emphasized to Sergeant Fear that these treasures—both windows and ledgers—were not to be touched. Fear gathered they could use the table and chairs, and that was the limit of the Master's munificence.

"About seeing Seb? Providing him with an alibi?"

"Possibly. Very likely, in fact. Still, there's something else. She has that view . . . but she claims to have been reading."

"What was she reading, Sir?"

"Hmm? Oh, it was a P. D. James. That newest one of hers—the one about the plastic surgeon."

"That's suggestive, isn't it? Maybe she likes playing detective, if she's a crime novel fan."

"That occurred to me, too. Damned silly game to play, if so. Silly, and dangerous." Fleetingly, he thought of Portia. "I warned her, but people her age, they always know so much more than the previous generation, have you noticed?"

"Trouble is, I think my Emma and Devin will know more than me. I'm certain of it. Anyway, Sir, maybe this Saffron, maybe she was just embarrassed to be caught spying on her boyfriend. Pride, you know."

"I had thought of that, too. You're right, that's probably it. I'll work on her a bit more later, and make it safe for her to tell me somehow."

"By the way, Sir. As I passed by Geraldo Valentiano's room, it looked to me as if he might be packing."

St. Just heaved a great, somewhat theatrical sigh, his head and shoulders dropping in an attitude of despair. Then he looked up at his sergeant and said:

"All right. Time for another little chat with him. He needs to know that simian charm of his has already worn thin. Then let's see who's in the SCR, shall we?"

As they were leaving, passing through the main library to reach the corridor to the stairs, they passed a Japanese student at work at one of the library's computers. He wore a Burberry scarf, tattered jeans, and an expression of the most intense concentration.

St. Just had earlier asked Portia about him when he'd met her in passing. He seemed ever-present.

"He's always there," she'd confirmed. "Always. He's been around ten years and apparently he just won't leave. We don't think he eats or sleeps, except perhaps for brief moments at the computer. Pay him no mind; no one else does."

"What's he doing?"

"We think he's either inventing a new video game or remapping the double helix. No one really knows, and everyone is afraid to approach him. He thinks one is trying to steal his thesis if one does, you see. As if anyone could understand his thesis, including his tutor, who professes himself baffled. Kurokawa Masaki is his name, and he's either a genius or a maniac. The tutor thinks he might be set to crack the code of the Universe, so he leaves him alone. Either way, it's best to not disturb him."

ALL MY BAGS ARE PACKED

GERALDO VALENTIANO WAS, AS reported, packing, folding his tailor-made shirts into a leather bag of butter-soft leather, and hanging his jackets inside a Louis Vuitton garment bag. He looked up briefly as the policemen entered (the door had stood open), gave them the once-over, and carried on with his task. His face betrayed not an ounce of concern.

"I think I just mentioned to you, Sir, that you were to remain here. We'll probably need you for the inquest."

Geraldo shrugged. "So I'll return for the inquest."

St. Just persisted. "I hope you're not planning to ignore an official police request? That could get … complicated."

"Could make you look guilty, like," volunteered Sergeant Fear. "Like you were fleeing justice."

"Fleeing justice," mimicked Geraldo. "What an old-time concept. Justice. Is a man not allowed to pack his luggage in this country?"

"As long as that's all you do," said St. Just. "Were you planning on growing a beard, then?" He indicated the shaving kit already packed into the bag.

Geraldo Valentiano looked at him. "I might."

"One question, Sir. Well, let's make it two. Lexy was overheard asking for the payment of some money you owed her."

Geraldo just looked stonily across the room.

"Well?" said St. Just.

"Oh. Was that a question?" said Geraldo. Then, off St. Just's look, he said, "Well, yes, I got in a tight spot at the tables one night. She bailed me out. Just twenty-five thousand pounds—no big deal. I was going to repay it—she knew I was good for it."

"I see," said St. Just slowly. "Yes. All right, second question: You've told one of my officers that when Lexy's room was broken into, you were playing tennis, is that right?"

"I was. An innocent pastime, no? The thing I like about tennis is that when you're in the thick of it, it takes your mind off everything else. You stop thinking, like."

Hardly a novel experience for you, I'd wager. Sergeant Fear fairly snorted his frustration. What more did St. Just hope to learn from this swarthy oaf?

"Who were you playing with, if not Lexy?"

Geraldo gave one of his eloquent shrugs.

"India. She was very keen. And quite a good…" Here he paused, lifting an eyebrow sardonically. "She is quite a good player. If you catch my meaning."

St. Just looked at him coldly.

"Will that be all, Inspector? It looks like I have some unpacking to do."

"What was that about?" fumed Sergeant Fear as they walked away from Geraldo's room. "Is he really trying to imply he's having some kind of affair with Lady Bassett?" Fear, having taken quite a shine to India, was in full chivalrous mode at hearing her honor maligned.

"I'd say he was. Implying, that is. It may or may not be true, of course, but it's a convenient alibi for them both, isn't it? Tennis, followed by . . . whatever." Sergeant Fear, with an effort, managed to stifle his horrified protests. "Let's see who's downstairs."

They came across Karl Dunning in the SCR. He was reading the Financial Times, closely following the type on its light salmon-pink pages as if deciphering an ancient rune.

"Ah, just the man I wanted to see," said St. Just, taking a seat across from him. "I wanted to get some insight from you. My feeling is that you're rather an insightful man."

"Flattery will get you everywhere, Inspector," said Karl, putting aside the paper. "What is it you want to know?"

"Nothing specific. Something general, rather. What was your sense of Lexy? I mean to say, what kind of person was she, beyond what was apparent?"

"You're on to that, are you? You must be, to ask the question."

"She seemed to manage rather well," said St. Just, "for a woman who was, technically, unemployed. She also apparently wasn't shy about asking for repayment from anyone who might owe her."

Sergeant Fear, at a loss, looked from one man to the other.

"Everyone talks about how flighty she was," said Karl Dunning. "Hermione goes on and on about how man-mad she was, but Hermione rather revels at times in her reputation as a crackpot spinster, don't you agree? Anyway, all of what Hermione says may be true, but it doesn't entirely match my experience of Lexy. She and I stumbled somehow into a conversation about the stock market, and I saw a different side of the woman, I can tell you. She was able lucidly to discuss the reasons behind the financial meltdowns in Iceland and on Wall Street, making her one of the few people alive who can. She wanted my advice, she said, but I'm not sure she really needed it. It was more like she wanted confirmation of what she'd already decided on for herself."

"Financial advice?"

"Yes. She had some money to invest, wanted to know what I'd do with 'a small windfall.' I told her I'd lend her a book I had with me. It was actually a book I'd co-authored on the subject, in point of fact."

"You were on friendly terms with Lexy, it seems."

For the first time, the amiable Karl showed a flintier surface. "I was lending her a book, Inspector, not asking her to run away with me."

"A windfall, you say. She wasn't specific about the amount? Or where it came from?"

Karl Dunning shook his head. "I didn't get the impression it was any large amount, although I realize 'large' is a relative term to an already wealthy person. She called it her 'mad money' and told me she wanted a flutter with some of the riskier stocks. But what I was saying—she liked to pretend she knew little about 'men's business,' as she called it, gazing up at you from under flickering eyelashes the while, but the questions she asked were spot on. I got the impression of a sharp mind in operation— sharp when it came to money, certainly. But at the same time, she was expending a lot of useless energy trying to cover up her knowledge. In discussing the economy, she'd use a phrase like 'collateral debt obligations' or 'sales-to-income stream,' realize what she'd said, and try to pretend she was just mouthing terms, like she didn't know what the terms meant. She knew. Do you see what I mean? It was like some tortuous Victorian-era style of flirtation. And why waste it on me? Force of habit, I guess. But she could talk the jargon with the best stockbroker."

———

"That was interesting," St. Just said to Sergeant Fear as they walked along the corridor from the SCR towards the long gallery above the Fellows' Garden.

"You think he's a reliable witness, Sir?"

"I do. For one thing, I don't know why he'd lie about such a thing. It's really nothing to us whether Lexy could balance a bank statement or not. What's interesting is that she felt it necessary to hide it. That Lexy was not as thick as she liked to pretend. That she was two personalities, if you like. I thought Mr. Dunning might be the person to ask. He may keep a low profile and let his wife do the talking, but I got the impression of a man who doesn't miss much. I don't think his wife is quite as silly as she appears, either. Like Lexy, she might be clever but only in certain ways. Certainly she's clever at getting her own way. Could be the man's had long practice with women who aren't quite the way the world perceives them."

They had reached the long gallery. Looking through one of the glassed-in archways, St. Just could see the back of a particular head of glossy dark hair, the thick, straight strands of which were tied back low on a long, graceful neck. The tilt of the narrow head made it recognizably Portia's.

Plus, he knew what she was up to.

Sergeant Fear followed his gaze and tactfully said, "Right. I'll get onto HQ about when we might expect to see some of those background reports."

Portia was sitting on the garden bench, in the same spot that had been occupied not that long ago by Lexy Laurant.

"How morbid, you'll be thinking," she greeted him.

St. Just raised a quizzical eyebrow.

"Actually," she explained, "I was doing a little unofficial investigating."

"Thought you might be. I've warned you before about that."

"I was trying," she went on, "to see what she could see from here. Maybe that night she saw something she should not have seen. You know—something that put her in danger. Drug smuggling or something."

St. Just looked around him at the gardens, the buildings, and the pale blue sky corrugated with narrow strips of white cloud. Peering down on them from above were two gargoyles, one at each end of the gallery roof. Only they saw, only they heard, thought St. Just. That little fellow with the claws and the pointed ears and the long tail. He saw Lexy walk away to her death.

He sat beside Portia and took her hand in his.

"I would much prefer having a little less help on this investigation," he said. "But if you really are trying to see things from her angle, you'll have to slump a bit. She was quite a small woman, you know. Short and petite, unlike my Portia. So zaftig."

Portia gave him a dig in the ribcage that could have sent him flying. If ever there were a woman to whom the word zaftig could not apply, it was Portia.

"What?" he said. "Luckily for you I like a woman with meat on her bones."

"Shut up," she instructed him. She slumped down several inches and panned the area slowly from left to right. St. Just sat quietly, breathing deep of the complex perfume of the garden, and of the light scent Portia wore, a flowery fragrance, perhaps mixed with a little vanilla. The air lay warm and moist against his face.

"Nothing," she said at last. "If anything, I have a more restricted view than before. The walls, the trees…she had to have been staring at the statue of the founder. Granted, he's an eyeful."

They both cast a baleful eye on Titus Barron, founder of St. Michael's. He stared out from across the centuries wearing his snug-fitting doublet, with his cloak tossed rakishly across his shoulders and his legs encased in hose. He was posed ballerina-like to display shapely ankles to best effect—ankles that no doubt had helped attract the wealthy merchant's widow he had taken as his bride, nicely shoring up his already substantial fortune. Bloodthirsty even by the standards of his day, he had been instrumental in pushing through King Henry's infamous divorce from Catherine, and had been amply rewarded for his efforts.

At the moment, a pigeon was perched on the feather in his cap.

"Granted," said Portia. "It's not taken from the life, but from some late-Victorian sculptor's idea of how a fine gentleman of that era must have looked."

They stared at Titus awhile longer, but nothing about the sixteenth-century founder, or the pigeon, suggested to them how a twenty-first century woman might have come to meet her violent death under his self-satisfied gaze. The Fellows' Garden, walled on all sides, seemed an oasis of calm.

"Anyway," Portia continued, "one has to say there was not a lot to hold her attention, although I suppose the fountain's rather nice."

"Is it always turned on, the fountain?"

She shook her head. "It's on a timer so it shuts off at ten. A compromise in another case of the Bursar v. the Master, the former wanting it turned off at all times to save money."

Together they watched the fine mist play against the light and air.

"She was apparently in an emotional state," said St. Just. "She may not have been looking at anything in particular, if you follow."

"Yes, I do. In any event, she evidently got bored after a while, and wandered off towards the boathouse and the river. I wonder why—was it just aimless wandering, or did she go there with a purpose, to meet someone?"

"I have wondered the same. Some party from completely outside our group of suspects, someone from her life in London, perhaps … an old flame, perhaps. She had been a single woman for some time. We're of course looking into that angle, but it seems unlikely someone not connected with the college would be guilty of this crime. Do you know: Was there much in the way of gossip about her?"

"Oh, yes, she was fodder for the gossip magazines of a glossier sort," said Portia. "Always photographed doing something glamorous, and managing to look better than the average mortal as she did it."

"Was she generally photographed with an escort of some kind?"

"Oh, generally. But it was her clothing that was of interest. The men tended not to be in the picture. Literally."

"Yes, well, we'll have to look into all that, I suppose. Disrupt a few lives, perhaps needlessly. It's jolly hard to imagine someone following her from London to lurk about in the grounds all weekend, awaiting the chance to strike. It requires a degree of lunacy, that kind of patience and planning—a sustained rage as well. One would think there would have been signs of that all along in the outward behavior of our killer, if this was indeed a crime of passion or revenge. That should make our job all the easier. But ... "

"But?"

"But somehow I should be very much surprised to find that kind of solution. For one thing, this crime speaks of an intimate knowledge of this college's doings, or at least its doings during this kind of old members' knees-up. Without that knowledge, there is too much left to chance in the crime. Far easier, in fact, to believe in the passing lunatic or addict doing her in for the thrill of it. And that kind of crime is mercifully rare in this city. Without robbery as a motive ... "

"I wonder ... she had no purse, no evening bag? She had one when I saw her on the stairs."

"One was found next to the body. It contained a little jeweled, mirrored container of face powder, a handkerchief, and a comb. The key to her room, and a ten-pound note. That was all."

"Face powder, but no lipstick?"

"Actually, a lipstick was found here, by the bench," he told her. "They're testing but the assumption is it was hers. It matched the design of the container of face powder."

"Hmm. I suppose that also speaks to the degree of her upset—that she dropped it or it fell out of her purse somehow, and she didn't notice."

St. Just nodded, and said, "Again, the circumstances—barring that she was killed by someone who just happened upon her— the circumstances argue for someone with some knowledge of the layout of this college. If they came here deliberately to meet her, to quarrel with her, to kill her, some knowledge of the setup is indicated."

"There was a quarrel, you think?"

"No, come to that, I do not. The physical evidence suggests she was surprised. There was no struggle to speak of; she was quickly overcome."

"Pity there was no one on the river to see," said Portia.

"It was getting too dark for most. Yes. Getting too late, and the boathouse is well out of the way for a puntful of tourists to wander off course and discover. The last punt rented out that night from any of the hire services went out at eight from Silver Street and was safely returned an hour later. We're asking the boat club and the colleges if any of their keener rowers would have been out practicing, like young Seb, but if they had they'd have been out of their usual range, perhaps in violation of the myriad of regulations that govern use of the river. And there are very few students around, anyway, as you know. The river is never quite deserted but at night, this time of year…"

"Fishermen?"

"We've got inquiries afoot. Or afloat, in this case. But if anyone saw anything we'll get a response from the appeal to the public that's appearing in tomorrow's paper. It will bring out the eccentrics in a town famous for its eccentrics, but it has to be done."

Just then the pigeon flew away, first having left a deposit on Titus Barron to mark its visit.

INNOCENT ABROAD

St. Just left Portia some time later and walked back towards the incident room to see what news, if any, might have come in. In the college's entrance hall, the Reverend Otis had just pushed through the main door, carrying an enormous mixed bouquet of wildflowers.

"So cheering, don't you think?" he asked the detective, with a little bleat of happiness. "I thought we needed something to dispel the gloom."

St. Just nodded and said, "I wondered if I could have a word."

"Certainly." The Reverend Otis smiled kindly at the detective, if a little reservedly. His eyes, already magnified behind thick spectacles, grew rounder. It was like being scrutinized by a friendly but inquisitive sheep.

"I wondered when you would get around to talking with me," said the Reverend Otis. "I have watched every Commander Adam Dalgliesh episode, you know. I have them on tape. So I know how these things go. All the suspects have to be interviewed until someone gives the game away."

St. Just, wishing real investigations were as easy, merely smiled and indicated that the Reverend should take a seat on the ancient wooden bench at one side of the entrance hall.

"The problem is, of course," said the Reverend Otis, settling onto the bench and placing the bouquet beside him, "that I know nothing that can help you."

"Just your impressions would be helpful," said St. Just. "I would imagine that in your line of work you gain some particular facility for picking up on the nuances." Thank God, he thought, the Master can't overhear me.

The otherwise humble Dean seemed to take this as his due. He dipped his balding head in acknowledgement and said, "That is a large part of my sacred calling, yes. Not giving advice, as some tend to think. But listening, noticing, and advising only when asked."

"Your impressions of what transpired this weekend, then. Was there anything leading up to the time of the murder that struck you as unusual?"

"That's just it—you've put your finger on the problem. There was nothing that seemed particularly out of place to me. I have thought and thought about it, you see. We have held these re-unions before, of course. Sometimes there is a bit of ... competition among the participants. These are all extremely clever people, you know. This particular group, being so successful—my impression was that there was less posturing than usual. They all had less to prove, perhaps."

St. Just asked, "Was that true in the case of Lexy Laurant, as well?"

"Ah," said the Reverend Otis. "Well." He looked at St. Just, bewildered anew, perhaps, by the fact of a murder having been committed on his watch.

St. Just said, "There was some tension there, was there not? I rather gather that Lexy was in competition with Lady Bassett, trying to gain the attention of Sir James."

The bewilderment on the older man's face deepened.

"Whoever told you that?" he asked, in his slow, gentle voice. St. Just had to lean in to hear him clearly. "No, no. Not at all. My impression was definitely that Lexy had other fish to fry. Sir James' hold on her had weakened considerably. Divorce is never pleasant and never the best option, but I did wonder how two such different personalities as Lexy and Sir James had ever come together in the first place. She was ... a bit frivolous; he was far more serious-minded by nature. I think she had come to realize this for herself. I overheard her call him a dried-up stick."

The same phrase used by Gwennap, thought St. Just.

"Really?" he said. "But surely that could be taken as anger, not indifference?"

The Reverend Otis shrugged. You might very well think that.

"Regardless," he said. "He was simply too serious a personality for Lexy. An author, you know. A creative artist. And quite a good one, too, don't misunderstand. Terribly serious with it all, is what I mean to convey. Some of his later works met with increasing puzzlement amongst the reading public. I daresay he felt the same...the works were disjointed somehow. Experimental and daring, I suppose. But Cygnus and the Northern Cross, along with one or two others, were spiffing good yarns. Pity about the title—difficult to remember. Perhaps they'll change it if and when it's filmed. No doubt they will."

"You seem to know a great deal about his career."

The Reverend Otis blushed.

"I am writing a novel myself. A children's book. It's a detective story, actually, with Biblical characters. I don't suppose you'd like to—? No, no, I can see you're rather busy right now. Anyway, I subscribe to a newsletter that keeps me up to date on all this sort of thing: happenings in the literary world. Do you know, Inspector, I even thought I had a theory about all this. You see, when I first saw Lexy in the Fellows' Garden, I thought she was with Geraldo. Well, quite naturally, one would, wouldn't one?"

"I don't follow."

"Sir James' back was turned, as he was looking at the fountain when I first saw him. And viewed from the back, he and Geraldo look remarkably alike. They both have sleek dark hair, although Sir James is losing his in front. But from the back they look identical—trim, well-built, dark-haired men. You do see what I mean, don't you?"

The Reverend Otis blethered on a bit in this vein. St. Just looked at him. Was it possible that some of the other witnesses had in fact seen Lexy not with Sir James, but, fleetingly, with Geraldo? Would Geraldo lie about that, simply to distance himself as completely from the case as possible? Were Sir James and Geraldo in cahoots somehow?

Just then, the door opened, and Sebastian entered the hall. St. Just realized his mistake in conducting this interview in such a highly trafficked area. But Seb merely nodded and headed up-stairs, taking the steps two at a time.

"Ah, youth," said the Reverend. "It's been years since I've been able to do that without courting the danger of tumbling straight back down. But then, to be honest, I never had that sort of com-mitment to sports. Seb has the reputation for being a bit of a lad, but he works extremely hard, you know. I see him going to and from the boathouse all the time, or coming in late from the labo-ratory. It's so heartening to see that kind of dedication among the young people. Chemistry can't be the easiest subject. It certainly wouldn't be in my case."

"Mine either, I'm afraid." Privately, St. Just wondered. Wouldn't Seb be more likely to be coming in late from a party? He'd gained no impression of him as a scholar—the "bit of a lad" reputation seemed more fitting. St. Just was beginning to think the Reverend Otis might be one of those kind people forever blinded to the faults of others. What was it Portia had said? Something about how he needed a constant eye kept on him or he'd be swindled every time he set foot outside the college.

"When is the last time you saw Lexy?" St. Just asked him.

"At dinner. Just after, in fact. She was in the garden."

"The garden is always kept locked to outsiders at night? The Master mentioned something about a donkey."

"Such a sweet creature. After curfew, yes, the oak door that leads into the grounds is bolted and locked by the Porter. Until then, it is open to all. Until ten o'clock, that is. The students know better than to use it as a shortcut into the building, however. Not too helpful to your investigation, I'm afraid. Anyone would be free to come and go before ten."

———

Parting from the Reverend Otis a few minutes later, St. Just made his way towards the incident room upstairs. As he walked through the main library area to the makeshift police headquarters in the reference room, he found Sir James working at one of the room's large tables ranged against the walls.

"Progress?" he asked him.

"No. Maybe. Of a sort." Sir James, removing his glasses, tiredly pinched the bridge of his nose between thumb and forefinger. "Just trying to take my mind off things, really. I don't think any writer ever has a clue if progress is being made. There is a lot of faith involved. Putting one foot in front of another and hoping for the best at the end of the road."

"Surely you must be used to that … uncertainty … by now?"

Sir James shook his head. "It's a strange kind of pressure and it never goes away. People, after all, have put down their ten pounds or more sterling to be entertained. One feels obligated to, at a minimum, reveal the secrets of the Universe, if not the key to all happiness. Which of course no one can—at least, not for ten pounds. It's just the pressure the author places on himself somehow."

Politely signaling the end of his interest in the conversation, Sir James began to turn back towards his work. St. Just said his farewells and moved on. He next spotted Sebastian Burrows hunched over a laptop at one of the oak study carrels that occupied the center of the room, the computer plugged into an outlet built into the desk for that purpose. The room was chilly, and Seb wore a black-and-white Arab scarf wrapped several times around his neck. St. Just thought it might be a fashion statement rather than a sign Sebastian was thinking of joining the PLO.

He saw the Inspector approaching and, shutting the lid of the laptop, sat back in his chair, arms crossed.

"Any luck, Inspector?"

"Yes, as a matter of fact. I think we're getting somewhere."

In fact, he doubted this very much, but Sebastian's reaction was interesting. He became still. It was an unnatural stillness, as if his muscles were gathering themselves for flight, and as if his hearing had suddenly become particularly acute.

"Really?" In what must have been a painful reminder of an adolescence not that far back in his past, Seb's voice cracked. He cleared his throat and tried again at a lower register. "Really? And how is that?" Now he sounded like Bette Davis announcing a bumpy night.

"You will be told all in good time," said St. Just in his most avuncular manner. There, he thought. Enough to keep Seb on his toes without scaring the bejesus out of him, rendering him useless to the investigation. "You know, you have a very loyal girlfriend."

"Who, Saffron?" He shrugged. "Yeah. She's all right. But she's more my friend than a girlfriend, you know."

"Oh, yes, I know your generation likes to make these fine distinctions. But you are sleeping with her, aren't you?"

"What's that to do with you?" demanded Sebastian, not unreasonably, thought St. Just.

"I'll offer you a bit of advice," St. Just said. "You may not think that makes Saffron your girlfriend, but I would be willing to bet she thinks it does. She is in love with you, if you didn't know it. And my impression is she'd do anything for you. Why, she might even lie for you, Sebastian. Do you think she'd do that, Seb?" He leaned onto the oak desk. "Do you think she'd lie for you?" he asked softly.

A mulish expression blunted the soft planes of Sebastian's face, a face which had not yet hardened into that of the man he would become. St. Just stood so close he could see the little spot of blood where Seb had cut his chin shaving, and could smell his stupendously dreadful, musky aftershave.

Sebastian looked away. He began to play with the cord of his computer, winding it 'round and 'round his index finger, then unwinding it in the other direction.

"Leave that and look at me," said St. Just sharply. The ever-present Japanese student near the window looked about, annoyed, to see what was the matter. "If you know something germane to this case," St. Just went on, "you'd best tell me now. If Saffron knows something, she'd be wise to tell us, even if it means turning her back on you. She probably won't, of course. She doesn't know yet how expendable she is, does she?"

Just then, Sebastian cocked his head sharply. It was exactly as if he'd heard his name called. The student by the window muttered something under his breath. But the room was silent. Nonetheless, Sebastian began gathering his things together, to the evident relief of Kurokawa Masaki.

St. Just made a mental note that he'd have to speak with Masaki as well. He seemed nearly oblivious, and tearing him away from his computer would take an effort, but one never knew.

Sebastian, now standing, turned to the Inspector.

"I don't know anything about your murder. Now, let me be."

St. Just let him be. For now.

St. Just decided a walk by the river might offer its usual restorative powers. But he wanted to get away from the City proper. Too much traffic, and too many suicidal bicyclists made it less than enjoyable. After sending someone to locate the number, he placed a call to Sebastian's coach, who told him where he might this day be found. Then St. Just got in his car and headed out to where the college boathouses were lined up along the river.

"During the summer I have a different gig," the man had explained on the phone. "The regular teams usually aren't around. The May Bumps are just over, of course. Plenty of other schools and rowing clubs needing a coach, though."

The Lent or May Bumps races, when the colleges competed against each other—the May Bumps so-called even though held in June—were the payoff to all the training of the previous months. All the going down to the river and hauling the boat in and out of frigid water. All the careful monitoring of the proper intake of protein and fat in the diet. All the single-minded resolve and dedication that could make the difference between exhilarating win or ignominious defeat. St. Just had been a rower for his college, but after twenty years he'd forgotten much of the lingo, and nearly all the pain of training. Only the exhilaration of being on the water, the wind in his hair, and the sun or rain in his eyes, remained in memory.

The coach proved to be a man of indeterminate middle age, his leathery skin criss-crossed with veins and broken blood vessels. He had the permanent squint of a man who'd tried to peer through sheets of downpour far too often.

Their ensuing conversation was punctuated by supportive if ragged cries of "Olly, olly" issuing sporadically from what looked to be a somewhat inebriated group picnicking along the banks. An eight skimmed by, commanded by a tiny cox screaming at top of her lungs: "Come on, you lard-arsed useless buggers! Power ten in two!" St. Just wasn't sure about the rowers, but that would probably make him row faster.

"You were asking about Sebastian," said the coach, who had introduced himself as Jason Wright. He paused in his examination of an oar collar. "Now I wondered at that. I wondered a great deal." Again the squint, as if peering out over fathomless seas, rather than the narrow, snaking River Cam, looking today as placid as a glass of water. "Of course, I know what's happened over there at St. Mike's. The whole town is abuzz with it. I will tell you this: Sebastian may not be the most honest kid you'll find, but he's no killer."

"All right. But how can you be so sure?"

"I just am. For one thing, he's not a stupid kid. Spoiled, head-strong, a bit full of himself—yes. But he'll grow out of those things. Thing is ..."

"Yes?"

"It's a suspicion I've had, merely. Things overheard. Young folk, they don't notice you're around, so you get to hear things maybe not intended for your ears, right?"

"Go on," said St. Just.

MAKING A LIST

By early afternoon Monday, the air had grown muggy, the clouds fat with unshed rain. St. Just and Sergeant Fear were in the CID offices of the police station, slowly recovering from an execrable lunch in the canteen. St. Just thought the police kitchen staff might have something to teach the St. Mike's chef on how to obtain unusual and nearly inedible cuts of meat.

St. Just had earlier faced down the media, an ordeal he anticipated much like a dental appointment: a necessary and uncomfortable thing to get through so that real life could resume. He had told the reporters as little as he could get away with and then quickly called a halt when questioning wandered into the absurd: "Is it true the police fear a Jack-the-Ripper-type serial killer is on the loose in Cambridge?" ("Absolutely not.") "Is it true the victim was the love child of the Duke of Edinburgh?" ("You must be joking.") From where, he wondered, did they get their rubbish? He understood too well the tactic of trying to provoke a reaction so they could fashion a story from his denials. "The detective in charge of the case strongly denies that the victim was pregnant"—thus firmly planting in the public's mind the idea that she was pregnant and there was a police cover-up afoot.

All was silence now, the members of the media having scuttled off to see what kind of sensation they could create out of no information whatsoever, but as the two policemen had returned from the canteen, a child somewhere in the station's waiting area had been pitching a tantrum, repeatedly screaming something that sounded to St. Just like "Baba Bear!" He couldn't see the child, but clearly she had a future in opera. Turning a corner they came upon her, a tiny thing of perhaps three years, crowned with a mop of riotous red curls, living up to her stereotype as a tempestuous redhead. St. Just smiled and the girl, immediately diverted from her sorrows, abandoned the tantrum to eye him closely with a rapt, if moist, regard. Her mother, who had been folded over trying to reason with the child, looked up at St. Just in no little astonishment. Sergeant Fear, who had seen the St. Just effect on children and animals many times, grinned proprietarily. Too bad we can't clone him and bring him home, he thought.

Now St. Just said to him, "Bring me some coffee, please, Sergeant, and then let's see what's turned up here."

They had retreated to the station to retrieve the reports they'd been told had just come in—reports St. Just wanted to review away from the prying eyes of the college. He had a sense at St. Mike's of being constantly watched, a sense he attributed partly to the eerie, unblinking gaze of the gargoyles adorning the roofs of the buildings.

He tapped the fingers of one hand against the pile of folders and papers that awaited him on his blotter. St. Just often wondered why he had been issued a blotter, an item normally useful in part to protect the surface of a desk. His desk was so scarred and battered it was hard to imagine what further damage could be done to it, unless someone set it on fire and dropped it from a plane. The same could be said for the station walls, decorated in gray on dark gray, the paint perhaps purchased in a fire sale, and the matching filing cabinets tilted rakishly against one wall.

He grabbed the top item from the stack as Sergeant Fear returned.

"The coffee isn't ready yet, Sir. I brought you an energy drink for now, instead."

"Energy drink?"

Cautiously, St. Just accepted the little bottle of drink, as if something so named might explode in his hand. "Pow-Wee," he saw it was called. Reading the label on the bottle, he noted its contents promised to improve his performance, increase his reaction speed, and enhance his vigilance. Why, he'd have the case solved in no time. He took a tentative sip.

"First things first," he said. "Ask Brummond to check the call notification settings on Sebastian's phone. Have Brummond call you right back with his findings. Then I want you to dial Sebastian's number, while Brummond is still standing there with Sebastian. And I want to hear from Brummond on the result. Got that?"

Fear did as asked. St. Just resumed his reading. Five minutes later, the phone rang. It was Brummond reporting back. St. Just listened, said, "That's what I thought," and rang off.

To Sergeant Fear he said, "Next, get William Trinity, the St. Mike's porter, on the phone for me. I need the results of the locker search." Once connected, he again listened a few moments, nodding. Again he rang off. Turning to his sergeant, he said:

"Our Sebastian has been funneling booze into the college—one hundred proof or more."

"He's a bootlegger?"

"Something like that. He and a few friends have been busy cooking up some kind of hootch in the chemistry lab. I thought something unusual was up with Seb's cell phone, and I was right. When you dialed Sebastian's number just now, Brummond couldn't hear a thing, although the phone was set on ring, not vibrate. You ever hear of the Mosquito, Sergeant?"

Sergeant Fear allowed as he had not.

"It's a ring tone young people use to put one past the oldies like you and me. It's a sound that can only be heard by someone under the age of thirty or so. I started to notice how anyone in that age group seemed to be hearing something out of my range, some sudden and irritating noise—Kurokawa Masaki, the kid who was always in the library, for one, as well as some of the kitchen staff. It was how Sebastian and his business associates communicated: the arrival of a shipment, or a customer, or the stage of production—whatever. Sebastian was operating his business mainly out of the boathouse, where there was plenty of storage, and to which he had access at all hours. However, our investigation has been putting a real damper on his trade. Generally, he transported his shipments by boat. It's extremely good-quality alcohol, says Vice."

"Well, it is Cambridge, Sir. Think of the kind of equipment he'd have access to." Fear paused. "Is it really a case for Vice?"

"Not really. I was afraid..." He'd been afraid it was hard drugs. This—this was still not "nice," it was still dangerous, but... Sergeant Fear seemed to read his mind.

"It's a little less than hard crime, and a little more than a childish prank. It's not as if no one ever died from acute alcohol poisoning."

"Exactly. More or less befitting the supreme lack of judgment you might expect to find in this age group. We can't ignore it, nor shall we. But right now..."

St. Just turned his attention again to the stack before him.

"Let's see," he said. "Appeals to the public for information have thus far proven fruitless, it would seem—once again, we only seem to attract the deeply insane but it's too vital a step to skip over. But—" and he pulled out a thick folder, "—this is just in from our stunningly efficient colleagues across the pond. Let's have a look." St. Just flipped through the pages for several minutes. "Well, well. Our Texan friend has a little violence in his past, it seems. Something about a shooting... yes, he was out hunting and managed to nip one of his fellow hunters in the earlobe. This sounds familiar, somehow. Didn't one of their vice-presidents suffer from a similar bad aim? Anyway, the wounded fellow was angry enough about it to press charges. Claimed Augie Cramb aimed for him on purpose. Boundary dispute... something about cows... fences. Looks like Cramb bought his way out of it. Yes, well, it was years ago but something to keep in mind, eh, Sergeant? He might have a hair-trigger temper, as well."

He reached for the next collection of stapled papers.

"Mr. and Mrs. Dunning, now. Nothing criminal here, unless you count having more money than God criminal, which some do. His seems to be a classic rags-to-riches story. Might be worth making sure the riches part is all above board. She has two children of a seemingly monumental dullness from a previous marriage—both doing something on Wall Street. Hedge funds. Good God. Always makes me think of topiary. Still, if it's criminal, that's probably par for the course these days. Not our onion, I shouldn't think.

"Next up ... Ah. Geraldo Valentiano." He paused, scanning several pages, then said, "This is interesting. He was at Cambridge but at a different college: Selwyn. I wonder why he didn't think to mention that? Again, pots of money, but he seems to have been born to it. A parent in the shipping business who makes Aristotle Onassis look like a tuna boat captain. In fact, I'd say there's considerably less money now than when Geraldo was born to it. What do you think, Sergeant? Recreational drug use? Gambling debts? He's certainly the louche type to be found haunting the casinos, and he admits being in debt to Lexy. Have an ask-around, will you, to see how far in debt he really is? As to drugs ... well, I saw no signs of anything like addiction."

"I'd say he's too mindful of his own skin to let himself get hooked," said Sergeant Fear.

"And I would agree with you. Still, if he's in the trade, it's easy to end up on the wrong end of a drug deal, and lose money where the idea was to make money. God knows there's a market for that kind of thing around the University. It helps keep Vice in business."

Sergeant Fear's mobile erupted just then in a blast of Ride of the Valkyries.

St. Just looked over at his flustered Sergeant, who appeared to be trying to pat his heart back into place.

"Emma?" St. Just asked mildly. One of Emma's many talents was for programming her father's mobile until all the combined forces of the police IT department could not de-program it. Her parents suspected their preternaturally precocious child was using nursery school as a cover for replicating the Manhattan Project.

"It's my wife. She'll be wanting to know when I'm coming home tonight." St. Just shrugged at the implied question; Sergeant Fear sent the call into voicemail as St. Just drew another sheaf of papers towards him. It was a thin sheaf this time.

"Tell your family I'm sorry," said St. Just, "but needs must." His forehead creased in a distracted frown. "Wasn't there something about a disguise in the Ride of the Valkyries?"

Sergeant Fear shrugged: Beats me. St. Just was not an opera fan, either, but something about the song triggered a memory of impersonations or substitutions. He'd have to look it up.

In need of a pencil, he began tugging at the left drawer of his desk. It always behaved as if it were permanently welded shut; St. Just had learned through trial and error it could only be opened by using an initial sharp downward pressure followed by a mighty tug, all this combined with a great deal of swearing. Sergeant Fear, used to this performance and knowing better than to intervene, stood by quietly observing. The curses, it seemed, had to be in a certain order, like an incantation. Eventually the drawer, with a screech and a groan, flew out of its opening, flipped out of St. Just's hands, and landed with a resounding thud on the floor, spilling most of its contents. An exasperated St. Just decided to leave it for now. At least he had his pencil.

"Now here we have Sebastian Burrows," he continued. "Not a lot here, but of course, he hasn't been with us on the planet all that long, either." St. Just unfolded a piece of paper that proved to be a news clipping in which Sebastian was identified as James' son. "Now, we know that's not precisely true. A little more digging called for there." He held up an official document. "Birth certificate. He was born Sebastian Augustus Windwell Burrows. The date on the certificate fits with what we know of India's adventures at the college."

He pulled a foolscap folder towards him and peeked inside.

"Sir James Bassett and his lady wife, India." He riffled through the papers. "Member of the Hawks' Club, et cetera. That's right—as I recall he was wearing the Club tie. Captained the University's Hare and Hounds Club."

"Horses again," said Sergeant Fear.

St. Just, not listening, went on.

"Took to novel writing early on; doesn't seem to have had a proper career. It looks like India has some family money of her own, but in general they're not where they were financially a year ago."

"Which of us is?" asked Sergeant Fear.

"Excellent point, Sergeant. The economy has affected everyone, high and low. It does look as if they have a holiday home at Southwald. Nice for them." He read aloud, now quoting from a newspaper clipping: "'The publication of Why Not Helene? helped put Sir James on the literary map.' Really. I remember reading that book. I still have it somewhere. It's partly autobiographical, I would have said—about his boyhood. Well-written but he rather whinges on about how much he—the main character—hated public school."

"I wouldn't know about that, Sir."

"Public schools are highly overrated," said St. Just, who was well aware his Sergeant was guilty on occasion of reverse snobbery. "Next up, the Master and his friends at the college." St. Just flipped through another sheaf of pages collected in a folder titled St. Michael's Officials. "Blameless existences, all of them, I'm sure. The same goes for Hermione Jax." He noted that Hermione lived in one of those pricey mock-Tudor enclaves that had sprung up in the Cambridge suburbs in recent years. A strange choice for a single woman, but perhaps she liked being surrounded by children's tricycles and other signs of family life.

He threw the folder back on his desk. The more he tried to tighten the lens of the investigation, the more the motive and the killer remained stubbornly blurred.

He said, "The staff—we have to go into all of that, of course, but I would be willing to bet we'll find nothing there. They've all been around for years, as we've been told, and I'd warrant the Bursar is ruthless in his background vetting. And if one of them had suddenly gone off his or her nut, the Bursar would probably be the first to know."

"It's not getting us very far, is it, Sir?"

"Do you think so, Sergeant? Well, then there's the victim. And it's her background that may hold the clue, more so than the rest of this." He waved a hand over the mess of papers now scattered on his desk. The details on Lexy Laurant had been collected in a pink foolscap folder, possibly by a team member of a heretofore unsuspected sentimental disposition. St. Just pulled out the contents and these he read with care. Sergeant Fear settled back more deeply into his chair. This might take awhile.

"Right," said St. Just after half an hour had passed. "Piles of money there, too, but we knew that. They're all from money, which is why they were invited by the Bursar and Master in the first place." He drew a pad of paper towards him. "Right," he said again. "Now, what have we got? We'll need that timeline of who was where, when. Or where they say they were, when. How far along are you with that?"

Just then they were interrupted by a PC carrying yet another sheaf of papers to add to the pile. St. Just scanned the new input quickly and said, "Confirmed: traces of prescription drugs in Lexy's body."

"But, did they find anything like that in her room?"

"Good point. I don't believe so." St. Just riffled back through an older stack of pages. "No. Traces only."

"There should have been a container. Even an empty one. Unless she just chucked it in the river or something, which seems a bit unlikely, doesn't it, Sir?"

"Hmm."

St. Just turned to the newspaper and magazine clippings someone had helpfully assembled. An enormous pile of articles amounted to a monument to Lexy and her life of frenzied and expensive nightclub hopping. Lexy, sporting her signature hairstyle, had appeared with monotonous regularity in magazines and newspapers. The red-top papers had loved her, but so had the more staid publications. Even St. Just, hardly a celebrity hound, had recognized her.

Here now were photo after photo of her smiling with a fierce gaiety belied by her flat, lifeless gaze. She looked bored. Worse, St. Just thought she looked lonely. In one recent photo, Geraldo stood beside her, and a younger, more vibrant version of Lexy stood on his other side. It looked as if he had one arm around each woman. As a fair summing up of the situation, St. Just felt the photographer could not have done better. Geraldo would always have one eye out for a replacement. No wonder Lexy looked so ... lost. She chose her companions unwisely, which was, reflected St. Just, the key to living a lonely life of desperation.

He sat and thought. Sergeant Fear, long accustomed to waiting out these silences, waited as patiently as he could. He began to unwrap a boiled sweet but the crinkling sound of the cellophane seemed to fill the room. At last St. Just said, "The question we have to ask ourselves, Sergeant, is whether an element of chance was in the pattern of the evening, or of the entire weekend—chance of which the murderer took advantage—or if some design was at work. Was this an impulsive act, or a carefully planned one?"

Sergeant Fear, suspecting another of St. Just's rhetorical questions, simply looked at the older detective with what he hoped was a look of intent alertness.

St. Just, noticing the expression, wondered if his sergeant weren't still suffering the aftereffects of their canteen lunch. Picking up his hard-won pencil, St. Just scribbled for a few moments and leaned back in his chair. He had drawn a rough sketch of the SCR and a rougher sketch of the college grounds. Along one side of the page he had written a list of names.

"Now, Sergeant, by some point in time that night, they were all gathered together in the SCR, according to their corroborated statements. If our killer was among them, and I feel certain he or she was, then Lexy was killed between the time witnesses last saw her—nine-sixteen, as Malenfant would have it—and the time they all generally agree they'd gathered together—nine thirty-five at the outside, say. Not a large window of opportunity, but more than large enough for someone acting quickly. Her body was found at nine-fifty or as near to as makes no difference. Agreed?"

Sergeant Fear nodded. "That all sounds right."

"Sounds all wrong to me, but I can't put my finger on why. Leave it for now . . . Get Malenfant on the phone for me, will you? Oh, and I'll need to ask Portia if she remembers yet who besides the Bursar was left in Hall when she herself left. That can help give us a starting point for our timeline."

Sergeant Fear's call having gone through, he handed over the receiver. Accordion music could be heard playing in the background.

Malenfant said, in answer to St. Just's question, "It depends on how heavy a meal she had. But the stomach starts to empty in ten minutes."

"Hang on." St. Just rifled quickly through the reports, then said into the phone, "Our suspects claim not to have noticed how much she ate. They were busy talking."

"Can't help you then, Arthur."

St. Just heard a woman's voice, soft and sultry, a Brigitte Bardot va-va-voom of a voice. She might have been saying, "Don't forget to get bread at the store," but in French everything sounded so much more exciting. The woman's voice became muffled as

Malenfant apparently held the phone against his chest. Then he came back on the line.

"If there's nothing else? I would help you if I could, but time of death can't be determined as exactly as we'd like. Not unless someone witnesses the crime, or the murderer tells us he happened to check his watch just before he strangled her."

"They are never that thoughtful, our murderers," said St. Just.

With a final wheeze of the accordion, Malenfant was gone. St. Just sat back in his chair, the better to study the ceiling. At last he said, "The manner of death is highly suggestive, don't you think?"

"Ye-s-s-s..." said Sergeant Fear, cautiously.

"She was stunned first, before she was killed. Supposedly a 'humane' death, like one might use to slaughter livestock. But was it humane—did someone, regretting their crime in advance, deliberately choose what seemed a 'kind' method? Or was the method chosen to ensure there would be no cock-ups—no way for Lexy to fight for her life? To scratch her attacker, perhaps, giving us skin samples from under her nails? Was it simply to prevent blood splatter, that she was hit just hard enough to do no more than stun? I think the answers to these questions would tell us a lot about our killer, if only we could ask."

"The psychology of the crime, like?"

"Exactly like. From what we know, she was a harmless enough soul, for all her failings—no threat to anyone but herself, perhaps. If she was killed cold-bloodedly, as the case may have been, we have an extremely dangerous killer on our hands. One who, having gotten away with it, would have no compunction about killing again, the next time someone got in her or his way, for any reason.

"Let us take, for example, India. A horsewoman, and, like her son, physically fit, given over to outdoor pursuits. A woman comfortable holding the reins of a horse, and holding a horse's reins so many years would make one strong—more to the point, make one's hands strong. We can't discount her. The only question is, to what degree did she see Lexy as a threat to her, to her marriage?"

Before St. Just's eyes now arose the specter of Hermione springing from the shadows, wielding a deadly scull. Not impossible, of course, despite Lexy's advantage of youth.

"Might India," he said aloud, following his earlier thought, "along with even the older Hermione, have had the advantage over the younger but more ethereal Lexy in a struggle to the death? Because if the blow to the head had failed to connect, if Lexy had not been hit forcefully enough to be rendered helpless, the killer had to be prepared and able to deal with an awake, enraged, and frightened victim, pumped full of adrenaline. One would have to be sure of one's physical superiority in case of such an eventuality."

He drummed his fingers on the battered desk in frustration. Some memory flitted at the edge of his mind, a memory connected somehow with the little gargoyle overlooking the Fellows' Garden, the evil little fellow who was all claws and pointed ears, the fellow who had a water spout where his mouth should be. He'd been clutching a club or mace, perhaps even an oar or some kind of boat paddle. It was difficult to say, time having eroded the stone, blurring the edges. Much like my thinking. St. Just shook his head. It would come to him.

"What I don't see," he went on slowly, "is how the break-in to her room plays into this. A break-in where nothing was taken, she claimed, although a prescription container does seem to be missing. Sergeant," and here Fear, who had let his mind wander as he pondered the theftless break-in, sat up straighter, "if you were trying to hide something, would you use a frequently used room—hide it in plain sight, à la Edgar Allen Poe—or would you use a room you thought would be empty? Yes, the timing of the break-in is very suggestive. A break-in where nothing was taken," he repeated. "What does that say to you?"

Fear shrugged. "They didn't find what they wanted?"

"That's one explanation, yes. The other is that she didn't want to admit what was taken. Find out who normally would have occupied her room. We'll need to eliminate their fingerprints."

"Fingerprints?" asked Sergeant Fear. St. Just explained what he wanted.

As the sergeant repeated the orders into his mobile, the gargoyle came creeping back into St. Just's mind, watching him and Portia as they watched the pigeon consecrate the statue of Titus Barron.

"Oh, and one other thing," he said to Fear when he'd rung off. "We'll probably need someone standing by to dredge up that river. Don't forget to call your wife."

As St. Just was reaching for his own phone to call Portia, the instrument began to ring. An ordinary ring, no instruments blaring, no mosquito buzz (which he wouldn't have been able to hear in any event), but not an ordinary call. As it turned out, an immediate full-scale dredging of the river was unnecessary. Divers already dispatched to St. Mike's had been able to recover an object of interest amongst the usual jetsam found in a busy river, news of which object they dispatched with all haste to St. Just.

DESPERATE MEASURES

St. Just and Sergeant Fear pulled up to the college, the sergeant, as if celebrating his liberation from enforced stillness, exuberantly spraying gravel as he spun the car to a full stop. Constable Brummond ran out to greet them. Expecting no more than an update on the river discovery, St. Just was puzzled by the look of alarm on the constable's face.

"Come quickly, Sir. The ambulance is on its way."

"Ambulance?" said St. Just and Sergeant Fear together.

Brummond didn't stop to explain, but led the way up the main staircase. With a sickening certainty, St. Just began to realize where he was leading them.

A bedder stood outside the oak door, a button-faced woman of perhaps fifty years, gray-haired, red-eyed, and weeping into her dustcloth. Automatically, St. Just pulled a pristine handkerchief from his suit jacket and pressed it into the woman's hand.

"She was a good girl!" she loudly informed St. Just. "There was no harm in her."

"Saffron. Yes, she was," said St. Just.

"Folk just had to look past all the makeup and earrings and such," she went on. "That was just her playing at being grown up. She was no more than a child!" St. Just noticed the woman was gripping an exercise book. Someone had decorated it in metallic swirls and flowers.

"What is that you have there?"

She looked down at her hands as if the object had leapt into them. Quickly, she handed it to St. Just.

"She always kept this under her pillow. It was her diary, I reckon. When I was ... trying to help her just now ... I don't know how I come to be holding it." She added quickly, "I never read it. I respect their privacy, I do that."

"What is your name, please?"

"Marigold. Marigold Arkwright."

"Marigold, this is important. Was she able to say anything to you?"

She shook her head. "Not really. She was delirious, calling for Sebastian, and for her father."

Brummond signaled him over and whispered. Turning to Sergeant Fear, St. Just said, "Call someone to stay with Ms. Arkwright. Don't leave her. She's in shock. Now, Brummond, what's all this about?" St. Just followed him into Saffron's room.

———

St. Just and Sergeant Fear waited in their temporary office off the main library, giving the team space to work in Saffron's small room. St. Just read her latest entries in the exercise book. Closing it, he smacked the pages against the desk and said:

"The silly child. The bedder had that right. No more than a child. Of all the numbty-headed things to do ..."

"Suicide, Sir?"

St. Just shook his head. "Murder. There were chocolates by her bed, and an opened bottle of cola, and I'd lay odds we'll find one or both have been tampered with. She's been snooping. 'Detecting.' It's all in here," he pointed to the garish little book. "It's partly a diary or journal, all right, but she's taken real events and tried to turn them into one of her favorite detective stories. She writes about what she saw the night of the murder, which was three different people in the vicinity of the boathouse. Three people who said they were somewhere else. We're narrowing it down, Sergeant. Narrowing it down."

"Where did the stuff come from, Sir? The poison, or the drugs?"

"Any drug taken in great quantity is a poison, Sergeant. We may know more when they're through going over Lexy's room. But let me clear up one mystery for you now. Sebastian admitted to Brummond he was on occasion using some of the empty college rooms for overflow storage for his illegal trade. They're comparing prints from his room with the unexplained prints they found in Lexy's room to be sure. I think we'll find some of the prints belong to Sebastian, some to the room's usual occupant. The prints he could easily explain away, of course. But now, according to Brummond, Sebastian hasn't been seen since he saw a team going over Lexy's room yet again. Apparently, he's gone missing ... and just as we find the girl like that, surrounded by a regular pharmacopeia. It is not looking good for our Sebastian, although he swears he had nothing to do with Lexy's missing drugs."

"I don't get it, Sir. Why would Sebastian be mixed up in something like this anyway?"

"Why would the golden-haired boy lower himself to this kind of scheme? At a guess, it's Seb's way of being independent of the parents. That's normally done by taking a paying job, of course, but Seb is one who would hold himself above the dull nine-to-five routine. That's for losers like you and me, Sergeant."

Just then, Constable Brummond stuck his head through the open door.

"They're leaving now, Sir."

"Good. Dispatch someone to bring me the package they found in the river." To Fear he added, "At least now we know who did it."

We do?

"Give me"—St. Just looked at his watch and back at Brummond—"exactly three minutes. Go down right now and tell the members of the media to gather downstairs in the entrance hall—now. I'll meet them there."

"How much are you going to tell them?" asked Sergeant Fear.

"Whatever I can think up in three minutes."

Fear didn't have time to puzzle over this statement.

"Tell them," St. Just went on, "that I'll be briefing them on important developments—make sure they understand anyone who is late is not being allowed in. While I'm talking to the media, tell the alumni guests and the Master, the Bursar, and the Reverend Otis: five sharp for sherry in the SCR. No excuses, no exceptions."

As Brummond left, St. Just turned to Sergeant Fear.

"Now, Sergeant, I have a special assignment for you."

He told him. Fear looked at his chief as if he'd gone mad, but slowly nodded his assent, thinking he'd get Brummond to go do the dirty work. Wasn't that what delegation was for?

St. Just, as if he could read his mind (one of his most annoying talents, in his sergeant's reckoning), said, "Oh, no you don't, Sergeant. Brummond already has his hands full."

IDENTITY PARADE

THEY WERE ALL THERE when he got to the SCR just after five. All the old members, along with Constance Dunning, Geraldo Valentiano, the Reverend Otis, Master Marburger, and Mr. Bowles, were crowded around the mullioned windows, murmuring worriedly amongst themselves, watching as the still, shrouded little form was removed from the college and lifted into the waiting ambulance. There were a lot of "My God"s and "This can't be happening"s. There was even some gentle sobbing and a shrill, hysterical questioning, this coming from India Bassett. It seemed to be aimed at her husband who, white and shaken, looked helplessly at his wife. Outside, pandemonium had broken out as members of the media shouted questions and brained each other with their video cameras as they struggled to get the best shot of a shrouded corpse. The scene would be replayed endlessly that night, often in slow motion, and accompanied by shocked, gasping voiceovers from Gwennap's various colleagues in the news world.

St. Just looked about the room, taking them all in. All his suspects. There were James and India, of course, they of class and privilege, oblivious to anyone's happiness but their own, oblivious most of all to their son and his doings. There was Hermione Jax, the kind of woman for whom the words "harmless eccentric" were coined. But was she harmless? Geraldo Valentiano, bolstered by an impenetrable belief in his own charms of seduction, living only for his own pleasure. The Master, the Bursar, and the Dean, the holy—or was it the unholy—trinity? Mr. and Mrs. Dunning, Karl and Constance. A clever man, who had known Lexy well; his wife, a woman expert at getting her own way. Gwennap Pengelly, Lexy's old rival for the attentions of men. Augie Cramb of Texas, a man with violence in his past, and a past that included a monumental failure to impress Lexy. Sebastian, spoiled but neglected, was the only one connected with the case not there. And Saffron, of course.

Predictably, Constance Dunning was first to speak.

"Well, I don't know about you, but I've had quite enough." Turning slowly, she bestowed her lemony gaze upon them all. Today she wore a gold and purple tunic appliquéd around the hem with dolphins frolicking in a stylized sea. The garment, unlike the couture creation he had seen her wear previously, looked amateurishly handmade and the dolphins cross-eyed, but that was difficult to say: He would have to verify this against his limited experience of folk art. Altogether it looked more like something Hermione would wear in a show of dolphin solidarity.

"That's two people we've seen go out of here feet first," Constance was running on. "We've already re-booked our flight—I just knew something like this was going to happen. I told my husband last night something like this would happen, didn't I, Karl?"

Karl seemed to understand that questions such as this when directed at him were emblematic and not requiring his full participation. Constance Dunning continued:

"We had to reschedule our plane at no little expense, and who's going to pay for that, I'd like to know? Anyway," and she turned to face St. Just, "we'll be leaving tomorrow, Detective Chief Inspector. You can't hold us here further, and that's a fact. I have spoken at length with the American Embassy." The emphasis on the last words could not have been greater had she claimed to have spoken with the Almighty. She looked around triumphantly, as if to suggest that at any moment a team of storm troopers dispatched by the embassy might appear to rescue her from her hostage situation in the SCR. "So don't try to stop us," she concluded.

"I'm sure that will be fine," said St. Just quietly. He watched with some amusement as she deflated, turning a bewildered face to her husband. "However," St. Just continued, "if you'll indulge me just awhile longer, I think we can unravel this skein for you before you leave."

"But you have your suspect … these kids were obviously mixed up in this. And now she's paid … the ultimate price."

"It's the murderer I want," said St. Just.

"But Seb is—"

"You'd be advised to keep your trap shut. Ma'am." They all turned in surprise in the direction of the harsh voice. Augie Cramb, much like James, looked pale, shaken, and at the end of his Texan rope.

"Your fatherly show of protectiveness becomes you, Sir, but I would advise you to get a rein on your temper," warned St. Just. "Otherwise, we can continue this conversation in much less opulent surroundings."

Augie Cramb subsided.

"Father?" asked the unstoppable Mrs. Dunning.

"If anyone's been a father to Sebastian, I have," cut in James gruffly. "I've fed and clothed him; I've tried to keep him in the right path. And where were you? Riding around playing cowboy on some dude ranch, without a care in the world, and without sending a penny of support."

"She told me to leave him—and her—alone," said Augie Cramb. "I tried. But I knew he would be here and realized I wanted to see him. That's only natural, especially after all these years. I have no other children."

"James, please," said India to her husband, but tentatively, as if expecting to be ignored.

"No, India," said Sir James. "I've seen what he's been up to. He thinks he can just swan in here after all these years and play the benevolent and understanding parent. The prodigal parent, in fact. But he has no idea. Seb was always a handful. But now this... wanted for murder! My God..."

"Now, who said anything about Sebastian and murder, Sir?" said St. Just. "It's early days, early days. Calm yourself. Now—"

"Father?" repeated Constance Dunning. "You mean to say Augie Cramb is Seb's father?"

Augie answered without looking at her, addressing instead some point midway on the fireplace mantle. "Yes, dammit. I am

Seb's natural father. Not that it's got anything to do with any of this." Turning to St. Just he said, "How did you find out?"

"You mean apart from the fact your son inherited your physique, and your love of rowing? That part was simple observation—it was the genealogical research to back it up that took all of five minutes. Seb's middle name on his birth certificate is Augustus. What were the chances someone born in 1988 would be given such an unusual, old-fashioned name? Coincidence? Sebastian Augustus Windwell Burrows. The name Augustus appears nowhere in the Bassett family tree, although it's rife with Sebastians and Windwells. India must have had some feeling that Seb at least deserved to have his real father's name, in some form, if not his real father."

St. Just paused, turning to look about him. India sat nodding, eyes averted. When she raised her gaze, a look of complete understanding passed between her and her husband. She did not look at Augustus Cramb, as he was known to the U.S. Department of State, which had issued his passport. Hermione gave her walking stick a tentative thump. Geraldo's face held a sneer of truculent boredom. When would the subject turn to him?

Sir James nodded in St. Just's direction.

"This is all very well, but of course it has no bearing on what should be of most concern to you. I'll ask that you spare my wife, and me, any more public revelations along these lines. They are not pertinent."

"Very well," said St. Just. "Let's find a topic you all might find more pertinent. Let's see. When you were in the Fellows' Garden, Sir James, you were perfectly situated to see the rest of the group pass by overhead, going through the gallery walk. Your testimony can help us fine-tune our timetable. Would you mind walking through with me again what you saw on the night of the murder? Whom did you see pass by up there, and in what order?"

James, evidently exasperated but grateful for the change in subject, said, "Really, I've no idea. I was focused on Lexy, of course. A group of people went by, all of them in black robes, which makes it even harder to be sure. I really can't say, except that I do remember Hermione Jax going by; in fact I think she waved at me."

"That is correct," nodded Hermione.

"And Portia De'Ath—she's a Visiting Fellow here, as you know. I think she saw me, and I think she was one of the last out. Or maybe it was the Bursar who was last out . . . but I tell you, I didn't have my focus trained there. I was trying to reassure and calm Lexy."

"That's all right, Sir. Your recollection is quite good for our purposes. Now, after you saw the Bursar pass by, how long was it before you joined the others in the SCR?"

"Oh, less than a minute, I'm sure. Thirty seconds, perhaps. When I saw him I realized I might be unconscionably late. There was no persuading Lexy to join us. I knew from long experience it was best to leave her alone to get a grip on herself. So I left her—rather too abruptly for politeness, I'm afraid. But it seemed best."

"Quite sensible of you. Now, when you got to the SCR, who was there?"

"I've given this some more thought, you know. I can only say for certain that India, the Bursar, and Ms. De'Ath were there. The Master and the Reverend Otis, I'm quite certain." The Master lowered his head in acknowledgement. "Mrs. Dunning. I think that's all but again—"

"You can't be sure," St. Just finished for him. "Right, that's understood. Sir. Now ... I suppose the only other question I have for you is this: How foolish did you feel standing there for five minutes or more, talking animatedly to an inflatable doll?"

TAKEN INTO ACCOUNT

THE ROOM HAD SUDDENLY gone quite still. Only the muted noise of people shifting uncomfortably in their seats and the soft patter of a long-anticipated rain against the window disturbed the quiet. Finally, and again predictably, the silence was broken by Mrs. Dunning.

"I told you, Karl. There would be some sort of deviant sexual practice behind all of this. It's those boarding schools, you know. They are veritable breeding grounds of vice and corruption. I don't suppose they can help themselves, poor mites. Why, in the States, we would never ship our young—"

But even her husband, in his gentle way, seemed to have heard enough. "Do be quiet, Constance. That's not what he means at all. Is it, Inspector?"

"No, of course not. No, indeed it is not. The inflatable doll— shall we give her a name, Sir James? 'Alibi,' perhaps? Yes, well. Because this alibi doll was not in use for some irregular or perverted practice—at least, not in the usual sense of that term. Nor as part of an undergraduate prank, which kind of thing has gone on here for ages. 'She' was there as a placeholder for Lexy. Lexy, who had already been dead some long minutes. Lexy, whose mortal body already lay near the boathouse."

Sir James spluttered into speech. "You must be mad. Lexy and I had been divorced for years. All passion spent on my side, I assure you. Why, then, would I engage in such a preposterous performance as you are suggesting? In order to kill someone who meant nothing to me? You are mad, I say."

St. Just, whose eye seemed to be caught by something outside the window, did not reply immediately. When he turned, a look of the utmost exhaustion etched his handsome features. He said:

"She meant nothing to you, that is true. But what was new, what had changed, was that you finally meant nothing to her. She had at last outgrown her juvenile attachment to you. At last, she had dropped the torch she had carried for so long. Suddenly, she was no longer willing to do whatever you asked of her, in her desperate need to be loved and admired. Just as bad—for you—once her infatuation faded, she began taking a closer look at her financial affairs vis-à-vis you. More to the point, you took a closer look at those finances. The case had altered. And so she had to be killed."

James Bassett cast his eyes about the room, looking in vain for support. He only found wide-eyed incredulity. "You're mad," he repeated.

"At first I thought the fact you two were distant cousins played into this," said St. Just. "That there might be some family inheritance that could not be altered by the divorce. You know, some form of entailment, so common amongst the titled families. Or perhaps there was some stock you had held in common, once worthless, now worth millions. Her canny way with a portfolio—I thought that might have something to do with this. Perhaps you were jealous of what she'd done with her share? Perhaps there was an option due to expire and if she exercised that option, it could mean your ruin, because of some lingering loophole in the divorce papers?

"But no, we found nothing like that in going over your finances and legal filings, or hers. No business partnership in common, no lingering ties of family inheritance.

"Still, looking at the current situation from a different angle: Could it be that far from mooning about over James, as you were all used to seeing her do, Lexy had in fact chosen this weekend to finally dump him? She was moving on, and a lot of details she had been neglecting, she finally began paying attention to.

"Now, Sir James must have known this day would come, but in the past it hadn't mattered so much to him. It hadn't mattered at all, in fact. He had money; his wife had money. But one day he woke up to find his portfolio larded with one bad investment after another—as so many of us have done lately, albeit on a smaller scale, given the state of the economy. But in Sir James' case, these percentage losses amounted to enormous sums. So, the case had indeed altered. And about the same time, his wealthy ex-wife was cutting him loose—emotionally—at last."

St. Just turned to the topic of his speech.

"The tragedy, for you, Sir James, was that Lexy was over you. She was free of you. It was rather a final turn of the screw, wasn't it? Geraldo here was a fling, a symbol, if you like—she was at least trying to enjoy herself, choosing one of the world's best-known ladies' men to finally kick over the traces."

Geraldo acknowledged the compliment with a grave bow of his head. Even playboys, apparently, had standards of greatness.

"Well, that's a jolly interesting theory, Inspector," said Sir James. "I killed Lexy because I've had rather a bad run in the stock market? Who, as you say, has not watched their stocks plummet lately? You have no evidence of motive whatsoever. Really, what has this country come to?"

"I wonder that myself," said St. Just quietly, just a trace of menace in his voice. A wiser man would have paid attention to the menace.

"I have half a dozen witnesses or more who give me an alibi," Sir James ploughed ahead. "Doll, indeed. You'd be laughed out of court. Where's this doll then? Where's your evidence?"

"I'm so glad you asked," said St. Just. "We'll get to that in a minute. Right now, I'm talking about your motive. As I say, the divorce papers on file revealed nothing of interest. And I assumed that the success of your books, and one in particular, meant that any problems you may have had in recent years were mitigated—years your investments were performing badly, both yours and your wife's. Your wife, to whose money you've had frequent recourse nonetheless to maintain your extravagant way of life. One wonders how soon even India, devoted as she is, would have tired of propping you up?"

India looked away, but not quickly enough to hide a fleetingly guilty look. St. Just sighed. Again addressing Sir James, he said:

"'We were children together once,'" you said of Lexy. "That wasn't strictly true—Lexy was the child, you were several years older. But to a romantic like Lexy, old friendships meant everything. Everyone spoke of her dog-like devotion to you, but only one of you—the Reverend Otis—recognized that what was in her sad eyes was not love, nor even mourning for a lost love, but a sort of pity. Pity for you. She had stopped wanting you at last. She, I believe, had finally recognized the man you were."

"You believe." Sir James practically shouted his contempt. "I repeat, where's your proof?"

"And I'll repeat that I'm very glad you asked and I'll get to that in a minute. Now, what was strange about your finances was this: About the time the money should have begun to roll in from your book, with talk of its being made into a film and so on, the money just continued to roll out. That could have been explained by a delay in paying the royalties—I understand publishers wait to see the level of returns on a book before issuing a cheque to its author. All right, that made sense, but where was the advance for this famous book? Oh, wait, that's right! The advance would have been paid years ago, because you sold the book to this publisher years ago. But…what about those royalty cheques? When might you expect to see some cash for your efforts—cash over and above the advance monies? Well, I'm happy to say that a call to your publisher set us straight."

St. Just's eyes narrowed, as if scanning a far horizon. He's going in for the kill, thought Sergeant Fear, fairly bristling with anticipation.

"We had a most pleasant chat today with someone in the accounting office of your publisher, didn't we, Sergeant Fear? I spoke with Mrs. Pennyfinger, a helpful and extremely competent woman who's been employed by your publisher for many years. She told me your now-famous book had been published and promptly 'sank without a trace'—her exact words. She told me you didn't even earn out your small advance. But then, some time later, the book developed a cult following on the Internet, a completely unforeseen circumstance. Well, not completely un-foreseen, because the publisher had retained the rights to come out with a reprint of the book, which they promptly did. A large reprint, at that. And even that print run was not enough to meet demand, because the book was going to be made into a film now—the Reverend Otis knew about that from his reading of a newsletter about the publishing industry. How ironic for you: A book that met universally with seawalls of indifference suddenly becomes a bestseller.

"Now, you might all be thinking what a lucky man Sir James was, to have life breathed into his creation a second time. But here is where it got interesting. Mrs. Pennyfinger told the police that payment had started going out some months ago, but your name, Sir James, was not on the cheques issued by the publisher. Instead, the royalties were going to the person to whom lifetime rights had been legally assigned: your wife at the time, Lexy. Now known, of course, as Lexy Laurant.

"And who had made this momentous decision, and who had signed the paperwork? You yourself, Sir James."

LIGHTING DOWN

"What was it?" St. Just drove on, relentlessly. "A birthday present? Anniversary? A bribe to get rid of her? Or some sentimental gift that cost you nothing—after all, you knew what the book was worth then, which was nothing much. You fobbed it off on her, but I'd be willing to bet that's not how she saw it. Lexy would have seen it as the sublime romantic gesture: You knew her well. During your divorce, you still thought the book was worthless and you were frantic anyway to get rid of Lexy and marry India. You probably thought you had been clever but then suddenly—the book became worth serious money. And just when you needed serious money.

"That money from your book—it could save you. Now, you might once have been able to swindle Lexy into assigning the rights back to you, but no longer. The veil had fallen from those famous blue eyes, had it not? I'm sure you reasoned—and this just fed your rage—that it was your book, not hers, for all that you had signed it away. It must have been absolutely galling, Sir

James. The book was yours. And now this silly gesture, the gesture that Lexy had no doubt thought at one time to be so sensitive and loving, had come back to haunt you in a big way."

"All right," said Sir James. "I'd assigned her lifetime rights while we were married, and they weren't part of the divorce settlement. So what? What does this have to do with poor Lexy being murdered? What proof do you have? You couldn't possibly—"

"Now, it's proof you want?" St. Just turned and pulled from his briefcase an evidence bag. Holding it aloft, they could see it contained a puddled mass of plastic. "Your doll, I believe, Sir?" He held up a second evidence bag. "And a wig for your doll. Partial to blondes, are we?" He nodded in India's direction. "But let us not forget: Lexy was a blonde—famous, in fact, for her hair. The Lexy Cut, they call it. All the rage among the ladies. Do you know, Sir James, it did occur to me that you and your wife might be in on this together—that it was India in a wig that everyone saw talking with you in the Garden, providing you an alibi. But India was seen in the SCR right after dinner, so that wasn't possible."

St. Just shook the bag in Sir James' direction. "We found these items—as you very well know, Sir James—in the river, inside a rubbish bag, the whole wrapped tightly with tape, and weighed down with a large stone. Funny kind of thing to find in the river, don't you think?"

"Leftovers from an undergraduate prank, that's all. What rubbish you are talking."

"A first-year caper, you say? High-spirited youngsters larking about, you think?"

"Quite obviously. I'm surprised I have to point this out to the police."

"We're always grateful for input from the public; you've no idea. So, you're saying that when the lab tests the prints that are all over the plastic here—"

"There can't be pr—" Sir James began, then bit off the end of the sentence. But not quickly enough. St. Just let the silence hang in the air for several long moments.

"What's that you say, Sir James? There can't be prints—because the killer wore gloves? And just how would you know that, Sir? Still, no matter. The saliva found in and around the valve, used, of course, by the killer to inflate the doll—well, that's as good as it gets. As good as prints, maybe better, I'm told. Ah! I see, Sir, you hadn't thought of that."

And from the look of him, he hadn't. Sir James glanced around at the others, stricken, as the meaning of St. Just's words spread through the SCR like the sound of a muffled underground detonation.

"Well, I never," spluttered Mrs. Dunning. Her husband shushed her with a quick gesture. The Master, the Bursar, and the Reverend Otis, who had remained huddled together throughout these revelations, continued to look on silently, their mouths forming three perfect circles of astonishment.

"So," continued St. Just, "let us reconstruct what really happened that night, shall we? And perhaps you'll put me right if you think I've strayed too far off course, Sir?

"Now, many people told me they saw you talking with Lexy after dinner the night of the murder, or they saw Lexy talking with you, or some version of either. They reported seeing, in other words, a conversation, a communication, between two people, one of them standing, the other—Lexy—sitting on a bench in the Fellows' Garden. These witnesses reported what must be true, what they had seen to be true, but in fact they saw only the back of a blonde woman's head—a rather famously blonde head. A woman whose hairstyle was so well-known, so much a part of her 'signature' look, it has been universally copied. Whose hairstyle has been made into wigs sold throughout the country, in fact—a fact of which our killer took full advantage. Nothing easier than to find a Lexy wig in shops, is there, Sir? I do hope you got a receipt? Never mind, you can be sure we'll find the shop."

Sir James, a look of distain stamped on his features, looked stonily ahead. His wife India, St. Just noticed, was not standing quite as close to her husband as she had been moments earlier.

"And to make things even easier for you," St. Just continued, "this woman—like all the men and women at dinner—was wearing a black academic gown. The alumni group was like an unkindness of ravens, or a murder of crows, wasn't it? All of them covered in black. There was no way you could anticipate what dress Lexy might wear to dinner, Sir James, but there was of course no need. She'd be wearing an academic gown over her dress, concealing its color and style. From the back, as I say, all that could be seen was the back of a blonde woman's head, and the top of a black gown covering her shoulders. She could have been anyone, really—or, more to the point: anything."

"But I distinctly saw Lexy move," interjected Hermione. "She was trembling—maybe shivering or crying. Upset."

"Yes, I remember you told me and I later wondered how that could be true, but it was in the end so easy to explain. What simpler than for Sir James to give his "dummy" a little nudge or two with his foot? It wouldn't take much to create the illusion of movement—trembling, as you described it."

Hermione seemed to think back over what she had seen, and slowly nodded. Reluctantly, she stole a look at Sir James. Incredible. And him a blueblood. Aloud she said, "I did tell you. Sir James' family have been allowed to breed too closely, and for generations."

St. Just acknowledged what she had said with a nod. The scheme was madness itself, the scheme of a desperate madman. But it could so nearly have worked.

"Our alumni witnesses heard no conversation," he went on, turning again to Sir James, "because of the glassed-in arches of the gallery, but they saw your lips move. You then told them you'd been talking with Lexy. They believed they saw Lexy in conversation because that is what it looked like, and that is what they'd been told by the estimable Sir James. That you were talking to a plastic doll—a man of your stature and dignity—would never in a million years have occurred to any of them.

"The college chef, in an unexpected bonus for you, actually overheard you talking. She also saw you walk away and leave 'Lexy.' Did you smell the chef's cigarette smoke—is that what told you you were being watched? In any event, you left 'Lexy' and came back to clear away the traces once the chef had gone back inside.

"As to the real Lexy—she was already dead. You'd killed her right after dinner. You'd arranged to meet her by the boathouse on some pretext or other—I imagine the boathouse held some romantic attachment from your old rowing days—and then you killed her and left her body there to be found by Sebastian. Then you raced back to the Fellows' Garden, where you planted her lipstick to bolster the impression she had sat there. You'd earlier, before dinner, hidden the dummy under the stone bench—if by remote chance it had been found, you could indeed have claimed an undergraduate prank. You'd dressed it in a wig and gown. The gown was simple: You borrowed it, one of dozens, from a peg in the entrance hall. As I say, you killed Lexy, then ran back to position yourself to await the trickle of people leaving the Hall. You had to make sure you were seen 'talking' with Lexy. Next, you waited until the last straggler had passed through the gallery walkway, and the chef had left. You let the air out of the dummy, stuffed it and the wig inside your shirt—your voluminous gown aided in all this concealment—and raced to join the others, putting the borrowed gown back on its peg as you ran."

"How long do I have to stand here and listen to these ridiculous police fantasies?"

"Not much longer, Sir James, do you have to stand there and listen to the truth. Just a little while longer, now. Next, you stood about sipping your port and your coffee—waiting. You wanted the body found quickly, not the next morning, and so you timed things for young Sebastian to find it. Your alibi, if you will pardon the pun, had to be 'water tight.' You knew Seb's routine and were relying on him not to deviate too far from it, to return on the dot.

"When Seb obligingly raised the alarm, you—leaping into your role of concerned step-parent—ran out to the river. As a still-fit member of the Hare and Hounds Club—the University running club—the distances you had to cover that night, back and forth, would present no problem whatsoever. At the river, you deep-sixed the doll and wig using a bag and tape you'd secreted near the boathouse earlier. You did this just in case having the police on the premises made it impossible for you to hide this evidence inside the college, or in the remote case the police immediately ordered a search of anyone's person. There would be no explaining that dummy and wig, would there? From this point we can pick up the story again from eyewitness accounts. You were racing back to the SCR for 'help' when you encountered the others on their way. They hadn't stayed to wait for you as commanded, but no matter. You ordered someone to get help; Augie Cramb punched in 999 on the mobile.

"All done. I wondered why the body of Lexy hadn't been tossed into the river—it seemed the best way for a killer to try to destroy whatever evidence there might be. But of course, the last place you wanted to direct our attention was the river, wasn't it, Sir?"

But Sir James, who suddenly looked as deflated as "Lexy," seemed to have chosen an enraged silence as the best course. St. Just let him tread water, hopefully to drown, while he himself pondered his next move.

"She'd recognized you for the freeloader you were," St. Just said. "When you asked her to revert back the rights to your book—you did ask, didn't you, Sir?—she finally had the gumption to say no, those rights were hers. So—and I'm guessing, here—you let the conversation drop, pretended it was a thing of no matter, perhaps casually asked her if she were going to be attending this weekend get-together. One way or the other, you lured her here. And she couldn't resist maybe a final little revenge—the chance to appear with her handsome, famous boyfriend on her arm. To prove how much she didn't care. You probably knew she couldn't resist—you knew her ramshackle personality so well. You lured her, as I say—to her death. This was carefully researched, planned, and premeditated, this crime. And so I shall tell the court."

St. Just sighed then, a vexed exhalation.

"Everyone thought of Lexy as a victim," he said, "but when you examine what we were told about her, there was a side to her character that doesn't go with true victimhood. We were told she was relentless, even ruthless, in her pursuit of James when they first met—although that ruthlessness may have backfired, as it so often does, given the brevity of the marriage that followed, and James' early revolt. We were also told by more than one of you that Lexy brought Mr. Valentiano along this weekend only for show—to show James she no longer cared."

"For show?" asked Geraldo, offended. Clearly, using people, women in particular, was his prerogative. He was not used to the shoe being on the other foot.

St. Just nodded. "For show. That speaks of a willingness to use people in rather a cold-blooded manner, does it not? Where is the victimhood in that? I think people tended to misread Lexy, on several levels. As I say, we were told by many that she brought Mr. Valentiano along to show Sir James she no longer cared. Now, just allow the possibility that she truly did no longer care."

"I don't follow," said Hermione.

"It's a subtle but important difference," said St. Just. "If she really had lost all interest in James, if she'd given up the struggle to captivate him, it means we've been reading the situation wrong from the beginning. For all we know, she may have grown to actively dislike or even hate him."

James' eyes sought out his wife's, beseechingly. She, this time, averted her gaze. Her face held a crushed, closed-in expression, as if it were all quite more than she could bear. Maybe, like Lexy, she wasn't so much in love with him any more. Maybe she knew St. Just was right.

Besides, having a murderer in the family was going to be frightfully difficult to explain away, even despite the already low standards of the Bassett family. Hermione was right—they were all barking.

"Really," said Sir James. Making an effort, he seemed to be recovering some of his aplomb, thought St. Just, perhaps thinking he was in trouble, but not trouble so deep a good barrister with a shovel couldn't fix things. "It would make an entertaining case. If only you had witnesses. But we just saw your witness being carried out, didn't we?"

Another little slip. Good. "First, what makes you think Saffron was a witness? But let's talk about her now, shall we? Let me tell all of you what I think happened. Then you tell me if you agree. How's that?"

Hermione, who had not taken her eyes off St. Just, nodded as if mesmerized.

"Saffron, it so happens, kept a diary, and on the night of the murder, having an almost unobstructed view from her room, she saw three people near the boathouse. Sir James, Geraldo, and Augie Cramb. She did a little 'private investigating,' and talked to all three of you. But only one of you was terrified enough at having been seen as to react as you did, Sir James. I think you misread her motives: You thought she was trying on a spot of blackmail.

"You went to see Saffron," continued St. Just, "and you brought chocolates with you. Chocolates that had been poisoned with an overdose of Lexy's tablets—the tablets you stole from her and later diluted for injection. I think you knew Lexy's reliance on drugs—it was probably getting to be an open secret—and you wanted to keep her unbalanced this weekend, even send her into a downward spiral if you could. Take advantage of her vulnerability. We found traces of the needle marks in the remaining chocolates where you injected them, undoubtedly using one of the needles India required for her insulin.

"Now, the Master and Bursar and so on would not expect Saffron to open the door when she'd sported her oak—they would respect the tradition and not dream of knocking. The other visitors of this weekend were strangers to her. Only the police, or Seb, or the stepfather or mother of her beloved Seb, would she be willing to speak with. But it wasn't Lady Bassett or Seb who had been seen talking with the fake Lexy. It was you. India had a real alibi for the whole time. So, as it happens, did Seb."

"Oh, come on, Inspector. You'll have to do better than this," Sir James said, his eyes now cold with dislike.

"All right, I will," said St. Just, smiling. "Would you get Saffron Sellers on your mobile, Sergeant?" he asked, his voice suddenly loud, filling the room.

The group exchanged glances, mystified. Had they heard him correctly? Sir James made a strange whickering sound, like a horse smelling smoke in its stables.

"But she's dead," said Hermione Jax, in a shocked voice. "We saw them … taking her … away." Already outraged at the indecency of a criminal investigation taking place within the hallowed grounds of St. Mike's, perhaps she believed St. Just quite capable of holding a séance in the SCR.

"You saw something that looked like a woman's body being stretchered out," said St. Just. "My Sergeant, happily, was able to find us an alibi doll of our own, in one of the more risqué Cambridge shops this afternoon. Saffron, I am happy to tell you, is fine and is expected to make a full recovery. So fine, she was able to tell the police about the chocolates given her by Sir James, about what she saw … about everything she knew, in fact. The real Saffron, who was found by the bedder in good time to save her—and who was in any case on a slimming regime, so she tells us, and so ate only a few of the chocolates—was taken to hospital from a side entrance to the college earlier today while I kept the members of the media entertained in the main entrance hall."

Sir James looked wildly round, as if the answer to his dilemma might be found hiding behind the sofa cushions or in the overhead chandelier. Finally, his eyes came to rest on St. Just's face.

Sergeant Fear permitted himself a triumphant twang! of the elastic against his notebook. Got him!

It was difficult to say later exactly what happened next, but the slight sound seemed to galvanize Sir James. The mask of benign but exasperated tolerance vanished, and in its place his face held an expression of the purest malice, like one of the gargoyles overlooking the Fellows' Garden. He made a move towards the exit.

Sergeant Fear stood and in one smooth unbroken movement threw aside his notebook and dove for the other man's ankles. There followed a loudly chaotic scuffle involving what looked to be several sets of arms and legs, one set clad in the finest Savile Row had on offer, the other in dark blue from Marks and Sparks. A blue-clad arm swung wildly and a fist connected sharply, followed by an anguished shout, just as the kerfuffle of limbs was increased by four. This was St. Just adding his elongated bulk to the skirmish. A moment later found Sir James contained in a chokehold, still struggling but, against the two policemen, starting to give up the fight.

EPILOGUE

"ALL THIS OVER A book?" asked Portia.

"I think that's the part that pushed him over the edge," replied St. Just. "I've had recent experience of writers and their egos, as have you. His book, all his hard work—the fruit of his genius, as I'm sure he thought of it—was finally being acknowledged, and this cursed woman he'd dumped years before refused to relinquish the rights. If it had been—I don't know, a piece of furniture or something, silverware or a painting, it might have been different. But his book—a book which is suddenly in huge demand, with movie rights being fought over by the studios. It was his birthday present to her once, he's finally admitted, and he thought the book was essentially worthless—worth a few thousand, at best. He'd actually, he says, forgotten all about it."

"Until it—and its author—became famous."

"Exactly."

"Thank God, Saffron is all right. Couldn't you have told me, though?"

"I'm sorry, darling." He reached across the table to pour her a conciliatory glass of wine. They were in her rooms in college, eating another of the gourmet meals she'd managed to prepare in incremental stages, taking advantage of outbursts of quiet in the chaotic student kitchen and combining them with the use of her own tiny kitchen. She had called into service three hot plates, borrowed various implements from the college chef, and raced several times up and down the hall to the communal microwave. At one point she had returned to her rooms wailing, "That blasted cat nearly got away with my scallops!" before vanishing once again into her kitchen.

Now she surveyed with satisfaction the result of her labors. They would start with the rescued roasted scallops served with a vermouth sauce, moving on to slow-roasted lamb flavored with rosemary, fried zucchini, and scallion potato puree. To finish, a Tarte Tatin. She thought of it as her Inspector Nankervis Special.

"Sorry," he repeated. "The murderer had to feel absolutely safe; cocky gets them every time."

Portia gave him a mocking smile. "Don't I know it?"

"It stood to reason that whoever stole Lexy's tablets also tried to silence Saffron with an overdose of those same tablets. The idea being to stress Lexy out and leave her strung out, without her usual defenses. Maybe hoping to wear her down to where she'd sign back the rights to his book, so he could avoid having to commit the murder he'd already planned—just in case."

"She did seem to be unraveling a bit as the weekend wore on."

St. Just nodded. "He may also have intended the tablets as a backup—in case he couldn't get her alone, he'd try an overdose made to look like accident or suicide. But in any event the tactic of stressing her out didn't work; it may even have backfired, making her more stubborn and difficult to deal with."

"Saffron told you what she'd seen," said Portia. "What exactly was it she'd seen?"

"She saw three people walk to the boathouse that night. She knew one of them was the killer. She just didn't know which one."

"What was she after? Was it a spot of blackmail?"

"No, I really don't think that's in Saffron's makeup. The realization she held the key to a real-life crime was what sent all common sense flying out the window. She wanted to investigate on her own and come to the police with a fait accompli. Does this sound like anyone you know?"

"I'm sure I don't know what you're talking about," said Portia.

"Really. Anyway, both Augie and Geraldo now admit she approached them. They didn't want to say anything because they'd not told the police they'd been near the boathouse, and Saffron's evidence would, they knew, make them look guilty. They just couldn't decide whether to own up to what was actually just a little walkabout for fresh air, or to stay quiet. Maybe they'd both have paid for her silence if asked; we'll never know. We've found Seb, by the way. Rather, he turned himself in when he saw the reports and the camera footage on the telly—he thought he'd had a hand in driving Saffron to suicide. He had no idea it was a murder attempt by Sir James, trying to silence her. If the bedder hadn't come by when she did, if Saffron had taken even a slightly larger dose, he'd have succeeded. That is what's frightening to contemplate."

"It was awfully handy, having all those television crews out there, just as her 'body' was being carried out."

"Hmm." He took a sip of his wine. "Reporters got wind of the story somehow. Gosh, I wonder who tipped them off? Surely not Gwenn Pengelly? Anyway, the news footage drove Sebastian to make a clean breast of things—he'd already admitted he was running a private distillery, and making a tidy sum from supplying undergraduate parties. He also broke into Lexy's room, by the way: He hadn't realized the weekend visitors would be given those rooms, and some of his equipment was stashed in there. He had to retrieve it. He was so shaken he probably thought he'd had something to do with Lexy's death as well, but we soon convinced him otherwise.

"It's a shame, really. Seb was not so much a bad kid as a foolish one. His mother's gone into overdrive to get the authorities to overlook the whole episode—it may be the first real attention she's shown him in years. We shall see..."

"I've been thinking of what you said," said Portia. "We all got it so wrong, didn't we? We saw exactly what we saw, but our interpretation was off. For example, I told you Lexy's eyes kept following Sir James. Absolutely true. But quite possibly she was trying to recall what she had ever seen in him in the first place."

St. Just nodded, smiling. "I really choose to believe Lexy, for all her silliness and wiles, would have changed, given time. Finally prying herself away from Sir James was a sign she was headed in the right direction. If only someone had realized her unhappiness, not to mention her addiction, and gotten her some real help. Geraldo was useless for that role, but if she'd lived, who knows? She might have met someone who didn't view her only as an attractive, rich, advantageous match, however temporary."

"Sir James—he took an awful chance."

"Not really. He planned things to the minute, and I think we'll find he did a bit of research on establishing time of death." He paused, thinking of Malenfant's grisly little lecture from France—breaking away from his game of boules or his café lounging or his mistress—on the temperature of the brain and how the eyes of a dead person are the first to "go." He had rattled off something about Rouleaux or boxcar formation in the eyes, as well as a mention of potassium levels.

"Suffice it to say," St. Just said aloud, "time of death cannot be determined precisely to the minute, although I daresay scientists are working on that. Sir James could easily have gotten away with pretending she was alive when she had in fact been dead about twenty minutes."

Outside, although well after nine-thirty, dusk was just showing at the edges of the day. It would be Lighting Up soon—a phrase he'd never hear again without thinking of Lexy Laurant, the woman who could light up a room. A shadow emerged from the trees just then, resolving into the forms of India and Geraldo. She was leaning against the wide trunk of an old shade tree, head flung back in accepted romantic heroine fashion, as Geraldo leaned in close, murmuring something—no doubt sweet nothings—his arms pinning her in place. She didn't seem to mind.

As if reading his thoughts, a talent Portia seemed to have developed rather quickly in their relationship, she said, "I wonder how India's going to cope? Stiff upper lip and all that, but that can carry one only so far. The scandal is what's going to kill someone like her."

He turned from the window and smiled, lifting his glass in a toast.

"Oh, I daresay she'll get over it."

———

It was late afternoon on a cold Spring day—freezing cold, the sun a silver-white disc against a sky nearly stripped of clouds by a steady wind. The river was choppy enough for there to have been discussion of postponing the race, but in the end it was decided to carry on regardless. Crowds, the largest on record, lined the Thames for the University Boat Race from Putney to Mortlake.

Sebastian Burrows was in the Blue Boat. What he couldn't get over, what he couldn't quite believe himself, was that not only was he in the Blue Boat, he was the stroke. All the months of training had finally led to this. All the early-morning practices, where he had often passed couples in dinner jackets and long dresses just coming home from a night of partying. All the weekends spent freezing on the Fens, enduring the bleak monotony of training on the River Great Ouse. All the punishing sessions on the erg. Before the race was over, he knew his lungs would be searing, his brain scrambling for oxygen, his legs surging with lactate. It wasn't uncommon for rowers to pass out at the end of a race.

Augie Cramb, he knew, would be waiting on the bridge to see Cambridge "beat the bejesus out of Oxford," as Augie put it.

Augie had probably been standing on the bridge all day to keep his place. His mother said she couldn't make it. But never mind that. That much Sebastian was used to.

He knew he was lucky. Far, far luckier than he deserved, and he was smart enough to be thankful. They hadn't sent him down, for one thing. That Inspector had fixed it, but only, he'd said, because Seb had turned himself in. Because he'd come back for Saffron's sake. The whole scheme with the alcohol he'd now put firmly in his past. The Inspector said it would stay that way if Seb kept out of trouble—otherwise St. Just would come down on him like the hounds of hell. Seb believed him. That expression about the iron hand in the velvet glove: That, he thought, was St. Just.

They were getting ready to start the race. The Light Blues were heavier than their rivals this year. The heavier boat was thought to have an edge, but that wasn't a given. They were good this year, thought Sebastian. Really, really good. They could do this. Barring an accident, barring a clash. If the wind would cooperate. He flexed his arms, resettled his hands on the oar. He stole a sideways look at Oxford. God, but those guys were tall. Then, remembering what the coach had said about positive thinking: Wimps! he telegraphed. Wankers!

The noise was deafening, the excited crowd already screaming in anticipation. Television helicopters roared overhead. A flotilla of assorted support vessels bobbed about, ready to add to the cacophony. All his senses were on high alert as he waited, trying to focus on nothing but the first stroke.

He looked at Saffron, sitting behind the cox-box. She looked back calmly, adjusting her microphone, waiting for the signal.

Suddenly the wind pushed the boat about and her hand shot up to warn the umpire they weren't ready. The boat straightened, she lowered her hand.

Into the microphone she said, "Okay, we're straight. Oxford's hand is up ... Now his hand is down. Boys, we're ready."

She gave Seb a slow wink. She'd broken off with him in Michaelmas Term and he'd spent most of Lent Term trying to win her back. She had changed, or perhaps he had, but the events surrounding the murder of Lexy Laurant seemed to have fundamentally altered Saffron. She was less girl, more woman now. And to possess her seemed to Sebastian the only thing in life worth achieving.

Sometimes, as just now, he thought maybe he was still in with a chance, but then he'd see her walking down Jesus Lane or King's Parade with some tall, handsome bloke or other. She was suddenly very popular, was Saffy. It was driving him crazy.

Don't think about that now.

He took a deep breath.

Concentrate on the first stroke.

He heard the umpire shout, "ATTENTION ... GO!"

And they were off.

THE END

BOOK CLUB QUESTIONS FOR
DEATH AT THE ALMA MATER

1. St. Michael's College is as much a character in Death at the Alma Mater as are the fictional characters. What other detective or mystery novels can you name where a place or an institution played this role?

2. The characters in the book reunite after some years for an alumni gathering, and the atmosphere is tense from the start. How does this compare with reunions—academic or family— you may have attended?

3. In what ways have the old members of St. Mike's changed over the years? How have they remained the same?

4. Sebastian (Seb) Burrows, a young student, seems to be a "golden lad" but also to be a driven and unhappy soul. What did you learn about his background that may have played a part in shaping his character?

5. Discuss Augie Cramb's role in the story. Are you sympathetic to his quest, or do you think he should have left the past alone?

6. How well has Hermione Jax managed to escape the role in life that was assigned to her?

7. Lady Bassett is described as a man's woman—physically unremarkable yet possessed of a magnetic charm. Have you met women like her in your life? What do you think is their appeal?

8. Geraldo Valentiano is the quintessential roué. What do you think is the basis for the perennial attractiveness of a man like Geraldo?

9. In what ways is Lexy Laurant different from or similar to her old rival Lady Bassett?

10. Discuss the role of the River Cam in the story. What does it symbolize to you?

11. DCI St. Just is portrayed as a decent, hard-working, yet shrewd public servant. Does he remind of you of other fictional detectives? How is he the same, or different?

12. The academic setting, such as that of Death at the Alma Mater, has long been a favorite for detective, mystery, and/or comic novelists. What other novels by what authors have you read with such a setting? What do you think is the appeal of the academic setting for these authors?

ABOUT THE AUTHOR

G. M. Malliet worked as a journalist and copywriter for national and international news publications and public broadcasters. She attended Oxford University and holds a graduate degree from the University of Cambridge.

Malliet's first novel, Death of a Cozy, Writer won the the Malice Domestic Grant, the 2008 Agatha Award for Best First Novel, and a silver medal for the IPPY awards in the category of Mystery/Suspense/Thriller. It was chosen by Kirkus Reviews as a Best Book of 2008, nominated for a Left Coast Crime award (best police procedural), short-listed for the Macavity Award for Best First Mystery, nominated for the Anthony Award for Best First Novel, and was a finalist for the David G. Sasher, Sr. Award for Best Mystery Novel.

Visit her online at http://gmmalliet.com.

WWW.MIDNIGHTINKBOOKS.COM

From the gritty streets of New York City to sacred tombs in the Middle East, it's always midnight somewhere. Join us online at any hour for fresh new voices in mystery fiction.

At midnightinkbooks.com you'll also find our author blog, new and upcoming books, events, book club questions, excerpts, mystery resources, and more.

MIDNIGHT INK ORDERING INFORMATION

Order Online:
- Visit our website www.midnightinkbooks.com, select your books, and order them on our secure server.

Order by Phone:
- Call toll-free within the U.S. and Canada at 1-888-NITE-INK (1-888-648-3465)
- We accept VISA, MasterCard, and American Express

Order by Mail:
Send the full price of your order (MN residents add 6.785% sales tax) in U.S. funds, plus postage & handling to:

Midnight Ink
2143 Wooddale Drive, Dept. 978-0-7387-1967-2
Woodbury, MN 55125-2989

Postage & Handling:

Standard (U.S., Mexico & Canada). If your order is:
$24.99 and under, add $4.00
$25.00 and over, FREE STANDARD SHIPPING

AK, HI, PR: $16.00 for one book plus $3.00 for each additional book.

International Orders (airmail only):
$16.00 for one book plus $3.00 for each additional book

Orders are processed within 2 business days. Please allow for normal shipping time.
Postage and handling rates subject to change.